Mariel's throat constricted
as they reached the corner of
Hereford Street. She dreaded entering the
house, facing her mother's unabashed
joy at her impending marriage
and her father's palpable relief.

Her spirits sank lower and lower as she and Penny neared
the end of the road.

When they were within steps of the town house, its door
opened and a man emerged.

He turned toward them and the sun illuminated his face.
"Mariel?"

She froze.

This man was the one person she thought never to see
again, never wished to see again. He was the man to whom
she'd been secretly betrothed, the man who had inhabited
her thoughts.

The man who had deserted her.

Leo Fitzmanning.

* * *

A Not So R...
Harlequin® Hi...

Author Note

One of the delights of my writing career was collaborating with Amanda McCabe and Deb Marlowe on *The Diamonds of Welbourne Manor* anthology. We'd known each other and been friends even before our Harlequin days. In fact, we went on a Regency tour of England together, visiting Mayfair and Brighton and Bath, seeing all the Regency-era houses and museums. One of our highlights was a venture on our own through Hyde Park.

It was such a great thrill to be invited to do the anthology together. We were given carte blanche to create it any way we wished.

The three of us gathered for a weekend of history and brainstorming at Historic Williamsburg, Virginia, where we created The Fitzmanning Miscellany, the group of siblings and half siblings who became the heroes and heroines of our novellas and the connected books.

These characters just leaped from our imaginations that day, as if they were real people waiting for us to knock on their door and interview them. *A Not So Respectable Gentleman?* is Leo's story and, sadly, the last of the Welbourne Manor series. It has been such a pleasure.

The Welbourne Manor books:

The Diamonds of Welbourne Manor anthology
Snowbound and Seduced by Amanda McCabe
The Shy Duchess by Amanda McCabe
How to Marry A Rake by Deb Marlowe
A Not So Respectable Gentleman? by Diane Gaston

DIANE GASTON

A NOT SO RESPECTABLE GENTLEMAN?

HARLEQUIN®
entertain, enrich, inspire™

Recycling programs
for this product may
not exist in your area.

ISBN-13: 978-0-373-29701-6

A NOT SO RESPECTABLE GENTLEMAN?

Copyright © 2012 by Diane Perkins

www.Harlequin.com

Printed in U.S.A.

Available from Harlequin® Historical and
DIANE GASTON

**Did you know that some of these novels are also
available as ebooks? Visit www.Harlequin.com.**

And in Harlequin Historical *Undone!* ebooks

*Three Soldiers

To Amanda McCabe and Deb Marlowe,
my fellow creators of *The Diamonds of Welbourne Manor*
and its heroes and heroines, the Fitzmanning Miscellany

Prologue

Spring 1826

*F*lames.

White hot, blinding red and orange and blue. Flames roaring like a dragon, weaving through the stable, crawling up the walls, devouring everything in its path.

Leo Fitzmanning still saw the flames, felt their heat, heard the screams of his horses, as he entered the mahogany-shelved library of a London town house. The scent of smoke lingered in his nostrils and his muscles ached from battling the fire for nearly two days.

One moment of inattention, one second of carelessness, had cost him his stable and two outbuildings. He'd failed to notice the peg holding the lantern had become loose. The lantern fell, spreading flames in an instant.

He blinked the vision away and faced the man he'd waited nearly a month to see.

Mr Cecil Covendale rose from the chair and extended his hand across the paper-cluttered desk. 'Good day, Fitzmanning.' His manner seemed affable. That was a good sign. 'How are you faring since the fire? You appear uninjured.'

News apparently travelled swiftly the ten miles between Welbourne Manor, on the outskirts of Richmond, and Mayfair.

'Only minor burns, sir.' He accepted the older man's handshake.

The stables, his horses and two outbuildings would cost a great deal to replace, a fact of which Covendale was, no doubt, aware.

'Word is you almost lost the house.' Covendale's expression showed only concern, not the disdain Leo expected in response to his failed enterprise. 'What a pity that would have been.'

Not for those who would rejoice at seeing Welbourne Manor destroyed. *Recompense for its scandalous past,* they would say, although Leo aspired to revise its reputation. To Leo and his siblings, Welbourne Manor was a beloved place. He would never have forgiven himself if he'd lost their safe haven, the house where they spent their unconventional childhood.

'The house is untouched.' Leo shrugged. 'The rest can be rebuilt.'

If one had the money, that is. Would Covendale guess nearly all Leo's funds had been invested in the stud farm, now nothing but ashes?

His mind reeled with all the tasks he'd left undone by keeping this appointment. Finding stables for the few surviving horses. Making arrangements for his stable workers, who had suddenly lost the roof over their heads and all their worldly possessions. He'd left them at the Manor, raking through the ashes, making certain that no glowing embers hid beneath the debris, hungry for more destruction. He ought to be working beside them, preparing to rebuild.

But nothing would have kept him from this appointment with Covendale. The man had already put him off for weeks. Some matters were even more important than Welbourne Manor.

'I presume you know why I wished to speak with you,' Leo began.

The smile faded from Covendale's face. 'I do indeed.'

Hairs rose on the back of Leo's neck. Why the change in expression? 'Your daughter told you?'

'She did.' Covendale lowered himself into his chair. He did not ask Leo to sit.

Leo's muscles stiffened. 'Then you know I have come to ask your permission to marry her.'

'I do.' Covendale sighed and shook his head as if in dismay. 'How do I proceed?'

Leo heard the fire's roar again. 'I assure you, the loss of my stable is only a minor setback. Your daughter will want for nothing.'

Leo would recoup his losses, he vowed. He'd borrow the money from his brother if he had to. Rebuild his stables to be grander. Make his stud farm even more prosperous, more respected.

'Perhaps.' Covendale winced. 'But—'

Leo cut him off. 'Are you concerned about her inheritance? I have no need of her inheritance.'

Mariel's great-aunt had bequeathed her a considerable fortune, to be bestowed upon her at age twenty-five if she remained unmarried, sooner if she married with her father's approval. If her marriage did not meet her father's approval, however, the fortune would be forfeited to some obscure and frivolous charity.

Leo pressed on. 'I ask your approval of our marriage only because I will not have Mariel give up her money for me.'

Leo and Mariel had discussed this. She'd insisted

her father would never approve of Leo. They'd considered running off to Scotland, but even though Mariel did not care about the money she stood to lose by eloping, she did care about the scandal it would cause her family, especially her younger sisters. Leo also had no wish for scandal. He planned to gain society's respect by producing the finest horses in England, even finer than his brother Stephen's horses. Furthermore, Leo would not take a penny of Mariel's money. It would always remain under her control.

He gave Covendale a steady look. 'I assure you, the money will remain in Mariel's hands. I will sign papers to that effect. We can make the arrangement before the marriage, if you like.'

Covendale raised a hand. 'Enough, Fitzmanning. This matter between you and my daughter has come as a complete surprise to me. I knew nothing of this—this—courtship before Mariel informed me why you sought an appointment.'

Leo had no defence for the secrecy, except that Mariel had desired it. 'Mariel and I have known each other since childhood, as you well know. She and my sisters have remained friends. We became reacquainted while she visited with them.'

In January, amidst Charlotte's wailing children and her barking pugs, Leo had found Mariel again. No longer was she the annoying girl with plaited hair who'd joined his sisters in trailing after him. Mariel had transformed into a woman so lovely that, for that first moment of glimpsing her again, he'd forgotten how to breathe. They met again at Charlotte's house and eventually contrived further meetings in secret. No one knew of their attachment, of the strong bond that quickly grew between them. No one knew that Mariel was the reason Leo left his brother's employ to establish his own stud farm. To make a loving, respectable home for her at Welbourne Manor.

Covendale waved a hand. 'Never mind that. When did you last speak with my daughter?'

It had been the day they'd discussed setting up this meeting. 'About a month ago.'

Since then there had been no opportunity to contact her. He'd thrown himself into setting up his farm to keep from missing her and to make the time fly.

Covendale glanced away, seeming to mull over something. He rubbed his face and turned back to Leo. 'A month can be a long time. Much can happen.'

Leo sprang towards the desk and came within inches of Covendale's nose. 'Has something happened to Mariel? I demand you tell me. Is she ill? Is she hurt?'

'Neither!' The man recoiled. 'She is betrothed!'

Leo stepped back. His brow knit in confusion. 'Betrothed? Yes. She is betrothed to me.'

'Not to you.' Covendale glanced away. 'She is betrothed to Lord Ashworth.'

Ashworth?

Edward Ashworth?

Ashworth had been a schoolmate of Leo's, an affable boy who'd grown into a decent man. He was titled, wealthy and well liked by everyone, the epitome of an ideal husband.

Covendale handed Leo a sheet of paper. 'It is all arranged. Here is the special licence. I could show you the marriage settlement papers….'

Mariel's and Ashworth's names were written legibly on the sheet of paper that allowed couples to marry elsewhere than a church and which waived the reading of the banns. The paper was signed by the Archbishop.

Leo shoved the paper back to Covendale. 'Does Mariel know of this?'

Covendale coughed. 'Of course she knows of it.'

'I would speak with her, sir. Send for her.' Mariel would never do this. Not without telling him.

'She is not here.' Her father raised his shoulders. 'She and her mother are in Herefordshire at Ashworth's estate.'

At Ashworth's estate?

Leo forced himself to meet and hold Covendale's gaze. Inside, his emotions flamed like the stable's burning rafters.

Why would she go there, if not...?

Covendale went on. 'Ashworth is a fine man, from a decent family. His is an old title. Mariel is not a foolish girl. She knows this is an excellent match for her. A real step up.' He made a mollifying gesture. 'You must look at this situation from my point of view. Do I approve your suit or the suit of a young man who possesses a title? Who will be better for my daughter?'

Leo glared at him. 'You cannot force Mariel to marry. She is of age.'

'I am not forcing her,' the man insisted. 'Her age is of issue, of course. That cannot be ignored. At twenty-one she's practically on the shelf. Her mother and I despaired of her ever making a good match. I believe she herself was becoming somewhat desperate—but, then, perhaps that is why she considered marrying you.'

Leo ignored that put-down. 'No. We pledged our devotion to each other.' Mariel's love was genuine. He would wager everything he possessed upon it.

Although most of what he possessed was now mere ashes.

Covendale clucked. 'Devotion? My poor, poor fellow. Devotion is fleeting. Whatever pretty words passed between you and my daughter are no match for what really matters.'

'And that is?' The fire again roared in Leo's ears.

Covendale shifted in his chair. 'A good name. Connections. Status in society.' He leaned closer. 'That is what my daughter desires and deserves. She will not have that if she marries you.'

So that was it? Good name? Status? Leo intended to build those things for himself. And he was not without connections. His father and King George had been fast friends, for God's sake.

Covendale smiled. 'Like all young women, she wishes to marry respectably.'

Leo's fists tightened. 'Have I ever conducted myself in any way that was not respectable?'

'Not that I've heard.' The man wagged his finger at Leo. 'With the exception of courting my daughter in secret.'

Leo burned as if the flames continued to surround him.

Covendale made another mollifying gesture. 'You must look at this situation rationally. Given a choice, Mariel cannot debase herself with—with a man of your birth.'

A bastard, he meant.

'Your father, for all his titles and high friends, flouted the manners of proper society. What is more, he and your equally scandalous mother reared you in a most amoral atmosphere....'

Was this explanation necessary? Leo had always lived with knowledge of his origins.

His father, the Duke of Manning, left his wife to set up housekeeping at Welbourne Manor with the equally married Countess of Linwall. They lived together for twenty years in unmarried, free-spirited bliss, producing Leo and his two sisters from their unsanctified union. His father's two legitimate sons, Nicholas, now the duke, and Stephen, a successful horse-breeder, spent nearly as much of their childhood at Welbourne Manor as Leo did. Also reared there was Justine, Leo's half-sister by a French woman his father bedded before meeting his mother.

Society called the lot of them The Fitzmanning Miscellany. But not to Leo's face, not if they wished to avoid broken bones.

Leo's hand curled into a fist. 'My brothers were reared at Welbourne Manor.' Except Brenner, his mother's legitimate son, the current Earl of Linwall. Leo and his siblings had not known Brenner until after their parents died. 'Do you consider them scandalous?'

'Of course I do!' Covendale exclaimed. 'But they are legitimate. Society accepts them for that reason alone. You, however, would not be accepted anywhere if not for the fact that your father was a duke. It was the only reason I ever allowed Mariel to befriend your sisters.'

Leo damned well knew society merely tolerated him. And his sisters. The difference between being the legitimate son and being the bastard had always been made crystal clear to him.

Truth be told, even his brothers treated him differently, albeit out of love for him. Nicholas and Stephen were forever trying to shield him from the consequences of his birth, to make it up to him for the shabby treatment by others. Their efforts were almost as painful as the barbs he'd endured as a schoolboy. Or the cuts, as an adult.

Society expected him to become a libertine like his

father, but he was determined to prove society wrong. From the time he'd been a mere lad, he'd made certain his behaviour was unblemished.

A man should be judged by his own character. And by his achievements. Leo intended to reach the pinnacle in both.

Mariel understood that. She'd supported him. Admired his drive. It had never mattered to her that his father had not been married to his mother. She'd loved *him*.

Leo faced Covendale and looked directly into his eyes. 'I do not believe any of this. This daughter you speak of is not the Mariel I know. She would not marry merely for a title. It is impossible.'

The older man pursed his lips. 'Well, there is also your financial situation. A stud farm is nothing to Ashworth's fortune. And now, with the fire, you have several buildings to replace, not to mention livestock. Even if we could ignore the vast inequality between your birth and that of Ashworth, you presently have nothing to offer my daughter.'

The fire. For all Leo's grand thoughts about achieving the pinnacle of respect, the ashes of his former dream revealed his failure.

Covendale turned all sympathy. 'I realise this is difficult for you. It is difficult for me that she left it to me to inform you, but I assure you, Ashworth came courting her and it has resulted in this.' He picked up the special licence.

Leo shook his head. 'She would have contacted me. Told me herself if her sentiments had changed.'

Her father held up a finger. 'It almost slipped my mind. Mariel did leave word for you. She wrote you a note.' Covendale opened a drawer and withdrew a sealed, folded sheet.

Leo took the paper from the man's hand and broke the seal.

It read:

> *Dear Leo,*
> *No time to write a proper note. I meant to be there*
> *in person, but Father will explain it all.*
> *Wishing nothing but good to you,*
> *Mariel*

It was written in her hand. The paper even smelled of her.

He crushed it in his fist. *Father will explain it all.*

'I'm sorry, boy,' Covendale said quietly.

The fire roared inside him again and flames filled his vision.

The special licence. Mariel's absence. Her note.

His failure.

There was no more denying it. She'd chosen respectability over him. A legitimate husband over a bastard one. And, without knowing, a wealthy man over a failure.

'I do not know what else to say to you,' Covendale said.

Leo barely heard him.

He thought about losing his horses, his stable. Losing Mariel was a thousand times worse. The pain was so intense he had to fight to remain upright. It was as if his insides were consumed by flames and what was left was ashes, a void that never could be refilled.

Respectability be damned. Stud farm be damned.

What had all his conscientious behaviour and hard work brought him? A pile of cinders.

Being jilted by Mariel.

He forced himself to rise to his full height. 'You are correct, sir. There is nothing more to say.' He nodded to Covendale. 'Good day.'

Leo turned and strode out of Covendale's library, out of the town house, into the grey afternoon drizzle.

And the emptiness that was now his life.

Chapter One

June, 1828—two years later

Loud pounding forced Leo from a dead sleep.

He opened his eyes and was stabbed by a sliver of sunlight, harbinger of a fine spring London day. He clapped his hands to his head.

Too much brandy. Now he was paying the price.

More pounding. A caller at his door.

Why the devil did Walker not send them away?

Walker was Leo's valet, but likely not out of bed himself. He and Leo had engaged in a bout of celebratory drinking after Leo returned from the card tables the previous night.

Walker might act as Leo's valet, but he looked nothing like a gentleman's gentleman. He'd been a ruffian from the Rookerie, caught by circumstance in Paris and hungry for a new life. Leo encountered him by accident and they had become more than gentleman and gentleman's man. They'd become friends…and now business partners.

The pounding resumed and Leo could just make out the voice of a man demanding to be admitted.

He groaned and roused himself from the bed, searching around the room for the clothes he'd shed the night before. The sound stopped and he sat back on the bed. Excellent. Walker would deal with it. Send the caller away.

Once, Leo would have been up and out to his stables at dawn. He'd have done a half day's work by this hour. He rubbed his face. That had been an age ago. A different lifetime. Being in London brought back the memory, but he'd carved out a new life for himself—from very rough rock, he might add—but it was a life that suited him surprisingly well.

Walker knocked and entered his bedchamber. 'Your family calls.'

His family? 'Which ones?'

'All of them.'

All six? His brothers *and* his sisters? 'What the devil do they want?'

'They would not tell me,' Walker replied.

Leo ran his hand through his hair. 'Why didn't you make some excuse? Say I was out?' It did Leo no credit that he'd avoided them for the fortnight he'd been in town, but he'd been busy. Besides, they'd never understand the direction his life had taken while he'd been away.

Walker cocked an eyebrow. 'I thought it unwise to engage in fisticuffs with a duke, an earl and one tiny, growling dog.'

Good God. His sister Charlotte brought one of her pugs.

'Very well. I will see them.' He pulled his shirt over his head. Walker brushed off his coat with his hand.

Leo's siblings had, no doubt, come with help to offer and would scold him for his behaviour, which had taken a downward path since last he'd been in London, although he trusted they'd never know the half of it. Let them believe the stories about him, that Leo was as much a libertine as his father had once been, but they would not know that Leo had faced situations their father would never have imagined facing.

He shoved his arms into the sleeves of the coat and pulled on his boots. 'I have the feeling I will not enjoy this.'

He left the bedchamber and entered the sitting room.

His brothers and sisters immediately turned to him. They stood in a circle. In fact, they'd even rearranged his seating into a circle.

'Leo!' Nicholas spoke first. As duke, he was head of the family. 'Good morning.'

Charlotte's pug yapped from under her arm.

Justine rushed over to him, clasping both his hands. 'Leo, how good it is to see you. You look dreadful.' She touched his cheek and spoke with some surprise.

'Indeed.' Brenner joined her.

He must look a sight. Unshaven. Rumpled clothes. Bloodshot eyes.

Brenner searched his face. 'Are you unwell?'

'Not at all,' Leo replied. 'Late night.'

Brenner and Justine comprised the most complex of his unusual sibling relations. She was his half-sister by his father, and Brenner, now Lord Linwall, was his half-brother by his mother. They were married to each other. Their love affair happened right after Leo's parents died.

Brenner flashed him one more worried look before wrapping his arms around Leo in a brotherly hug. The others swarmed around him. Charlotte burst into tears and wept against his chest. Nicholas and Stephen slapped him on the back. Even the pug raced around his feet and tried to jump up his legs. Only Annalise held back, but that was typical of her. She was observing the scene and would probably make a painting of it and call it *The Return of the Prodigal Son*.

Only he had no intention of returning to the well-meaning bosom of his family. He was just passing through, literally waiting for his ship to come in.

'What are you doing here?' he managed to ask.

Nicholas clapped his hands. 'Come. Let us all sit and we will tell you.'

One of the chairs was set just a little inside the circle. That was the one they left for him.

Nicholas leaned forwards. 'We are here out of concern for you.'

Of course they were. 'Concern?' They intended to fix things for him. Take care of him as they'd always done.

'We are so afraid for you, Leo!' Ever the dramatist, Charlotte punctuated this with a sob. 'What will become of you?' Her dog jumped onto her lap and licked her face.

This was all nonsense. 'What the devil are you talking about?'

Nicholas spoke. 'You are spending your time drinking, womanising and gambling.'

He certainly looked the part this morning.

'It won't do,' Nicholas went on. 'It is time you found some direction in your life.'

'Some useful occupation,' Stephen explained.

'Before it is too late,' Charlotte added.

It appeared that rumours of his rakish living had preceded him. To be sure, he often stayed up all night playing cards, but he womanised hardly at all and actually drank very little.

Except for this morning.

They could not know of his more clandestine dealings, one that nearly got him killed, and others that skirted the law and earned him a great deal of wealth.

Leo started to rise from his seat. 'I assure you, I am well able to handle myself.'

Brenner, who was seated next to him, put a hand on his shoulder and silently implored him to stay in the chair.

He sat back down. 'Do not trouble yourselves about me.'

'But we do,' whispered Annalise. 'I mean, we *must* trouble ourselves.'

Brenner took on a tone of reasonableness. 'We understood your need to get away, to travel. It was good for you to see something of the world, but now—'

'Now you are just drinking and gaming,' Justine broke in. 'You avoid the family. You avoid healthy pursuits.'

How easily they believed the worst of him. And how readily they assumed it was their job to fix him.

'You cannot know my pursuits.' He gritted his teeth.

'Oh, yes, we can.' Nicholas levelled his gaze at him. 'We have ways of finding out everything.'

Not everything, Leo thought. They obviously knew nothing about his investments. He'd wager a pony that they had never heard of what he and Walker had been through. And they'd never known the real reason he had fled England, why he still had no use for London society.

One after the other they begged him to change his life, to abandon his pursuit of pleasure. They implored him to *care* about something again, to invest his hopes and dreams in something.

He ought to tell them, but the shipment of goods he

was expecting was not precisely done to the letter of the law. Not that it would hurt anyone.

'The thing is…' Nicholas glanced towards Brenner, who nodded approval. 'We have a surprise for you.'

Stephen moved to the edge of his seat. 'We've rebuilt the stable at Welbourne Manor! And the outbuildings. Bigger and better than before. It is all ready for you. Complete with a fine breeding pair from my stables, already in residence at the Manor. Say the word—today, if you like—and I'll take you to Tattersall's to buy more horses. If you need money—'

Leo felt the blood rush to his face. 'No.'

Charlotte piped up. 'Nothing has changed at Welbourne Manor. Even the servants are the same. Halton, Signore Napoli, Thomas—'

'It is waiting for you,' Justine added. 'What do you say, Leo?'

Leo regarded each of them in turn. 'I sold Welbourne Manor to all of you. It is not mine any more. I no longer wish to breed horses. And I am not staying.'

'Leo—' Brenner began.

'No.' He spoke firmly. 'I do not need help. And I especially do not need for you to tell me what to do.'

'We are not…' Brenner protested.

It was no use to explain to them. He did not need them to help him. He did not need anyone. He'd proven it to himself. He had left the country after losing everything, and, almost out of nothing, built a solid fortune. Without a good name. Without top-lofty connections. What's more, he no longer sought the good opinion of the *ton*. He'd discovered self-reliance was more valuable than what society thought of him.

'I refuse to discuss this further.' Leo kept his voice firm. 'If you continue, I will walk out the door.' He softened. 'Tell me about yourselves. How are you faring? How many nieces and nephews do I have? I confess to have lost count.'

He only half listened as they proudly filled him in on their children, their lives. When they spoke, their faces glowed with contentment and deep satisfaction. They were happy and that gladdened him.

But their visit brought back memories. Of his dreams for Welbourne Manor, and a similar happiness that had almost been within his reach.

Late that night Leo again sat at a card table at a Mayfair gaming hell. Tucked among discreet buildings off St James's Street, the place buzzed with men's voices and women's laughter. Smoke from cheroots filled the air. Disquieting. Smoke always disquieted him.

Leo held excellent cards. Perhaps a run of luck would settle the restlessness that had plagued him ever since his siblings' visits.

'Did you hear about Kellford?' the man on his right at the whist table asked as he rearranged his cards.

Leo lifted his eyes from his own hand without any great interest in Baron Kellford. He'd known Kellford in Vienna. 'Your turn, sir.'

But the man clearly would not throw down his card before disgorging his precious *on dit*. Did he have a trump card or not?

Leo's opponent rearranged his hand. Again. 'The news is quite amusing.' Pressing his cards against his chest, the fellow looked from Leo to the other two men at the table. 'Kellford is soon to be flush in the pocket.' He leaned back, waiting for one of them to ask for more.

Leo's whist partner took the bait. 'Did he engage some unbreeched pup in a game of piquet?'

That would be like Kellford. Take advantage of some green lad in London for the first time.

'Oh, he did not win a hand at cards, but he will win a hand.' The man chuckled at his clever wordplay and finally threw down a card of the leading suit.

Leo trumped it.

Seemingly unconcerned with the loss, the man grinned. 'Kellford is betrothed. He's marrying an heiress.'

Poor woman. Leo collected the markers he'd won.

His partner shuffled for the next deal. 'I'm the one who needs an heiress. Who did Kellford find? Some squint-eyed daughter of a wealthy cit?'

'Not at all,' the man said. 'He's marrying Miss Covendale.'

Leo froze.

No. Mariel married Ashworth. Hadn't she? Leo spent two years on the Continent, travelling as far as he could to keep from hearing news of her marriage to Ashworth. On his first day in London, who did he glimpse on Oxford Street? Ashworth. He'd half expected to see Mariel at the man's side. What had happened?

More to the point, why marry Kellford?

The noise and smoke-filled rowdiness of the gaming hell receded, and in his mind's eye Leo saw Kellford, whip in hand, about to strike a cowering tavern maid from the hotel where they both happened to be staying. Leo had pulled the whip from the baron's hand and forced Kellford out of the hotel.

'Come now. I hired her!' Kellford had protested. 'I would have paid her well.'

Leo closed his eyes and saw Mariel's face instead of that nameless girl.

'Mariel Covendale?' Leo's partner leaned back. 'Men

have been trying to win her fortune for years. How the devil did Kellford manage such a coup?'

How indeed.

'I do not know.' The gossipmonger shook his head. 'But the first banns have been read. I wager before the knot is tied, I'll learn how he did it.'

The fourth man at the table piped up. 'I wager a pony you will not.'

As the three men placed bets with each other, Leo stood and scooped up his share of the winnings.

'What are you doing?' his partner cried. 'The set is unfinished.'

'I must leave.' Leo did not explain.

He hurried out to the street. The night was damp after a day of steady rain. The cobbles glistened under the lamplight and the sound of horses' hooves rang like bells.

Leo walked, hoping the night air would cool emotions he thought had vanished long ago.

Kellford had once boasted of being a devotee of the Marquis de Sade, the French debaucher so depraved even Napoleon had banned his books. 'The man was a genius,' Kellford had said of de Sade. 'A connoisseur of pleasure. Why should I not have pleasure if I wish it?'

Now all Leo could picture was Kellford engaging in pleasure with Mariel.

A coachman shouted a warning to Leo as he dashed across Piccadilly. He found himself wandering towards Grosvenor Square within blocks of Covendale's London town house. From an open window in one of the mansions, an orchestra played 'Bonnie Highland Laddie,' a Scottish reel. It was near the end of the Season and some member of the *ton* was undoubtedly hosting a ball.

Did Mariel attend? Leo wondered. *Was she dancing with Kellford?*

He turned away from the sound and swung back towards Grosvenor Square, staring past the buildings there as if looking directly into her house on Hereford Street.

Had her father approved this marriage? Surely Covendale had heard talk of Kellford's particular habits.

Or perhaps not. One disadvantage of living a respectable life was being unaware of how low deeply depraved men could sink.

Leo flexed his hand into a fist.

He'd vowed to have nothing more to do with Covendale or his daughter, but could he live with himself if he said nothing? If he'd save a Viennese tavern maid from Kellford's cruelty, surely he must save Mariel from it.

He turned around and headed back to his rooms.

No brandy this night. He wanted a clear head when he called upon Covendale first thing in the morning.

Chapter Two

'Do not walk so fast, Penny.' Mariel Covendale came to an exasperated halt on the pavement.

'Sorry, miss.' Her maid returned to her with head bowed.

Mariel sighed. 'No, I am sorry. I did not mean to snap at you. It is merely that I am in no great rush to return home.'

Penny, a petite but sturdy blonde, so pretty she would have been prime prey in any household with young sons about, looked at her softheartedly. 'Whatever you wish, miss.'

The maid deliberately slowed her steps. After a few minutes, she commented, 'You did not find anything to purchase. Not even fabric for your bridal clothes.' Penny sounded more disappointed than Mariel felt.

Mariel smiled. 'That is of no consequence.'

In truth, she'd not cared enough to make a purchase. She'd merely wished to escape the house and her parents for time alone. Time to think. So she'd risen early and taken Penny with her to the shops. They'd browsed for hours.

Penny's brow furrowed. 'I cannot help but worry for you, miss, the wedding so close and everything.'

Too close, Mariel thought.

They crossed Green Street and Penny pulled ahead again, but caught herself, turning back to Mariel with an apologetic glance.

The girl was really a dear and so devoted that Mariel had been tempted to make her a confidante.

Better to say nothing, though. Why burden her poor maid?

Instead she gazed up at the sky, unusually blue and cloudless this fine spring day. Yesterday's rains had washed the grey from London's skies. Weather always improved if one merely has patience.

Unfortunately Mariel saw only grey skies ahead for her. And she had no time for patience.

For Penny's sake, though, she forced her mood to brighten. 'It is a lovely day, I must admit. That is reason enough to dally.'

Penny gave her a quizzical look. 'If you do not mind me saying, miss, you are so very at ease about everything, but it is only three weeks until your wedding, and you have no bridal dress or new clothes or anything.'

So very at ease? That was amusing. Mariel must be a master of disguise if Penny thought her at ease. 'I have many dresses. I'm sure to have enough to wear.' She wanted no special bridal clothes. 'If you like, tomorrow we can search for lace and trim to make one of my gowns more suitable for the ceremony.'

It was as good an excuse as any to be out and about again and Penny was a creative seamstress.

'We could do that, miss,' the maid agreed.

Coming from the shops on New Bond Street, they

had meandered through Mayfair, passing by Grosvenor Square and the Rhedarium Gardens, but now they were within a short walk of the town house she shared with her parents.

If this wedding were not looming over her, she'd be happily anticipating summer months in their country house in Twickenham. She missed her younger sisters, although it was good they had not been old enough for the London Season and all the pressures it brought. At twenty-three, Mariel had seen many Seasons, had many proposals of marriage.

Only one mattered, though, but that proposal occurred when she'd been two years younger and foolish enough to believe in a man's promises.

Foolish enough for a broken heart.

Luckily her powers of disguise had hidden the effect of that episode well enough. No one but her father ever knew about her secret betrothal. Or her heartbreak. She'd even trained herself not to think of it.

Mariel's throat constricted as they reached the corner of Hereford Street. She dreaded entering the house, facing her mother's unabashed joy at her impending marriage and her father's palpable relief.

Her spirits sank lower and lower as she and Penny neared the end of the street.

When they were within steps of the town house, its door opened and a man emerged.

He turned towards them and the sun illuminated his face. 'Mariel?'

She froze.

This man was the one person she thought never to see again, never *wished* to see again. He was the man to whom she'd been secretly betrothed, the man who had just inhabited her thoughts.

The man who had deserted her.

Leo Fitzmanning.

He was as tall as ever, his hair as dark, his eyes that same enthralling hazel. His face had become leaner these last two years, more angular with tiny lines creasing the corners of his eyes.

She straightened, hoping her ability to mask her emotions held strong.

'Leo.' She made her tone flat. 'What a surprise.'

His thick dark brows knitted. 'I—I have come from your father. I called upon him.'

'My father?' Her voice rose in pitch. 'Why on earth would you wish to see my father?' She had not even known Leo was in London.

He paused before closing the distance between them and his hazel eyes pleaded. 'Will you walk with me?'

She glanced over at Penny, who was raptly attending this encounter. Mariel forced herself to face him again. 'I can think of no reason why I should.'

He reached out and almost touched her. Even though his hand made no contact, she felt its heat. 'Please, Mariel. Your father would not listen. I must speak with you. Not for my sake, but for yours.'

For her sake?

She ought to refuse. She ought to send him packing with a proper set-down. She ought to turn on her heel and walk into her house and leave him gaping in her wake.

Instead she said, 'Very well. But be brief.'

He offered her his arm, but rather than accept it, she turned to Penny. 'You must follow.'

Leo frowned. 'I need to speak with you alone.'

Mariel lifted her chin. 'Then speak softly so she does

not hear, but do not ask me to go with you unchaperoned.'

He nodded.

They crossed Park Lane and entered Hyde Park through the Cumberland gate. The park was in its full glory, lush with greenery and flowers and chirping birds.

He led her to one of the footpaths. It was too early in the afternoon for London society to gather in carriages and on horseback for the fashionable hour. The footpath was empty. Once Mariel would have relished finding a quiet place where they could be private for a few moments. She would have pretended that nothing existed in the world but the two of them. This day, however, it made her feel vulnerable. She was glad Penny walked a few steps behind them.

Off the path was a bench, situated in an alcove surrounded by shrubbery, making it more secluded than the path itself.

Leo gestured to the bench. 'Please, sit.'

'No.' Mariel checked to make certain Penny remained nearby. 'Speak to me here and be done with it.'

He was so close she could smell the scent that was uniquely his, the scent that brought back too many memories. Of happy days when she'd contrived to meet Leo in this park. They'd strolled through its gardens and kindled their romance.

He faced her again and she became acutely aware of the rhythm of his breathing and of the tension in his muscles as he stood before her. 'I will be blunt, because I have not time to speak with more delicacy.'

His tone surprised her.

'Please do be blunt,' she responded sarcastically.

She wanted to remain cold to him. She wanted not to care about anything he wished to say to her.

It was impossible.

Amidst the grass and shrubs and trees, his eyes turned green as he looked down on her. 'You must not marry Lord Kellford.'

She was taken aback. 'I am astonished you even know of my betrothal, let alone assume the right to speak of it.'

He averted his gaze for a moment. 'I know I have no right. I tried to explain to your father, but he failed to appreciate the seriousness of the situation.'

She made a scornful laugh. 'I assure you, my father takes this impending marriage very seriously. He is delighted at the match. Who would not be? Kellford is such a charming man.'

His eyes flashed. 'Kellford's charm is illusory.'

She lifted her chin. 'Is it? Still, he meets my father's approval.'

He riveted her with his gaze again. 'I tried to tell him the man Kellford is. Your father would not listen, but you must.'

A *frisson* of anxiety prickled her spine. With difficulty, she remained steady. 'If you have something to tell me about Kellford, say it now and be done with it.'

He glanced away. 'Believe me. I never would have chosen to speak this to you—'

His words cut like a sabre. He preferred to avoid her? As if she'd not realised that already. He'd avoided her for two years.

She folded her arms across her chest and pretended she did not feel like weeping. 'Tell me, so you do not have to stay a moment longer than is tolerable.'

His eyes darted back and flared with a heat she did not understand. 'I will make it brief.'

Mariel's patience wore thin. 'Please do.'

His eyes pinned her once more. 'What do you know of the Marquis de Sade?'

Was he changing the subject? 'I do not know the Marquis de Sade. What has he to do with Kellford?'

He shifted. 'You would not *know* him. And I suppose no gently bred young woman would have heard of him....'

'Then why mention him?' Why this roundaboutation? 'Do you have a point to this?'

'I dislike having to speak of it,' he snapped.

Enough. She turned to walk away.

He caught her by the arm and pulled her back. Their gazes met and Mariel felt as if every nerve in her body had been set afire. She saw in his eyes that he, too, was affected by the touch.

He released her immediately. 'The Marquis de Sade wrote many...books, which detailed scandalous acts, acts he is said to have engaged in himself.'

'Scandalous acts?' Where was this leading?

He nodded. 'Between...between men and women.' His eyes remained steady. 'De Sade derived carnal pleasure from inflicting pain on women. It was his way of satisfying manly desires.'

Mariel's cheeks burned. No man—not even Leo— had spoken to her of such matters before. 'I do not understand.'

He went on. 'For some men the pleasure that should come...in the normal way...only comes if they cause the woman pain.'

She'd heard that lovemaking—at least the first time—

could be painful, but he didn't seem to be talking about that. 'What pain?'

He did not waver. 'Some men use whips. Some burn with hot pokers. Others merely use their fists.' His cheek twitched. 'Sometimes the woman is bound by ropes or chains. Sometimes she is deprived of food or water.'

Her stomach roiled. 'Why do you say this to me?'

His features twisted in pain. 'Because Lord Kellford has boasted of such predilections. Because I have heard accounts about him. I have seen him use a whip—'

An icy wind swept through her. 'That is the information you needed to give me?'

'Yes.' His voice deepened. 'That is it.'

She glanced over at Penny, whose expression reflected the horror Mariel felt inside. Penny had heard it all.

Mariel had known Kellford to be a greedy, calculating man hiding behind a veneer of charm. Now she discovered he was depraved as well and that he would likely torture her. Hers would not merely be a wretched marriage, it would be a nightmare.

She turned from Leo and started to walk away.

Again he seized her, this time holding her with both his hands, making her face him, leaning down so he was inches from her face. 'You cannot marry him, Mariel. You cannot!'

He released her and she backed away from him, shaking her head, anger rising inside her like molten lava.

It was easier to be angry, much easier than feeling terror and despair. She fed the anger, like one fed a funeral pyre.

Why had Leo saddled her with this appalling information? Did he think it a kind gesture? A worthy errand? Would he depart from this lovely park feeling all self-righteous and noble? Might he even pretend this atoned for disappearing from her life and breaking her heart?

He had walked away from her without a word, as if she'd been nothing to him, and now he burdened her with this?

She felt ready to explode.

'Do you think you have helped me?' Her voice shook.

He seemed taken aback. 'Yes, of course. You can cry off. It is not too late.'

She gave him a scornful laugh. 'I can cry off.' Suddenly she advanced on him, coming so close she felt his breath on her face. 'You understand nothing, Leo.' Let him feel the impact of her wrath. 'I *have* to marry Kellford. Do you hear me? I have no choice.'

She swung around and strode off.

'What do you mean you have no choice?' he called after her. 'Mariel!'

She did not answer. She did not stop. She did not look back. She did not even look back to see if Penny followed. She rushed down the path and out of the park. Hurrying across Park Lane, she did not stop until she reached the door to her town house.

Out of breath, she leaned her forehead against the door and waited for Penny to catch up.

To herself she said, 'I have no choice, Leo. No choice at all.'

Chapter Three

Leo watched Mariel flee from him. Seeing her had shaken him more than he cared to admit. Her ginger-coloured eyes fascinated him as much as they'd done two years before. His fingers still itched to touch the chestnut hair, peeking from beneath her bonnet. And her lips? It had been all he could do to not taste of them once again.

He thought he'd banished her image from his mind, but the full glory of her flooded back to him. Her eyes sparkling with delight. Her smile lighting up his very soul. Had that all been illusion? She certainly seemed to find his presence distasteful to her now. Had she merely been pretending all that time ago?

It was a question that had once kept him awake at night and consumed his days. Finally he'd pushed it aside so well he'd thought he'd forgotten. One glimpse of her brought everything back.

But his emotions were not at issue here. No matter her feelings towards him, she must not marry Kellford.

Her words still rang in his ears. *I have to marry Kellford. Do you hear me? I have no choice.*

What did she mean *no choice*? Had Kellford compromised her? Good God, had the man already forced himself on her?

All manner of circumstances came to Leo's mind as he finally walked out of the park. He'd supposed this task relatively simple to discharge. Unpleasant, but simple. Merely call upon her father and warn him about Kellford and that would be the end of it. Cecil Covendale had not been pleased to see him; in fact, he'd been surly, as if he'd wished he could toss Leo out on his ear. Leo had minced no words. He'd explained precisely what Mariel faced if marrying Kellford. Covendale accused him of spreading falsehoods, ordered him to leave and never return.

Mariel had not assumed they were falsehoods, though. She'd believed him and still declared she must marry Kellford.

He must speak with her again, learn why she felt compelled to marry at all. She was only two years away from inheriting her fortune outright. It was madness for her to marry, let alone marry Kellford.

He crossed over to Hereford Street and glanced at Mariel's town house as he passed. Perhaps he should knock on the door again and insist she see him right now.

No. Her father would forbid him admittance. Leo needed to find some place where he might catch her alone and off guard.

The problem was, she did not attend the sorts of places that he frequented of late. Gaming hells. Taverns. Dank and dismal rooms in the Rookerie with Walker and the shipping partners. Mariel attended society functions, called upon society friends. With his newly acquired reputation, Leo was on no one's invitation list and would be an even more unwelcome caller.

He knew precisely how to rectify that problem, although it was a step he detested making. His brother Nicholas could get him invited anywhere. Who would refuse such a request of a duke? Nicholas would agree. As always, Nicholas would be delighted to help his bastard brother.

Leo walked the short distance to the ducal residence on Park Street. His knock was answered by a footman whom he did not recognise. The man's brows rose.

'Please tell his Grace his brother Leo desires a few moments of his time.' Leo handed the man his hat and gloves.

'I will see if his Grace is available.' The footman gestured to the drawing room off the hall. 'If you would care to wait…'

Leo strode into the drawing room, a room transformed from the gold-gilt furniture and rich brocades of his childhood into something warmer and more welcoming. The new duchess's influence, no doubt. Too fired up to sit, he wandered the room, noticing that the clock and some of the porcelain figurines were relics from his childhood.

As children they had not stayed in the Mayfair residence often, so it always had been a special treat. It had also been a place Leo had not felt at ease. He used to think about all the dukes and duchesses who'd once graced these rooms, including Nicholas and Stephen's mother. He wondered how she must have felt, knowing this house was sometimes occupied by her rival, Leo's mother, and her illegitimate children.

The footman appeared in the doorway. 'His Grace will see you now.'

Leo followed the man up the marble staircase to another more private drawing room, one where the girls had been allowed to practise the piano and where they all played at skittles.

Nicholas and his wife approached Leo as he entered the room.

'Leo! I hope this means you have had a change of heart.' Nicholas's tone, as always, was welcoming.

Nicholas's wife reached Leo first. It was evident she was expecting another child, news probably given to him the day before but not recalled.

'It is so wonderful to see you!' she cried, clasping his hands.

He leaned down to kiss her on the cheek. 'Emily. You look as beautiful as ever.' He glanced at her. 'I hope you are feeling well.'

'Very well, thank you.' She smiled.

Nicholas's expression turned serious. 'Are you in any trouble? You know I will help you in any way I can.'

Leo resented the assumption. 'No trouble. And if I were in trouble, I would not come running to my brothers.'

'No, you never did,' admitted Nicholas. 'But we always found out, did we not? And were there to help.'

Nicholas would never know what Leo had faced in the last two years and how well he'd managed on his own, but he gave his brother a grudging nod.

Nicholas clapped his hands. 'Then you have reconsidered our gift? Welbourne Manor is yours again for the asking. We can easily help you get back on your feet. Begin stocking your stables.'

Leo clamped his mouth shut lest he say something that would only lead to a shouting match.

Emily stepped in. 'Nicholas, enough!' She pulled at her husband's arm. 'Let us all sit down before you speak business.' She turned to Leo. 'We have tea. Let me pour you a cup.'

He lifted a hand. 'Thank you, no tea for me.'

She carefully lowered herself on a sofa and Nicholas sat beside her. Leo chose a chair adjacent to them.

Nicholas started. 'Why did you react to our plan as you did, Leo? You must know we are concerned about you. We would do anything for you.'

Leo stiffened. 'Your concern is unfounded.'

'But you disappeared for two years,' Nicholas went on.

'I wrote letters,' Leo protested. 'I kept you advised as to where I was.'

Nicholas shook his head. 'You told us nothing about what you were doing, you must admit. Then stories of your activities reached us, increasing our worry for you—'

Leo held up a hand. 'Those stories were greatly exaggerated, I am sure.'

He could agree that he had gone through a brief period of very heavy drinking, placing himself in dangerous situations from which he often had to resort to fisticuffs to escape. That period had been short-lived and he did not credit his heavy gambling as scandalous. All the other activities they could not know about.

Nicholas leaned forwards, worry lines appearing between his brows. 'I know that much can happen when you travel to new lands.' His duchess touched him and a look of understanding passed between them. 'You can tell me if anything happened to distress you.'

Nicholas was speaking about himself, Leo realised. Was he harbouring secrets of his own? 'Nicholas, believe me. Nothing of consequence happened to me.'

Meeting Walker had been important, of course, but

the crucial event in his life had happened before his travels. He'd never spoken of his secret betrothal to his siblings and, if Mariel had disclosed it, surely his siblings would have smothered him with their commiserations and battered him with their advice.

Which would still be the case today if he shared the truth of why he'd come to beg a favour of his brother, the duke.

Both Nicholas and Emily continued to gaze at him with sympathetic disbelief.

Leo lifted a hand. 'Stop looking at me like that! I did very well on my travels. It was a great adventure having no responsibilities. Quite freeing, in fact.'

Nicholas frowned. 'But you cannot live your life that way. You must let us help you secure your future. The plan for Welbourne Manor is a good one, is it not?'

Leo scraped a frustrated hand through his hair. 'Nick, I no longer wish to breed horses. I do not know how to convince you all of that fact.' That dream had been too connected to Mariel for him to pursue it now, and too connected to his misguided wish for society's acceptance.

'I cannot believe it,' Nicholas protested. 'You've loved horses since you were out of leading strings.'

'I still love horses.' Leo shrugged. 'I merely have no wish to breed them.' There were better ways to gain wealth and success, he'd discovered. More exciting ways.

'But—' Nicholas started.

Leo held up a hand. 'There is something I do need from you—'

His brother's demeanour changed. 'Anything, Leo. Anything.'

'I want to re-enter society.' How was he to put this?

'I will eventually wish to mix with members of the *ton* and I want to counteract the gossip that apparently has preceded me.' A bold-faced lie, of course.

This was a story Nicholas would believe, however.

'Of course. Of course.' Nicholas said. 'What can we do?'

'Take me along to society functions.' Ones that Mariel would also attend, he meant. 'I know I may not be welcome everywhere, but those where you think my presence would not be objectionable.'

Nicholas's eyes flashed. 'You are my brother. I dare say you'd better be accepted at any affair I condescend to attend.'

Nicholas would never accept the truth of Leo's situation. Or that it no longer mattered to Leo whether society accepted him or not. Leo wanted nothing to do with people who judged others by birth alone. If it weren't for needing access to Mariel, Leo would tell them all to go to the devil.

'I would be grateful, Nick.'

Emily brightened. 'Leo could accompany you to the ball tonight.'

'Indeed!' Nicholas clapped his hands. 'Come here at nine and we will go together.'

'Nine. I will be here.' He rose. 'I'll take my leave of you now, however.'

'No!' cried Emily. 'You have only just arrived. You must stay for dinner.'

Too many hours away. 'I cannot, but I appreciate the invitation.'

Nicholas helped Emily to her feet and she embraced Leo. 'Please know you are welcome in our house any time.'

Her sincerity touched him deeply. 'Thank you.'

Nicholas clapped him on the back. 'I will walk you to the door.'

It seemed an odd thing for a duke to do.

As they descended the staircase, Nicholas said, 'I am delighted that you asked for my help. I am very glad to give it.'

Leo felt a pang of guilt for so resenting what was offered him out of such brotherly affection.

'Do you have suitable clothes?' Nicholas asked. 'I'm sure I can fix it if you do not.'

If only such loving offerings were not so insulting. 'I have formal clothing,' he managed through gritted teeth. 'Where is this ball tonight, may I ask?'

'Lord Ashworth's,' Nicholas responded. 'Do you remember him?'

Ashworth's. Why did that irony not amuse him?

'I remember him.'

That evening as Leo and Nicholas stepped up to the doorway of the Ashworth ballroom, waiting to be announced, Leo immediately scanned the crowd, looking for Mariel.

Nicholas whispered to the Ashworth butler, who then announced, 'The Duke of Manning and Mr Leo Fitzmanning.'

The buzz of conversation ceased for a moment and all eyes turned their way. Leo supposed the silence was not merely the deference due a duke, but the shock at seeing the duke's bastard brother at his side.

Ashworth, whose girth had thickened since his youth, immediately stepped forwards from where he'd been standing to receive guests. 'Your Grace, how delightful you were able to come.'

A pretty young woman who'd been standing next

to Ashworth also approached Nicholas. 'I do hope the duchess is well, your Grace.'

'Very well, Lady Ashworth,' Nicholas replied. 'Simply not up to the rigours of a ball.'

Ashworth had married someone else, obviously.

Nicholas turned as if to present Leo, but Ashworth had already seized his hand. 'Leo! How delighted I am to see you!' The man pumped his arm enthusiastically. 'It has been an age and you have been abroad!'

Before Leo could form a response, Ashworth put an arm around his shoulder and brought him over to his wife. 'Pamela! Here is my dear friend!' It was kind of Ashworth to characterise him as such. 'May I present to you Leo Fitzmanning.'

Leo bowed. 'I am very pleased to meet you, Lady Ashworth.'

This woman, who might have been Mariel had events transpired as Leo thought they would, was a pretty doll-like creature who appeared as soft and affable as Ashworth himself.

'Mr Fitzmanning. How nice you could come.' Her words seemed as genuine as her husband's and in her expression there was no hint of censure for attending without an invitation.

At that moment other guests were announced and Leo left his host and hostess to their greeting tasks. Nicholas had been commandeered by some gentlemen now surrounding him, so Leo felt free to search for Mariel.

He moved through the crush of guests, nodding to those people who acknowledged him, noticing those who avoided looking his way. Though no one dared risk offending his brother by giving Leo the cut direct, he was aware of whispers about him in his wake.

The room was ablaze with candles and decorated with huge jardinières of flowers. Richly upholstered sofas and chairs were set against the walls and grouped for conversation. It had been a long time since he'd wandered through a Mayfair ballroom. Nothing had changed.

Except him.

In his travels he'd wandered through the worst parts of cities, the poorest parts, and often found people living with more dignity than some of these glittering guests, so quick to judge and disdain.

He heard a squeal. A rush of pink silk caught the corner of his eye.

His sister Charlotte advanced on him. 'Leo! You are here! I could not believe my eyes.' She seized his arm and dragged him with her. 'Come say hello to Drew. Justine and Brenner are here, too. Isn't it lovely?'

He had to admit it felt gratifying to be greeted with even more enthusiasm than Ashworth had shown. He received a brotherly embrace from Charlotte's husband, Drew, whom he'd known practically their whole lives, and answered Drew's many questions regarding his health, when he'd arrived, where he'd travelled from, why they had not seen him sooner.

Charlotte interrupted. 'Oh! Here is someone else you know, Leo. You must say hello.' She tugged him away from her husband.

And brought him face to face with Mariel.

Her dress was a deep-rose silk and a dark blue sash was tied at her waist. Matching blue ribbons adorned her hair, which was swept atop her head with curls framing her face. She was so lovely she seemed unreal.

She was obviously not delighted to see him, but even less delighted was the man at her side.

Lord Kellford.

Leo bowed. 'Miss Covendale.'

'Miss Covendale?' Charlotte cried. 'Since when do you call Mariel *Miss Covendale?*'

He shot Charlotte what he hoped was a dampening look. 'Since I am at a formal ball.' He turned back to Kellford and gave him a curt nod. 'Kellford.'

Kellford responded in kind. 'Fitzmanning.'

Mariel's eyes pleaded with him, as if she feared he would blurt out their long-held secrets. Did she think he would retaliate for her having spurned him? In any event, he was fairly certain she would not willingly speak to him privately, even if he could manage it.

Making matters worse, Mariel's father approached and on a flimsy pretext hustled her away. Leo turned back to Drew, asking him how his sister and nephew fared and about their estate, and pretending the brief exchange with Mariel meant nothing to him. A few moments later, Justine and Brenner appeared and were delighted to see him. He was soon enveloped by family, who remained near him the entire night, an armour he did not need. He could stand on his own anywhere, especially in the superficial gaiety of a Mayfair ballroom.

Kellford rarely left Mariel's side; Leo was beginning to despair of ever catching her alone.

Watching her altered something inside him, Leo had to admit. It would take some effort to turn his emotions to stone again. Still, he would never allow himself to be vulnerable to her smiles and promises. He must question, though, why he cared so much to discover why she must marry Kellford. And why he felt determined to prevent it.

He no longer believed he was merely playing the Good Samaritan.

Finally he spied her saying something to Kellford. She managed to walk away and leave the ballroom alone. Leo made an excuse to his family and followed her, taking care not to look obvious. He guessed she was bound for the ladies' retiring room, otherwise why would Kellford have let her go?

Catching a glimpse of her entering the room as another lady left, Leo retreated to a discreet corner where no one would notice him.

It seemed a great deal of time passed before she emerged again. Had she delayed on purpose to enjoy being free of her constant escort?

Leo quickly stepped from the shadows and seized her arm, pulling her out of sight of prying eyes.

'Leo! Let me go,' she whispered, trying to twist away.

He released her, but blocked her way back to the ballroom. 'Give me a moment.'

Her eyes darted. 'Someone will see us.'

'A moment,' he implored. 'Tell me the reason you feel you must marry. I'll fix it for you. Let me help you.'

Her face flushed with anger. 'You will fix it? Do not make me laugh, Leo. You have no right to even speak to me now.'

'I have no right?' he answered hotly. 'Because of the choice you made two years ago?'

'A choice I made?' Her brows knit in confusion.

'To marry Ashworth...' Leo had not wanted to pursue this matter.

'Marry Ashworth?' She gave a scornful laugh. 'Well, I obviously did not marry Ashworth. If I had, I would not be in this fix.'

It brought him back to the task at hand. 'Never mind. Tell me why you must marry Kellford.'

She stood so near his arms ached to hold her again.

He leaned closer, suddenly helpless against the need to taste her lips and recapture some of the youthful joy they'd shared.

Her eyes rose to his and her pupils widened. For a moment she did not move. He leaned closer.

'Leo,' she whispered, then pushed him aside. 'What does it matter? Move away. I must return to my charade.'

Her charade. She did not wish to marry Kellford, that was clear. And, like it or not, Leo had made the choice to help her. He'd not back out now.

At the moment, though, he could only watch her hurry back to the ballroom.

At the end of the evening as Leo rode back to the ducal town house with Nicholas, he asked, 'What event will everyone attend tomorrow night?'

'A party at Vauxhall Gardens hosted by Lord and Lady Elkins.' His brother stifled a yawn. 'But I will not attend. I prefer to stay home with Emily.' He glanced at Leo. 'Would you like to go in my stead? I can arrange that.'

'I would indeed.'

Anything was possible at Vauxhall Gardens.

Chapter Four

'Vauxhall Gardens?' Walker's brows rose.

'That is correct.' Leo opened a cabinet in his sitting room and pulled out a decanter of brandy. He poured himself a glass. 'I'll need a domino and a mask. Do you know where you might get one?'

The valet shrugged. 'I will find one, but what is this? A card game at Vauxhall Gardens?'

Leo lifted an empty glass in an invitation to pour some for Walker. 'Not precisely. It is a society event.'

Walker shook his head. 'Another society event? This is a change for you. May I ask why?'

Leo frowned, an image of Mariel flying into his mind, as well as one of Kellford brandishing a whip.

Walker's expression turned to one of concern. 'What is it, Fitz?'

Walker only acted the role of valet, which accounted for his plain speaking and familiar address. Few gentlemen—or servants, for that matter—would understand the sense of equality between the two men, born of mutual respect and one life-changing experience. Leo had fed Walker's thirst to better himself, teaching Walker to read and to speak like an educated man. Walker had shown Leo the skills he'd acquired to survive the Rookerie and provided the contacts that would make their present venture profitable. There was little they did not know about each other's lives.

Still, Leo had never told Walker about Mariel. His feelings for Mariel were a secret locked so deep inside him he did not know if he could ever dislodge them.

Walker's brows knit. 'Is this what your family asked of you? That you must rejoin society and attend its entertainments? And you are doing it?'

'No.' Leo lifted the glass of brandy to his lips. 'Although no doubt my family would be delighted by it. You know my opinion of society.' On the Continent he had learned that he needed only his wits and his courage to make money.

'Then what is this?' Walker circled with his finger. 'Why this visage of life and death, then? It must be more than some new scheme. If you are in trouble, you should let me in on it, you know.'

Leo smiled inside at the way the word *visage* dropped so easily off Walker's tongue. As did Walker's willingness to help, somewhat reminiscent of Nicholas's.

Leo took a sip of his brandy. He needed Walker's help, he was certain of that, and Walker was not as easy to fool as Nick. He was also not one to follow orders without an explanation. Walker had freed himself from blind adherence to orders.

Leo must stick close to the truth, but he had no intention of exposing what was still painfully raw.

'Do you recall Lord Kellford?' he finally asked.

Walker made a disgusted sound. 'The lout with the whip?'

'Precisely.' Leo lowered himself into one of the chairs. 'He is set to marry an...old family friend and I am determined to stop it. There is a masquerade party at Vauxhall tonight which I suspect he will attend. As will the lady.'

Walker stared at him and Leo had the distinct feeling the man was trying to decipher what Leo left unsaid. 'Does the lady know what he is?'

'I told her.' Leo tried to appear dispassionate. 'She insists she must marry him. I would like to discover why, what hold he has over her and then stop him.' Beneath his prosaic tone was a swirl of painful emotions. He took another sip of brandy. 'I shall see what I can discover as a guest at this Vauxhall affair. My brother will arrange my invitation.'

Walker sat in an adjacent chair. 'Then perhaps I can discover something from a different end. Shall I try to befriend some of his servants? See what they know?'

This was why Leo valued his valet-friend so much. Walker did not wait to be ordered about; he just acted.

'An excellent idea.' Leo smiled. 'After you find me a domino, that is.'

The music from Vauxhall reached Leo's ears just as the pleasure garden's entrance came into sight. Nicholas had insisted on providing the ducal carriage, and, if anyone witnessed it, Leo supposed arriving in such style could do nothing but help his acceptance as his brother's substitute.

As he moved through the garden's entrance, his domino billowed in the night's breeze and gathered between his legs, impeding his gait.

There could not be a sillier garment for a man, lots of black fabric fashioned into a hooded cloak, the accepted male costume for a masquerade. Once Leo put on his mask, the costume had advantages. No one would know who he was. He would be able to remain near Mariel without anyone suspecting his identity.

He knew she would attend. Before walking to his brother's house and donning his domino, he'd concealed himself near the Covendale town house and watched as Mariel and her parents climbed into Kellford's carriage. The evening remained light enough that Leo was able to clearly see her costume. Her dark green dress clung to her figure from neckline to hips. Gold-braid trim adorned the low square neckline and the long trumpet sleeves. Over the gown, she wore a matching hooded cape. How ironic she would dress as a medieval maiden, the quintessential damsel in distress.

Kellford, on the other hand, had exerted as much imagination as Leo. He, too, wore a black domino.

Leo hurried down the South Walk. Tall, stately elms shaded the area with its booths and the supper boxes. Ahead of him at some distance, Leo spied three triumphal arches and a painting of the Ruins of Palmyra so realistic it fooled many people into believing it was real. The three supper boxes reserved for the party hosted by Lord and Lady Elkins were located just before the arches.

His domino caught between his legs again and he slowed his pace, taking more notice of the gardens which seemed to show some tarnish since he'd last seen them. Or perhaps it was he who was tarnished.

He remembered his first look at Vauxhall, when still a schoolboy, the night his father and mother hosted a masquerade. He and his brothers had been allowed to attend until darkness fell and the drinking and carousing began in earnest.

A wave of grief washed over him. His parents had been blissfully happy, as scandalous as their liaison had been. They'd looked magnificent that night, costumed in powdered hair and shiny, colourful brocades, the fashionable dress of the last century. Surrounded by their equally scandalous friends and those few respectable ones who were loyal no matter what, they had been in their element. No one had enjoyed the pleasures and entertainments life had to offer better than his mother and father.

Perhaps they had enjoyed a masquerade in Venice before contracting the fever that killed them.

As Leo neared the supper boxes, so close to the ones his parents had secured that night, he stopped to put on his mask. He presented his invitation to the footman at the entrance. Because it was a masquerade, no guests were announced and Leo could slip into the crowd in perfect anonymity.

Almost immediately he found his sister Charlotte, dressed as a shepherdess, but he did not reveal himself to her. No, this night he'd take advantage of his disguise. He walked through the crush of people, searching for Mariel.

Finally the crowd parted, revealing her, as if gates had opened to display a treasure. Her hood and cape hung behind her shoulders. Her headdress was a roll of gold cloth, worn like a crown. She looked like a queen from a bygone age. He savoured the sight of her before moving closer.

He had no difficulty spotting Kellford or Mariel's parents, or the fact that Mariel was edging away from them. He stepped forwards to help her, deliberately pushing his way between her and Kellford and remaining in Kellford's way.

His ploy worked. She hurried away from them and let the crowd swallow her. Leo waited a moment before following her, confident he could find her no matter how many people obscured his view.

He was correct.

Darkness was falling fast, but he was able to glimpse her making her way out of the supper box. She covered her head with her hood and hurried towards the large gazebo in the centre of the gardens. The orchestra was still playing on its balcony, high above the area where guests danced to the music.

He continued, walking quickly, puzzled at what she was about. It was not safe for her to leave the protection of the supper boxes. In addition to revellers, Vauxhall Gardens attracted pickpockets and other rogues and miscreants who combed the gardens searching for easy prey.

She weaved her way around the dancers until she was on the other side of the gardens near the Grand Walk. She made her way to one of the trees that bordered the area and leaned against it.

He slowed his pace and stopped a few feet from her. 'Mariel?'

She started and then gave him a careful look. 'Leo.' Her tone was flat. Obviously his mask had not disguised him from her.

He came closer. 'It is not safe to walk alone here.'

'Indeed?' She lifted one shoulder. 'Do you not think walking alone is preferable to remaining on Kellford's arm? I confess, I do.'

He scowled. 'Is that why you ran off? To get away from him?'

She made a disparaging sound. 'Were you watching me, Leo?'

'I came in hopes of speaking with you,' he admitted.

She turned away to face the dancers twirling and

gliding like fairies in a dream. 'We can have nothing
to say to each other.'

'I need to know—'

She stopped him from speaking, putting her hand on
his arm and moving to the other side of the tree.

'What is it?' He glanced around.

She gestured with her chin. 'Kellford is looking for
me.'

Leo caught sight of him, perusing the crowd, moving closer to where they stood.

He grasped her arm. 'Let us make you more difficult to spot.' He pulled her into the crowd of dancers.

The orchestra played a French waltz and the dancers had formed two circles, one inside the other. Leo
led Mariel to the inner circle. He placed his hands on
her waist; her hands rested on his shoulders. Their eyes
met and locked together as they twirled with the circle
of dancers. The sky grew darker by the minute and everything and everyone surrounding them blurred.

Leo only saw Mariel.

Her face remained sombre, as did his own, he imagined. Did she feel the same emotions that were coursing
through him? Savouring. Yearning. Regretting.

How different their lives would have been had his
parents been respectably married. Had there been no
fire. They would have married. Had children. Built a
prosperous stud farm together. Had a lovely life.

What foolish fancy. He'd learned early that it was no
use to wish for what one could not change.

The orchestra stopped playing and a violinist began
playing a solo. Some of the dancers stopped to listen;
the others made their way back to their boxes or to the
booths selling food and wine.

Mariel averted her gaze. 'Thank you for coming

to my rescue, Leo. Another good deed you have performed.'

She sounded despairing and he ached for her.

He searched for Kellford and no longer saw him. 'Walk with me.' He extended his hand.

Mariel hesitated. She should never have danced with him, even if it meant being discovered by Kellford.

Oh, she was full of foolishness this night. She'd so abhorred Kellford's presence being forced on her in this beautiful place of fantasy and romance that she'd impulsively run from him.

Perhaps she had sensed Leo nearby, because she was not entirely surprised when he appeared in front of her. It has been foolish indeed to dance with him, to swirl to the sensual melody, to lose herself in Leo's warm hazel eyes, his gaze more piercing framed by his mask.

No, she should not walk with him. She must be sensible.

But his fingers beckoned. 'Please, Mariel?'

She glanced around, wondering what would happen if Kellford found her, especially with another man. Mariel had sensed the falseness of Kellford's gallantry even before Leo told her of the man's perversions. His actions towards her might speak to others of a solicitous lover, but Mariel had known all along that all he wanted was her money. His solicitousness was merely a means to control her every move.

She'd been clever enough to escape him this night. She'd find some excuse to offer him for disappearing from his side.

If only she could think of some way to rid herself of him entirely.

She stared at Leo's extended hand, temptation itself.

Before she knew it, she'd placed her hand in his and felt his warmth and strength through her glove. 'Do not take me back to the supper box.'

He nodded.

They stepped onto the gravel of the Grand Walk and, like so many other couples, strolled to the fountain. Beyond the fountain the paths led through trees as thick as a forest. The Dark Walk, they called it, a place where lovers could disappear and indulge in intimacies forbidden in the light.

They entered the Dark Walk and walked past the illusionist making cards appear and disappear at will. They continued and soon the darkness of a moonless night surrounded them. Then, all at once, the thousands of gas lamps strung throughout in the trees were lit and the night blazed with light.

Mariel gasped. It was as if they'd been lifted to the stars. She glanced at Leo and saw the wonder of the sight reflected in his eyes, as well. It had always been like this between them. An instant understanding. Conversing without needing to use words.

To be so close to him again made it seem as if no time had passed, as if they were still young and full of optimism, eager to lose themselves in the Dark Walk. In those days he would have pulled her into the privacy of the trees. He would have placed his lips on hers and she would have soared to the stars with happiness.

She shook herself. They were no longer young and full of optimism. They were no longer in love.

They came upon an area almost as private as in her imagination, a bench set in among the shrubbery, almost completely concealed from the path itself.

'Shall we sit a moment?' he asked.

She should resist the temptation of him, not succumb to old fantasies. She'd grown out of them. He'd forced her out of them.

Still, she sat.

They removed their masks, but did not speak.

Finally he broke their silence. 'Tell me now why you must marry Kellford.'

She stiffened. Why did he persist in asking her this? She could not confide in him.

'Because I will help you.' He seemed to answer her very thoughts. 'But I must know the problem.'

She turned away from him, not wanting to believe in him again. How could she?

But he persisted. 'What hold does Kellford have over you? Has he compromised you?'

She swung back. 'Compromised me!' The thought was appalling.

'Has he forced himself on you? Is that why?' He blanched. 'Good God. Has he gotten you—?'

'No!' She held up a hand. 'Do not insult me. Do you think I would tolerate his touch?'

His expression turned grim. 'I think him quite capable of forcing himself on you. If it is not that, then tell me what it is. You said you *must* marry him. Tell me the reason.'

Her anger flared. 'I cannot tell you, Leo. You know I cannot.'

'Whatever it is, I can help you.' His gaze remained steady. 'I have ways.'

This was so much like the Leo she once knew, the young man who believed they could create a bright future together. She wanted to shake her head lest he be an apparition.

But she could not let him hurt her again. Trust in

him? Impossible. 'You once made promises to me, Leo. We both know what happened to those promises.'

He was opening the old wounds, wounds she'd been able to ignore even if they'd never healed.

'Mariel.' His voice turned tight. 'You broke those promises.'

'*I* broke them?' It had been devastation when she'd heard nothing from him. 'You left me!'

'What did you expect? You were marrying Ashworth. You chose a title over a bastard. What happened to that plan, by the way?'

'Ashworth again. Why do you persist in saying I would marry Ashworth? I was betrothed to you.' She felt as if she were bleeding inside once again.

'Your father—' he began, but did not finish.

The blood drained from her face. Had her father sent Leo away? 'Do you mean you spoke to my father?'

'You know I did. You set the appointment.' He clenched his jaw. 'Surely you have not forgotten that we planned for me to speak with your father. He told me you had chosen Ashworth.'

'No.' She shook her head. 'You never kept that appointment. I assumed it was because of the fire. My father said you didn't keep it.'

'Your father said that?' A look of realisation came over his face.

Her father. She felt the blood drain from her. Her father had been manipulating her even then. 'Tell me what my father said to you.'

'That you chose Ashworth over me, because I was a bastard with nothing to offer you. Since my stables had just burned down, he was essentially correct.' His eyes narrowed. 'Were you at Ashworth's estate that day?'

'At Ashworth's estate?' She felt cold inside. 'No. I

was in Bath. With my mother. She wanted to take the waters.'

They sat close to each other, so close their faces were inches apart. She could see the shadow of a beard on his chin, the lines at the corners of his eyes, the shadows within him that spoke of his own pain.

'He told me you chose Ashworth because of his title,' he went on, speaking as much to himself as to her. 'Because he was respectable.'

She almost weakened, almost transferred her anger to her father, who owned plenty of it already. But Leo was not wholly innocent in this.

She lifted her chin. 'You believed those things mattered to me? Titles and such? Is that what you thought of me? Why did you not speak with me yourself, Leo? You left without a word. Without a word. At first I thought it was because of the fire, but even then it shocked me that you would not come to me so we could plan what to do together. It took me months and months to realise that you had no intention of returning to me.' She felt as if she were bleeding inside.

His face turned stony, but she sensed turbulent emotions inside him. 'I was convinced you did not want me.'

'You were *easily* convinced, apparently. Did you think so little of me, Leo?' She slid away from him and crossed her arms over her chest as if this would protect her heart. 'Even if you thought all that nonsense about Ashworth was true, you did not try to fight for me, did you? Or try to make me change my mind? You never gave me a chance. You just took it upon yourself to run off.'

Her words wounded him, she could tell by his face, but they were true.

He spoke quietly. 'I am not running away now. I want to help you.'

She desperately wanted help, but not from him. The pain of his leaving her still hurt too much.

Her own father had manoeuvred the situation, true—she must deal with that later—but it was Leo who'd chosen to leave.

She stood and tied her mask back on. 'I want to go back.'

He rose and donned his mask, as well.

They entered the crosswalk that led back to the other side of the gardens. She took long deep breaths, trying to calm herself lest tears dampen her mask and give away her emotions. The closer they came to the supper boxes, the more she cringed at having to return to Kellford's side and to pretend to her father that he had not set about the destruction of her happiness two years before this. At the moment, though, it was worse to be with Leo. She was enraged at him—and perilously close to falling into his arms.

He'd held her many times when they'd discussed marrying, when they declared their love, said they would overcome all obstacles together.

She remembered when she'd learned his stables had burned down and most of his horses were lost. She'd read it in the newspapers. When her father told her Leo never showed up for his appointment, she'd imagined it had been because of the fire. She waited and waited until days stretched into weeks and weeks into months. She waited even after learning Leo had left the country. He would send for her, she'd thought.

But he never did.

He'd promised he would marry her, and now he promised he would find a way to prevent her marriage.

It was too late to believe in him. It hurt too much to be wrong.

She walked at his side, not touching him, her cape wrapped around her like a shield against him.

One good thing about his sudden appearance in her life was she now felt roused to battle harder against this forced marriage. She did not need him for it. All she needed was to remain single for two more years and her inheritance would be hers, free and clear. No man could use it to rule her life. No man could keep her from protecting her mother and sisters.

Her father told her he owed Kellford a large gambling debt, one so large that their family would be ruined if he did not pay. Apparently Mariel was payment of the debt. Or rather, her fortune was. How much of that was a lie, like the lies he told her about Leo? She wanted the truth.

Then she would know what to do.

It was a start. A plan. And her time was better spent dwelling on how to escape this dreadful marriage than on fantasies and regrets about Leo Fitzmanning.

They reached the arches; the supper boxes were just on the other side.

'Do not remain with me,' she demanded of Leo.

He seized her arm before she could leave him. 'I cannot let you go until you tell me what hold Kellford has over you.'

This was becoming tedious. Why not tell him? Perhaps he would leave her alone if she did.

She turned so she could look directly into his eyes. 'Kellford threatens my family. He has the power to ruin my father, my mother, my sisters.' She spoke the words slowly so he would not miss their importance.

'Mariel—' he began.

'No more promises!' She pulled out of his grip. 'Do not stop me again, Leo. This time I am the one who is leaving. Right now.'

Chapter Five

❧❧❧❧

Once again Leo watched Mariel walk away, her dark green cape billowing behind her as she hurried back to the supper boxes. Once again she'd shaken him.

By God, he'd been thoroughly duped by her father. What an elaborate ruse the man had created, complete with a special licence, a story about Mariel's absence and Mariel's cryptic note. Enough to convince the bastard suitor he'd been thrown over for a man with a title. Leo had fallen for it, without a single question.

The realisation was like a dagger in the gut.

He deserved Mariel's anger. He'd not believed in her. He'd run away without a fight, so ready to believe her father's lies.

The dagger twisted. He might have gained happiness. She would have been spared pain. If only he had not been so easily misled, so abominably weak.

He straightened his spine. Never would he show such weakness again.

The truth sliced into him. He was responsible for her suffering. If he had done the right thing two years ago, she would not be betrothed to Kellford now. By God, he vowed he'd fix that. Even though such amends would not bring back what he'd lost. What he'd foolishly tossed away.

He slowly walked towards the supper box.

What was it that Kellford held over Mariel's family? The key was her father, Leo guessed. The bloody liar. What had Covendale done this time for which his daughter must pay?

Leo would find out. He'd begin a search for the answer this very night. Judicious questions posed in certain gaming hells should yield answers. Few secrets were safe in gaming hells, where men made it their business to discover what others were hiding. Leo's secret, his once-betrothal to Mariel, had, thankfully, never seen the light.

Leo re-entered the supper box, where the masked and costumed guests continued to laugh and flirt and imbibe too much wine. He distinctly heard his sister Charlotte's laugh above the others. Dear Charlotte. She'd certainly inherited their parents' capacity for enjoyment.

Keeping his distance lest his sister recognise him, Leo watched Mariel sidle through the crowd and pick up a glass of wine from a liveried servant carrying a tray. She made her way to the table of food and positioned herself in a nearby corner. Leo found a spot where he could keep her in view without being too obvious. She'd noticed him, though, tossing him one annoyed glance before pointedly ignoring him.

Not more than two minutes passed before Kellford bustled his way to the food table and placed paper-thin slices of ham on his plate.

Mariel marched up to him. 'There you are!' she snapped. 'If you insist upon being my escort, you might at least have remained by my side.'

Kellford nearly dropped his plate. 'Miss Covendale.'

He made a curt bow. 'I have been searching the Gardens for you.'

She laughed. 'Searching the Gardens? Do you think me such a fool that I would leave the party? No woman would leave the protection of her friends to venture into the Gardens alone.'

'Are you saying you were not alone?' Kellford put on an affable smile, but his voice rose. 'Come now, you were not with another man, were you?' This was jokingly said, but one look at Kellford's eyes showed he was not amused.

Mariel waved a hand dismissively. 'Do stop talking nonsense. You know very well I remained here all the time. It was you who left the boxes. I saw you. If you do not wish my company, please have the courtesy to say so. Do not merely sneak away.'

Clever girl. Leo smiled.

She lifted her chin and walked away from Kellford, seeking out Charlotte, who was delighted to see her.

Kellford was left scowling in her wake, but his posture conveyed uncertainty. Her ruse had been successful.

But how many more times could she thwart him? Once married, Kellford would undoubtedly have no further need to charm her.

Leo kept his eye on Mariel the rest of the night while she continued to portray an indignant, offended woman whenever Kellford came near her. It was a brilliant performance. From time to time she caught sight of Leo, but, at such times, the displeasure on her face was not play-acting.

The next morning Mariel rose early and rang for Penny to come help her dress.

'Did you enjoy yourself at Vauxhall Gardens?' the maid asked as she pinned up Mariel's hair.

Mariel had had a miserable time, but there was no reason to explain that to Penny. Worse, she'd spent the night tossing and turning. Whatever sleep she'd managed had been filled with dreams of walking through the Gardens with Leo. They were lovers again. They were joyous.

Then she would wake.

'The Gardens were lovely,' she finally managed to respond.

'I'd like to go there.' Penny sighed.

Mariel smiled at her maid's reflection in the mirror. 'Do you not have a beau who would take you there?' With Penny's beauty, she ought to have several willing to be her escort.

Penny blushed. 'Oh, miss! There is no one I like that way.'

'Indeed?' Mariel was surprised. 'None of our footmen? Or the others who work near here?'

The girl shook her head. 'I…I cannot like their attentions. They look at me so strangely. Like a hungry cat looks at a mouse.'

This Mariel did not doubt. 'Well, some day perhaps you will find a man who is to your liking.'

Penny stilled. 'Is Lord Kellford to your liking, miss?'

It was an impertinent question for a servant to ask, but Penny spoke with so much concern that Mariel refused to chastise her.

'No,' she responded. 'Lord Kellford is not to my liking at all.'

'He is a bad man, is he not?' Penny went on. 'I heard what that other man said of him.'

Leo, she meant. They had not spoken of that day Leo walked back into Mariel's life.

Mariel nodded. 'Kellford is bad, indeed.'

'Who was the man who told you about Lord Kellford?' Penny asked, obviously emboldened by Mariel's confidences.

But Mariel could not explain Leo to her lady's maid. She could not explain Leo to anyone.

'Someone I once knew,' she said, as if it was of no consequence. She quickly patted her hair. 'Are we done here? I believe I'll wear my blue morning dress if you would fetch it, please.'

Penny curtsied and hurried over to the clothes press. They spoke no more of Leo.

After Mariel finished dressing she went to the dining room to see if her father was still at breakfast. The room was empty, although the sideboard was set with food. She bit her lip, hoping her father had not gone out.

The scent of sausages and muffins made her mouth water, but she did not stop to eat. Instead she hurried to her father's library and knocked at the door.

'Who is it?' she heard him say.

Relieved to have found him, she walked in. 'It is Mariel, sir.'

'Ah, Mariel.' He attempted a smile, but she knew he was not pleased to see her. 'What do you want?'

'I wish to speak with you.' She approached his desk.

He glanced down at his papers. 'I have much to do.'

'You may do it later.' It was difficult for her to be civil to her father. She could not forgive the situation he had put her in. Or how his lies had ruined her chance for happiness.

He balled his hand into a fist. 'Do not speak to me

again of not wishing to marry Kellford. You must do so and that is enough. Talk until you are hoarse. You still must marry him.'

'I do not wish to argue with you.' She attempted a mollifying tone, strolling to the bookshelves and pretending to peruse the titles. 'I want some information.'

He sighed. 'What is it?'

Why did you lie and trick Leo? she wanted to say. *Why did you send him away, believing I cared nothing for him? Why would you wish to cause me such anguish?*

Worse, why had Leo so readily believed you and not me?

Her legs trembled. She needed to confine herself to the problem at hand. It was too late to change what had happened two years ago.

Forcing herself to remain calm, she ran her fingers over the leather bindings of the books. 'I want you to tell me exactly why I must marry Kellford. How is it he can ruin us? What does he know?'

Her father's face turned an angry red. He looked down again and rattled his papers. 'That is none of your affair. Suffice to know we will all be ruined if you do not marry him.'

'But that will not suffice, Father.' She walked back to his desk and faced him directly. 'I want to know all. Whatever you tell me need not go beyond this room, but you must tell me the whole.'

He lifted his chin and glared at her. 'I need do no such thing. And I'll brook no further impertinence from you. I am your father—'

She held up a hand. 'And I am your daughter, the daughter you are giving away in marriage to a monster.'

Her father gave a dry laugh. 'Come, come. He is not a monster. He is a charming man.'

She leaned closer to him. 'You know all about Lord Kellford, Father. He follows the practices of the Marquis de Sade. That makes him a monster, correct?'

Her father turned pale and guilt shone in his eyes.

She met his gaze and held it. 'Tell me what this is all about. Tell me and I'll not argue with you about this ever again.'

He glanced away and carefully stacked his papers.

'Tell me,' she insisted.

He squirmed. 'I owe him money.'

She rolled her eyes. 'You owe everyone money.' He'd already sold her mother's jewellery. And hers and her sisters', replacing them with paste. He'd sold everything they had of value and mortgaged their houses to pay his gambling debts. 'What else is it?'

He lifted his head and stared with vacant eyes. 'He knows what I did.'

Her alarm grew. 'What did you do?'

He swallowed. 'I stole money from my cousin.'

'From Cousin Doring?' The wealthy Earl of Doring had paid off her father's debts several times.

'He would not give me a loan.' Her father wiped his face. 'I begged him. I had money lenders pressing me for payment. I was desperate.'

Money lenders? Had he sunk that low? Low enough to steal, apparently.

She blew out a breath. 'How much?'

He cleared his throat. 'A thousand pounds.'

'A thousand pounds!' He'd gambled away a thousand pounds? On top of the debts he'd already amassed?

'How does Kellford know you stole this money?' she asked.

He shrugged his shoulders. 'He was the one who sent me to the money lenders. I…I'd already confided in him that Doring would not give me the funds to pay. I fear he became suspicious when I paid the whole. Next thing I knew he'd discovered my theft.'

Her father embroiled himself with such despicable characters? Money lenders *and* Kellford? He was beyond foolish. A liar and a fool.

What difference if Kellford knew of the theft? Surely Cousin Doring would not want the scandal. They could strike a bargain with him.

She put her hands on her hips. 'Well, it seems to me it is Kellford's word against yours about this theft. I think we should go to Cousin Doring and confess the whole. I will write a promissory note to pay him back when I come into my inheritance.'

'It will not work.' Her father's shoulders slumped. 'My cousin has already told me he does not care if I go to debtor's prison. He said he did not care if I hanged. He washed his hands of me. He said I was never to darken his door again.'

'I will go to him, then.'

He shook his head. 'Doring told me not to send you, your mother or sisters on my behalf. He said you could not influence him any more than I could.'

'But if I made a promise to pay the money back?' she insisted.

'No.' His voice rose. 'If you tell him what I did, he'll have me hanged. He was that angry. You must believe me!'

The risk was too great not to believe him. The stakes were his life and, at this moment more importantly, the well-being of her sisters and mother.

She sighed. 'What exactly did you do? How did you steal the money?'

Her father drummed nervously on his desk. 'I forged a note on Doring's bank, giving me the money. Doring never looks that carefully at his finances. I thought he'd be none the wiser and his men of business would assume he was merely giving me money again.' He paused. 'Kellford has the note in his safe.'

'Kellford has the banknote?' Her skin turned cold.

'I do not know how he did it, but I have seen the note in his hands. He threatens to confront Doring with it— in a public place, he says—and openly accuse me of theft.' His expression turned bleak. 'I will hang!'

Worse, her mother and two younger sisters would be plummeted into scandal and poverty, and there would be nothing Mariel could do about it until she turned twenty-five. Isabel was fourteen and Augusta was sixteen, almost ready for her Season. What chances in life would they have if such a scandal were attached to their name?

Unless Mariel married Kellford. 'So you offered me in return for Kellford's silence?'

He shook his head. 'He wanted to marry you. That was the bargain he struck with me. Marriage to you and the paper would remain in his safe for ever.'

'Why would he want to marry me?' she cried.

Her father grimaced. 'For your inheritance, Mariel. Why else?'

Countless men had tried to court her, even during these last two years. Those men had been after her money, as well, but surely those men did not derive pleasure from inflicting pain and were not extortionists.

She trembled as she glared at her father. 'Do you know what you have done to me, Father?'

He raised his hands. 'I had no choice. Surely you can see that.'

She leaned towards him again and deliberately lowered her voice. Otherwise she might have screamed at him. 'You chose to gamble, Father. You chose to amass debts you could not pay. You resorted to theft and put your family in jeopardy like this. How could you do this?'

He'd ruined her life. If only he'd not interfered two years ago. If only he had not lied.

If only…

Leo padded in bare feet from his bedchamber, yawning as he entered the drawing room, then stepped back into the hallway.

'Walker!' he called. 'Are you here?'

'Mwa?' Walker staggered out of his room, still in the clothes he wore the previous day and with the ashen look of a man who'd bitten the jug. Two jugs, perhaps.

Leo peered at him. 'Where were you last night?'

Walker winced. 'Do not shout.'

'I'm not shouting.' Leo entered the kitchen. 'Do we have anything to eat?'

'Do not speak to me of food.' Walker pressed his hands against his head.

Leo emerged from the kitchen, munching on a piece of bread. 'I discovered something last night. Covendale is deep in debt. Gambles.' He took another bite of bread. 'I could not discover if he owes Kellford, though.'

'Stop chewing so loud,' Walker mumbled. 'Don't know about that. Kellford's in deep with money lenders, though.'

'What?' Leo was taken aback. 'How did you learn that?'

Walker slumped into a chair. 'Drinking. Followed his valet to a tavern. Got him talking.'

'Excellent.' This was why he valued Walker. 'What did you learn?'

Walker pressed his head again. 'The valet is unhappy. Hates Kellford. Gossips like a woman. I've discovered what you need to know, I believe. Even have a solution.' He grinned up at Leo. 'How would you like to again become a thief?'

Lord Kellford stood in the office of Mr Carter of Messrs Carter and Company, No. 14 Old Cavendish Street.

'Payment is overdue, Lord Kellford,' Mr Carter intoned.

It was a humiliation to be spoken to in such a tone. And to be required to beg. 'A month's time is all I ask.' Kellford favoured Carter with his most charming smile.

'A month is a long time.' Carter looked at him over spectacles worn low on his nose. The money lender dressed like any cit, in plain coat and trousers, devoid of the tailoring that would have marked him a gentleman. It was unconscionable that he held Kellford under his thumb, like an insect about to be squashed.

'I shall have to demand more interest,' Carter drawled.

Kellford kept smiling. 'Do not fear. I am marrying an heiress in less than three weeks. In four weeks I shall pay you in full.'

'At twenty per cent, Kellford.'

'At twenty per cent.'

Carter nodded and waved Kellford out of the office like some inconsequential underling.

Infuriating.

How he'd like to slice that man in two. No. No. Better to kill him slowly. Flail him with chains. Burn him with hot irons. Unfortunate they did not live in medieval times. Think of the pleasure of placing Carter on a rack and slowly turning the wheel.

Kellford crossed into the hall and walked out the door. As soon as he stepped onto the street, the skies opened up with rain. Perfect.

After receiving Carter's summons, Kellford had taken an ordinary hackney coach to Old Cavendish Street. It would not do for a coach with his crest to be seen waiting in front of a money-lender's door.

He was soaked to the skin by the time he reached the line of hacks awaiting riders. 'Take me to Charles Street, Mayfair,' he demanded of the first coachman.

He climbed in and settled back against the cracked leather seat, closing his eyes.

Only a few weeks more of this degradation. He abhorred kowtowing to a manipulative money lender. When the Covendale chit's inheritance was in his hands, he'd be free of the man.

And he'd have plenty of money to spare, which was as it should be. He deserved the luxuries of life.

And the pleasures.

She had angered him the previous night, making him look the fool for chasing after her in Vauxhall Gardens. After she had spoken her marriage vows, he would teach her not to make a fool of him.

Ever.

Until then, he'd play the devoted future husband. He'd make sure the *ton* all knew about the dinner he was hosting the next night, the one honouring his prospective bride and her family. Perhaps it would quiet her prickly nerves when he impressed her with the finest delicacies and wines.

He rubbed his chin. Knowing his betrothed had such spirit made him want to break her like a wild horse.

Tame her.

Chapter Six

Mariel sat at Kellford's right at the long table laden with every delicacy that might impress. Kellford, at the head of the table, urged his twenty guests to try each dish, and, as if he were a besotted lover, offered a toast to her, calling himself the most fortunate man in the world.

She inwardly scoffed. If he thought himself the most fortunate, then surely she was the least. The only good fortune he wanted was her inheritance.

Her mother, happily oblivious to Mariel's frightful situation—and her husband's if his misdeed came to light—giddily pronounced everything a delight. Her father's behaviour proved even more appalling. Gone was the miserable demeanour he'd adopted when confessing all to Mariel; he now laughed appreciatively at Kellford's attempts at humour and chatted genially to the ladies seated on each side of him.

The table included some impressive guests, making Mariel wonder how many of these titled men were fooled by Kellford's gracious facade and how many knew his true nature. Worse, were any of these men like him? Did their wives endure the horrors Leo had described to her?

Kellford continued to lay on the charm as thick as plaster on a wall. She supposed some would think him a handsome man with his fair hair and pale blue eyes; that is, if they ignored the expression of disdain in those eyes and the hint of cruelty around his mouth. He was paying for this dinner on credit, she would wager. She'd be paying for it out of her inheritance, no doubt.

Not if she could help it, she vowed.

Although Mariel tried to avoid looking at him as much as possible, she watched everything else carefully. Impatiently, she looked for the opportunity she needed. The guests were busy talking and eating, the servants, serving. Now was the perfect time.

Damping down a flutter of nerves, she leaned over to Lord Kellford and spoke in a quiet, confidential voice. 'Sir, I fear I must use the ladies' retiring room.'

He looked perfectly solicitous. 'Are you ill?'

'No,' she replied. 'But it is a matter of some urgency.'

He glanced around at his guests as if assessing their reaction to their private conversation. The guests paid no attention to them.

The corner of his mouth turned up. 'Do you need for me to show you the way?'

'Not at all,' she assured him. 'I remember where it is.'

When she and her parents had arrived at Lord Kellford's town house, her mother requested a tour of the house, so Mariel knew precisely to which room she was headed.

She stood and addressed the guests. 'Please excuse me. I will return shortly.'

Most of them did not even trouble themselves to look up.

She exited the dining room in some haste and quickly found the room set up as the women's necessary. She went inside, but only long enough to find a lighted candle. Peeking out to make certain the hallway was empty, she tiptoed to the door of the library.

Her father had mentioned that Kellford kept the incriminating paper in his safe. Her father's safe was in the library, so it stood to reason Kellford's would be, too.

She opened the library door and stepped inside, closing it behind her.

Instantly she was seized from behind. She uttered a surprised cry and dropped the candle. Its flame was extinguished by the fall.

A man's hand covered her mouth. 'Be quiet. Do not make a sound.'

How could she mistake that voice?

'Leo?' she mumbled beneath his palm.

He freed her mouth, but still held her. 'Mariel?'

'What are you doing here?' she whispered.

Another man, dressed all in black and his face shrouded by a mask, stood behind the desk. Although there was a small candle in his hand, he almost blended into the shadows.

Leo's lips came very close to her ear. 'We have come for a paper incriminating your father.'

He knew about the paper? 'You are mad. The house is filled with people.'

'Perfect time to come.' His breath was warm against her cheek. 'Everyone is occupied.'

The other man turned back to the shelves behind the desk. Mariel's eyes adjusted to the dim light and she could see the man had found the safe.

Leo pulled her away from the door to a small alcove.

He loosened his hold on her. 'Why are *you* here? Are there others walking about?'

'They are all dining. I am alone.' She turned to face

him. 'Why are you searching for the paper? I've come for it, as well. What do you know about it? How did you learn of it?'

He, too, was masked and dressed in black. He held her closer, and the darkness felt like a blanket around them. Her heart skittered.

He murmured into her ear, 'You should know why. Never mind how we knew of it. You should not be here. What if Kellford discovers what you are doing?'

'He could hardly do worse to me than what I face after the marriage,' she retorted. He and his companion were risking far more than she. They would hang if caught. 'You have obviously broken into the house. You are trespassing, Leo. And stealing. Have your wits gone begging?'

He held her so close their bodies touched and, in spite of the situation and her anger at him, her senses flamed. Feeling malleable as putty, Mariel found temptation to melt into his embrace become nearly irresistible. He again placed his lips near her ear, and she yearned to turn her head and place her lips upon his.

'I said I would help you,' he murmured. 'Leave it to me.'

Mariel trembled at the whirlwind of emotion and sensation coursing through her. The darkness of the room fuelled the illusion that they were alone.

The man at the safe put the candle down on the desk; the sound caused enough distraction to jolt her back to reality.

She strained against his arms. 'What will you do with the paper if you find it?'

He released her, but reached up to cup her face. 'Give it to you, Mariel. What else?'

Perhaps it was the darkness or the danger with which

they flirted, but he seemed to possess her with his touch, warm her with the sound of his voice. Her body ached to be held by him again.

'Mariel,' he murmured.

His hand still rested on her arm; his thumb gently rubbed her skin, creating wonderful sparks that flashed through her.

He drew her closer, leaning down so that his lips were near to hers. Memories flooded her, memories of stolen kisses, hidden from everyone's view. The impulse to close the scant distance between them and again taste his lips was hard to resist.

She forced herself to step away from him, out of the alcove to where she could feel chaperoned by the other man. He seemed to be putting keys in the safe's lock.

'Do you have a key that will fit the lock?' she asked Leo.

'Not a key. A set of lock picks.' He still spoke in whispers. 'How did you intend to open the safe?'

'I would have used a hairpin.'

He smiled for a moment, then sobered. 'You must go back, Mariel. Someone might come looking for you, then we will all be in danger.' He took her arm and led her back to the door. 'Meet me in the park at eleven tomorrow. The same place where we talked the other day. I will give you the paper then.'

'Yes.' Her heart gladdened. It would be over by tomorrow. She would be free. Impulsively she flung her arms around him.

He held her very tight, so tight she could feel the length of his body against hers. The ache grew stronger.

He released her and, his gloved hand firmly on her arm, walked her over to the door. Opening it a crack, he peeked out. 'It is safe to leave.'

She hesitated. 'The candle I dropped—'

He put his hand on her back, urging her on. 'We will take care of it. Go now.'

She slipped out and hurried down the hallway back to the dining room.

Leo stared at the closed door as if it would give him one more glimpse of her. Her appearance in the room had shocked him. Holding her in his arms, feeling her body against his, had sent his senses reeling. His desire for her was unabated, even if he had ruined long ago any chance of spending the rest of his life with her, loving her each night, waking beside her each morning.

The wrenching pain he thought he'd buried deep inside him burst forth anew. He felt doubled over with it.

And it was only worsened by the knowledge that he could have prevented it.

He glanced over at Walker, who was trying one pick after another. This escapade of theirs was fraught with danger, but Leo would do anything to save Mariel from Kellford.

Walker tried another pick. 'That's it,' he whispered. The safe door opened.

Leo walked over to him. 'Let us have a look inside and be quick about it.'

His hopes rose. Kellford's garrulous valet had told Walker about the paper. They were moments from discovering it.

Mariel would be free. She would be safe.

The next day Mariel told her mother she was taking Penny with her to shop for wedding clothes. Her mother detested shopping, but cooed with excitement at Mariel's apparent interest in the wedding.

'Purchase anything you desire,' her mother said.

Her poor mother. Had not the sale of her jewellery taught her she must practise economy?

As Mariel left the house, she turned to Penny, 'Let us hurry.'

'Yes, miss.' Penny sounded puzzled.

Mariel usually stretched out her time away from the town house for as long as possible.

When they reached Oxford Street, she turned left instead of heading towards Bond Street.

Penny looked around in confusion. 'Where are we bound?'

'To the park.'

Penny faltered. 'We are not going to the shops?'

Mariel waited for her to catch up. 'I must beg you say nothing of this. I am meeting someone. The...the man I met before.' She looked down on Penny. 'It is of great importance.'

Penny's eyes widened. 'Yes, miss.'

They walked through the Cumberland gate and down the same path where Leo had led them before. When they reached the alcove with the bench, Leo was already there, pacing back and forth. Her heart quickened at the sight of him, tall and powerful. The memory of his body against hers returned, filling her with a unique excitement. He did, indeed, look as if he could perform impossible feats such as saving her from Kellford.

He turned and caught sight of her, but did not smile. 'Mariel.'

A *frisson* of anxiety ran up her back. She spoke to Penny. 'Would you mind standing where you did before?'

Staring at Leo, the maid nodded and stepped away from the alcove.

'We must speak quietly, Leo. I do not wish her to hear.' She walked with him to the bench, but did not sit. 'Do you have the paper?'

His frown deepened. 'I do not.'

Trepidation replaced hope. 'You did not bring it? You promised me, Leo.'

He put his hand to his forehead. 'We did not find it, Mariel. There was no bank draft in the safe. No paper showing your father's name. It was not there. We searched the desk. It was not there, either.'

'No!' Tears stung her eyes. 'Then Kellford is still able to threaten my family? I am still in his clutches?'

He stepped forwards and enfolded her in his arms. 'No, Mariel. I will find another way. I promise you.'

The sensations of the previous evening when he had held her returned with full force. His arms enveloped her; his masculine scent filled her nostrils; his hard, muscular body pressed against her. Worse, she almost fell under his spell. She almost believed him.

The memory of how deeply she had once believed in him, trusted him, known in her soul that they would be partners for life, flooded her. How wrong she'd been! He'd walked away from her when she'd never have done so to him. She would have followed him anywhere, given up anything, even the inheritance that had now become an albatross around her neck. She'd believed they could face any trial, any tribulation, as long as they were together.

And he had abandoned her without a word.

Her spirits plummeted to rock-hard ground and she pushed him away. 'It is no use.'

'Miss! Miss!' Penny ran back into the alcove. 'There is a man in the bushes. He is eavesdropping!'

'Oh, no!' If anyone saw them together—heard

them—it could make matters much worse. They might make enquiries about her father. Or tell Kellford—

Leo caught her arm. 'Do not fear. He is with me.' He turned. 'Walker!'

The man emerged from the shrubbery.

Mariel swung back to Leo. 'You had someone spying on me?'

'Not spying.' His gaze was earnest. 'Protecting. Walker was looking out in case you were followed. Or in case someone strolled nearby.'

She glanced away. She'd gone from believing the best to believing the worst of him and she could not seem to help herself.

Leo's companion bowed. 'Miss Covendale, ma'am.'

'Walker is my valet,' Leo explained.

'Your valet?' Her suspicions returned. This man did not have the appearance of a valet. On the contrary, he was nearly as tall as Leo and even more muscular. His face had the battered look of a pugilist and there was nothing servile in the way he carried himself.

Leo cocked his head. 'For want of any other description, I call him my valet. I suppose if we had been in the army, he'd be called my batman.'

It suddenly dawned on her who the man was. 'Did we almost meet last night, Mr Walker?'

He gave a deferential nod. 'Very perceptive of you, miss.'

She returned the courtesy. 'You were the other man.' The man who had picks to open a safe's lock.

Walker's gaze drifted to Penny and held for a moment before he turned back to Leo. 'Did you tell her of your plan?'

Mariel's hope stirred. 'You have another plan?'

Leo gestured towards Penny. 'Do you wish your maid to hear this discussion?'

Mariel lifted a shoulder. 'She knows enough of this ugly business already. She may hear whatever you have to say.'

Leo waved a hand. 'The plan Walker refers to poses too much of a risk. You need not concern yourself about it.'

Mariel's eyes narrowed. 'It is my life that is at stake. And that of my family.' She lifted her chin. 'Tell me the plan, Leo.'

'Mariel.' Leo shook his head. 'The plan requires too much of you. It puts you in danger.'

She put her hands on her hips. 'Am I not in danger already? Do me the courtesy of including me in any discussion of what might save me from Kellford.'

His eyes flashed at her words. 'It is not a good plan. Too much can go wrong.'

'I thought it was a good plan,' Walker chimed in.

Mariel fixed Leo with a glare. 'Tell me of it and let me decide.'

'You might as well tell her, Fitz,' Walker said.

Leo flashed him an annoyed look, before facing Mariel again. 'The idea is for you to confront Kellford. Tell him you do not believe that there is a forged banknote. Ask him to produce it for you or you will refuse to marry him. Then you coordinate with Walker and me the time you arrange to meet him. We'll know Kellford has the paper and we will take it from him.'

It was a brilliant idea. 'Do you actually think he would agree to show me the paper? Would he not merely refuse?'

His eyes found hers. 'You would have to convince

him. Stand up to him. He needs your money. He will not be able to refuse you.'

She easily set her mind on it. 'I will do it. The risk means nothing to me.' Anything to free herself of this marriage.

John Walker's attention wandered away from the discussion between Miss Covendale and Fitzmanning. His gaze slid to the pretty blonde standing near him, the one who'd warned of his presence.

She must be Miss Covendale's maid, he decided, although being a mere maid seemed too confining for such a beauty. She reminded him of a portrait he'd seen in Florence, a painting of timeless, ethereal beauty.

In addition to teaching him to read and write, Fitz had exposed him to such things as mathematics, science, literature and art. He'd easily perceived the usefulness of science and maths and literature, but art? What use was art? That Italian portrait taught him.

Like the portrait, this young woman had pale skin, huge brown eyes fringed with dark lashes, lips as pink as roses. Her thick, blonde curls were too luxurious to be contained by her bonnet.

His throat grew dry as he merely gazed upon her.

She turned to him and asked in a quiet voice, 'What are they talking about?'

Walker felt his cheeks burn at this scant notice from her.

He answered her in a low voice, 'Lord Kellford has a paper that would cause Miss Covendale's father harm. If we can take possession of the paper from him, she will not have to marry him.' He was surprised he could form so many words.

She turned away again, as if thinking on this, then

glanced back at him, her lovely brow furrowed. 'Will she truly be in danger?'

He took a step towards her, drawn to her as a magnet attracts metal. 'We will protect her.'

Her face relaxed and gratitude shone in her eyes.

He swallowed and extended his hand. 'I am John Walker.'

She put her small delicate hand in his. 'I am Penny Jenkins, Miss Covendale's maid.' She looked up at him with her wide brown eyes. 'Are you really a valet?'

He tried to smile. 'Among other things.'

'You do not look like a valet.'

He averted his gaze, well aware his appearance spoke of mean origins in the East End. He could hardly remember a time there when he had not needed to fight just to reach the next morning. Walker had yearned to escape. He had finally managed it, fleeing to the Continent and making his way to Paris. But he knew only thieving and fighting and nothing had changed but the city. Until Fitz happened upon a street fight, that is. Walker had been outnumbered and was taking a beating, but Fitz had come to his aid, fighting hard for a complete stranger. By the end of it one man lay dead and both he and Fitz were wounded. They'd gone to Fitz's rooms to recuperate. Walker never left. Fitz taught him to read and to think and to behave with decorum. Walker taught Leo how to survive the seamier side of life.

When Walker turned his gaze back to Miss Jenkins, though, he felt as if every sordid act he'd ever committed showed on his face.

She tilted her lovely head. 'I thought valets were all skinny men.'

His cheeks heated. Hers had been an admiring glance?

She transferred her attention back to her lady, who was at the moment listening to Fitz.

'We need a way for you to inform us of when and where the meeting will take place,' Fitz said.

Miss Covendale glanced over at her maid. 'Perhaps Penny can carry the message.'

Then Walker would see her again? His heart beat a little faster, but the young woman looked distressed.

'Do you object to that idea, Miss Jenkins?' he asked as Fitz and Miss Covendale continued talking.

Again her expression cleared. 'Oh, no. I am just so worried about her. I heard your employer say that Lord Kellford will hurt her. I cannot bear that thought.'

'Were you to go with her if she married?'

She shook her head unhappily. 'She will not allow it.' She lifted her gaze to him. 'But, if she marries Lord Kellford, somebody has to be there to help her. She cannot go alone.'

As if this sprite would be any match for Kellford's whips. More likely Miss Jenkins would merely become another of Kellford's victims.

Walker glanced over to Miss Covendale and Fitz. They dealt together as if she was a great deal more than an old family friend.

He asked Miss Jenkins, 'Do you know what there is between them?'

She shook her head. 'I do not even know who he is.'

'He is Leo Fitzmanning, the natural brother of the Duke of Manning.'

Her eyes widened and he assumed she would comment on Fitz's irregular birth. 'A duke's brother!' she exclaimed instead, clearly impressed.

'He is a good man,' Walker commented to no purpose.

What would this beauty think if she knew of *his*

birth? Walker knew nothing of his father. All he remembered of his mother was her leaving him alone at night in their dark, tiny room, with frightening sounds coming at him through the walls. He remembered her death, a slow, wasting ebbing away of her life.

Women in service might come from humble origins, but their employers demanded their reputations be unblemished. In comparison his reputation was a festering sore.

Like the Italian portrait, Penny Jenkins was something to admire from afar, not something he could aspire to possess.

Miss Covendale's voice rose. 'Penny, come. We are finished here.'

Fitz put his hand on Mariel's arm. 'You will send word to us?'

The way they looked at each other… Yes, Walker suspected something existed between them, something now fraught with complexity.

If Miss Jenkins looked at him with that same pent-up yearning, he would do anything for her.

Chapter Seven

After parting with Mariel, Leo and Walker took a path through the park to return to Leo's rooms on Jermyn Street. Walker, typically so alert, seemed preoccupied with watching his feet.

'Is something troubling you, Walker?' Leo asked.

His friend glanced up in surprise. 'No—no—nothing.'

There was much troubling Leo.

He was becoming more and more affected by Mariel with each moment he spent in her presence. She looked beautiful this morning in the fawn-coloured walking dress that highlighted her ginger-coloured eyes and chestnut hair. He knew that he had never stopped loving her, not even when he'd thought she'd rejected him.

His yearning for her now was nearly unbearable.

Sometimes he sensed the same yearning in her, but likely that was his own desire creating an illusion.

Not that it mattered. He'd changed in these last two years. He no longer wanted the things they'd planned together, a business the *ton* were bound to respect. He no longer cared what anyone thought. He wanted to be a success in his own eyes and to the devil with everyone else. Mariel still worried about her family being ruined and he could not deny that the disdain of society could ruin a woman's life.

Besides, she'd not forgiven him for leaving her—and well she should not, although he'd forgiven her the instant he realised it was his inconstancy, not hers, that had separated them. And to think now he was putting himself and Mariel at risk merely to protect the honour of her father, whose duplicity had already done irreparable injury to them both.

He'd prefer to solve the problem of Kellford alone, but in any event, he must resolve the problem quickly and keep Mariel safe. They should have conceived a plan to procure the incriminating banknote that did not involve her.

'Walker.' Leo's voice was harsh, as if Walker were privy to his thoughts. 'You should not have forced me to disclose that plan to Miss Covendale. I told you I wished to leave her out of it.'

Walker scoffed. 'How else were we supposed to find the paper? There's little more than two weeks before she's to wed the lout.'

They exited the park through the Stanhope gate and walked through the town houses to Piccadilly. When they reached Jermyn Street, a familiar figure walked towards them.

Leo's brother Stephen.

Stephen's face lit up when he saw Leo. 'Ah! How fortunate. I was disappointed not finding you at home.' He shook Leo's hand. 'Good to see you.'

Walker stepped back as befitted a valet.

'Hope you are well, Stephen.' Leo managed to sound reasonably glad to see his brother, although his emotions were so tied up with Mariel that the last thing he needed was a brother primed to come to his aid. 'Sorry to have missed your call.'

Stephen smiled. 'Nothing's missed. I'll go back with you.'

As they entered Leo's rooms, Walker said, 'Shall I bring some whisky, sir?'

Leo could use some spirits right now. 'Whisky, Stephen?'

His brother removed his hat and gloves. 'Delighted.'

'Have a seat.' Leo tried to sound cordial. 'I assume you have a purpose in calling upon me.'

By the time they were seated, Walker had produced a bottle and two glasses. He poured them each a drink and with a bow—as if he were a typical servant—he left the room.

'So, what is it, Stephen?' Better not to tarry.

His brother took a sip and raised his brows in appreciation of the flavour. 'I don't have a particular reason for calling, except to see how you are getting on.'

Leo was surprised. 'You are not going to try to give me new stables and an abundance of breeding stock?'

Stephen's expression brightened. 'Have you changed your mind?'

Leo put up a hand. 'No! Not in the least. I told you I am never breeding horses again.' That desire had truly passed.

Unlike his desire for Mariel.

Stephen settled back in his chair. 'So… How are you getting on?'

Leo sipped his drink. 'Splendidly.'

'Nicholas said you have been attending society functions.'

He'd been talking to Nicholas. Leo could imagine

their conversation. *How can we help our poor bastard brother?*

'Not many.'

'You are welcome to accompany Mae and me any time you wish. We receive almost as many invitations as Nicholas. I know he is refusing more of them now that Emily is getting closer to her time.'

Leo felt a stab of shame. Stephen's generosity was based on deep family affection. Leo understood that.

'I appreciate the offer.' He changed the subject. 'I trust Mae fares well? And the children?'

Stephen beamed. 'They fare excellently well…' Stephen went on to describe the latest antics of his children, whose lives Leo had almost entirely missed.

His nieces and nephews were a blur. He doubted he even had an accurate count. They were part of a world into which Leo did not fit.

'I say—' Stephen lifted his glass to his lips '—you ought to come visit us in Sussex. It would be like old times.'

Leo's days helping Stephen establish his stud farm had been productive ones and Leo had learned everything he'd needed to know to establish his own farm at Welbourne Manor. They'd been productive days, but it had been like living another man's life.

'We're only in town for the Season,' Stephen went on. 'I confess, I am eager to return.'

Leo raised his glass in a toast. 'To Sussex.'

Stephen's horse farm, smelling the stable smells, hearing the stable noises, touching the horses—that was a part of Leo's past. He'd moved on to explore and conquer new worlds and experiences. He'd grown in strength and character and wealth as a result. He experienced deep satisfaction over devising an investment scheme, carrying it out and having it succeed. His associates were in trade, trafficking and manufacture, hardly acceptable in the world in which he'd grown up.

The world that included Mariel.

Leo downed the rest of his whisky and stared into his empty glass.

'Leo?' Stephen's voice jarred him back to the present.

'Sorry.' Leo cleared his throat. 'Was I wool-gathering?'

Stephen looked at him with concern. 'Does something trouble you? Does it have something to do with why you wish to re-enter society?'

'I told you before—all of you—I am not *troubled*. There are no problems you need fix for me. It is time for me to re-enter society, that is all.'

Stephen persisted. 'Are you in the market for a wife?'

'No!' he snapped, then made himself laugh. 'Good God, no. I'm not ready to be leg-shackled.'

Stephen smiled. 'You say that now, but you will change your mind when the right woman comes along.'

Except she already had come along—and Leo had deserted her.

Stephen finished his drink and stood. 'I should be on my way.'

Leo stood, as well. He and Walker had some preparations to make. It would not be the first time they'd planned an ambush.

At the door, Stephen shook his hand again. 'Let me know if you need anything. Anything at all.' He held Leo's hand longer than necessary and gave him a direct look. 'It is good to see you, Leo. I am glad you are back.'

Suddenly Leo missed those days at Welbourne Manor when he and his brothers and sisters were free to laugh and play and enjoy life.

His brother crossed the threshold and stepped into the street. A moment later he was gone.

That afternoon Kellford called at the Covendale town house, as was expected of a betrothed gentleman. It would not be all tedium. He anticipated and rather relished another sparring match with his spirited heiress.

He'd driven his phaeton—Tilbury's latest design and the height of fashion, he was told. Having the best was important to him, even if he did not care a whit about horses or carriages.

Leaving his phaeton in the hands of his groom, Kellford knocked upon the town-house door. He was admitted by a footman and escorted to the drawing room where Mrs Covendale and her daughter were taking tea.

'Kellford, my dear boy, how good it is to see you,' Mrs Covendale chirped, extending her hands to him from the sofa where she sat, a piece of embroidery at her side.

'You look as lovely as ever, my good lady.' He leaned down to give her a kiss on the cheek, before turning to her daughter in a chair nearby. 'And you look quite fetching as well, Miss Covendale.'

The mother tittered. 'My gracious, you are to marry her, Kellford, you may call her Mariel.'

An honour Miss Covendale had not yet granted him. He smiled at her as if she'd not given him a slight. 'Only with your permission, my dear.'

Her face conveyed no emotion. 'Whatever pleases you, sir.'

He laughed inside. She had no idea what pleased him, but she would soon learn.

'Mariel it is, then.' He bowed to her.

'Please do be seated, Kellford.' Mrs Covendale patted the space next to her. 'Have a cup of tea with us and tell us whatever news you have heard in town.'

He sipped tea and regaled the mother with various bits of gossip he'd heard, thinking all the while that he would have preferred to marry into a titled family. Mariel, the mere granddaughter of a second son, was quite a bit below him, but she would have to do. Still, she was presentable, she was a challenge and, most of all, she would make him very rich.

He was fully cognisant of the fact that she did not want to marry him, but that did not trouble him over-much, not with a fortune as large as she would provide. It had been a stroke of luck when her father confided in him about his money problems. That information gave him what he needed to discover the man's crime and win the hand of this heiress.

She would eventually learn how fortunate she was to be married to a baron, but for now he would enjoy the challenge of winning her over. He was confident he could do so.

When he took his last sip of tea, he placed his cup on the table and addressed his reluctant bride. 'Mariel, my dear, I brought my phaeton and would derive great pleasure in taking you for a turn in the park.'

It was the fashionable hour and he rather wanted to be seen with her, to show the *ton* he had won the heiress, to rub their noses in it.

She stared at him, with that impassive expression of hers, before answering, 'Very well. Give me a moment to change.'

A short time later they pulled into Hyde Park and found a space among the other fashionable carriages circulating the paths. With his liveried groom standing on the back footboard, Kellford trusted his equipage showed to good advantage.

He had to admit that Mariel looked equally impressive in her dark blue carriage dress.

He greeted everyone he saw and was gratified to receive their admiring glances.

Eventually the crush of carriages thinned and there were fewer people to impress.

'Shall we leave the park, my dear?' he asked, glancing over at her.

To his surprise she replied, 'Not yet. There is something I wish to discuss with you.'

'My pleasure.' His interest was roused.

Her face turned deadly serious and she lowered her voice. 'My father told me that you have in your possession a banknote that proves he improperly appropriated money from his cousin.'

Kellford lifted his brows. Her father had told her of the banknote? How foolish of him. The man should have kept his mouth shut.

She blinked. 'Well, do you have the paper or not?'

He smiled. 'I have it, never fear.'

She shifted in her seat. 'How do I know you are not bluffing?'

He simply stared at her.

She glanced away and back. 'How do I know this is not some elaborate ruse to force me into marriage and to get your hands on my inheritance? For all I know you may have merely heard some piece of gossip and embellished it.'

She dared to question him?

His smile stayed fixed. 'Trust me on it…' he paused '…or not. It is your father and your family who will pay the consequences if you are wrong.'

Her smile matched his own. 'Or it is *you* who pays the consequences if I am right. Can you hold off your creditors until you find another heiress to coerce?'

He gripped the ribbons and his face flushed with anger. 'What do you propose, then? You want proof that your father is nothing better than a common thief?'

'That is precisely what I want,' she shot back. 'I want to see this banknote you claim to possess. I want to hold it in my hands and convince myself it is genuine and not a forgery.'

'Forgery?' he huffed. 'It is your father who commits forgery, not I!'

Her gaze did not waver. 'No, your crimes are extortion and—and—other offences.'

He forgot about the horses and seized her arm. 'You impertinent chit! You will be sorry for this!'

A tiny flash of fear appeared in her eyes. It aroused him.

She straightened. 'Take your hand off me or I shall scream. Your groom might be trained to ignore me, but there are others near enough to hear.'

A quick glance behind him revealed other carriages approaching. He opened his hand, retrieved the ribbons, flicking them to signal the horses to increase their pace.

'Will you show me the paper, or shall I break our engagement?' she persisted.

He collected himself. 'Very well.' He put on an ingratiating smile. 'I will bring it to the ball tomorrow night.'

'No.'

She dared to disagree with him?

She explained, 'It is too public a place. If this paper is real, I will not have anyone else discovering its contents.'

He feigned solicitousness. 'Shall I bring it directly to your father's door, then?'

She shook her head. 'My mother must know nothing of this. A private place, I think.' She glanced around the park. 'There.' She pointed. 'That bench over there. Meet me there at seven tomorrow morning.'

'Seven tomorrow morning?' His voice rose.

She might as well have said to meet her at dawn. Was she fancying this to be some sort of duel?

'No one will be about at that hour and it is but a short walk for me from my house.'

'Very well.' He could not believe he was allowing her to dictate to him, but she had guessed one thing correctly. He could not afford to have her cry off. Mr Carter and the other money lenders would refuse him more time, high interest rate or not.

They reached the Cumberland gate. Kellford did not even ask her if she wanted another turn in the park. He was eager to be rid of her. He drove her to her house and escorted her to the door.

Before she went in, he seized her arm once again. 'I will see you in the morning.' He spoke it as a threat.

Once safe inside, Mariel leaned against the door, taking deep breaths to stop her shaking. She'd done it! She'd convinced Kellford to bring her the paper and, even more, she'd matched wits with the man again and won. It felt extremely gratifying.

Perhaps she could succeed in ridding herself of the man and his menace to her father after all.

Perhaps she could simply rip up the paper once he placed it in her hands. Leo and his valet did not have to risk being caught as thieves.

That would be a better plan, she thought, but there

was something more satisfying about working together with Leo, even with his valet and with Penny. She quite liked the camaraderie of it all.

Besides, she would feel secure knowing Leo and Mr Walker waited in the shrubbery, just in case Kellford turned menacing, as he had today. No, she would proceed with the original plan. She was no longer alone in this.

Mariel giggled with excitement. She'd even managed to point to the exact spot Leo had suggested for her to meet Kellford.

She pulled off her gloves and ran up the stairs, removing her hat as she entered her bedchamber. Penny was not there. She pulled the bell cord and undid the buttons of her spencer and sat at her writing table to compose a note.

Penny arrived as she was finishing it. 'You rang for me, miss?'

'I have the note for you to deliver to Mr Fitzmanning, Penny.'

The girl's eyes widened. 'You arranged a meeting with Lord Kellford?'

By now Penny had overheard enough so that Mariel had filled her in on almost all the details of her situation—except those of her father's crime.

And Mariel's past history with Leo.

'They must receive it today.' She folded the envelope and sealed it with a wafer. 'Because I am meeting Kellford in the morning.'

Penny took the note and placed it in her pocket. 'When shall I deliver it?'

'As soon as possible, I think,' Mariel responded. 'But help me dress for dinner first.'

As Mariel changed into a dress suitable for dinner,

she was glad that Penny knew as much as she did. It had been so lonely handling everything by herself.

One worry nagged at her. She might adhere to the plan, but would Leo? He did not like this plan. He might take matters into his own hands somehow. Could she truly count on him to work with her?

He'd failed her once before….

Chapter Eight

Penny rushed out of the servants' entrance and hurried to the line of hackney coaches on Oxford Street.

'Jermyn Street, please,' she told the jarvey.

His brows rose and she felt herself blush. Did he think she was bound for some tryst? He was wrong!

She climbed in the coach and leaned back against the seat.

Hers was an important errand, one that might mean life and death to her lady.

When Penny had been little and living with her parents above the glove shop in Chelsea, she could often hear through the wall when their neighbour, Mr Baker, beat his wife. One day Mrs Baker's cries abruptly stopped. Her husband had killed her!

That must not happen to Miss Covendale.

So it was very important to bring the note to Mr Fitzmanning.

Penny was not sure what to think of Mr Fitzmanning. He seemed like a very formidable man and always upset Miss Covendale so. Something very bad must have happened between them in the past. Penny wished she knew what it was, but that was wrong of her. It was not her place to be curious about her lady's private matters.

She did already know a great deal. It was a very great privilege to be taken into her lady's confidence like she was. It was a great honour to be trusted with the important task of delivering the note to Mr Fitzmanning.

Would she see his valet?

Probably not, because valets usually stayed near bed-chambers. Lady's maids did, too. Mr Covendale's valet was a fussy little man who didn't like her at all. He was nothing at all like Mr Walker.

Mr Walker's face scared her a little. Not because it was ugly, though, because it wasn't ugly. He did have some scars and a broken nose, but that wasn't why, either. She only knew that she felt funny inside when she looked at him.

He stared at her like Edward, the footman, stared at her, but for some reason, it did not feel bad when Mr Walker did it. Maybe it was because Mr Walker looked sad.

She gazed out the window and saw that they were on Bond Street, not far from Piccadilly. Too nervous to even think any more, she watched out the window, counting the shops they passed, holding her breath when they turned on to Piccadilly at Burlington House.

When the hack turned onto Jermyn Street and stopped, Penny climbed out and paid the jarvey the two shillings Miss Covendale had given her. As the hack drove away, she walked slowly down the street until she came to the right door. Taking a deep breath, she knocked.

Mr Walker opened the door. 'Miss Jenkins.'

She curtsied, although she thought maybe she should not have, because he was a valet. 'Miss Covendale sent me with a note. Is—is Mr Fitzmanning at home? I must give it to him.'

Mr Walker's surprised expression remained fixed on his face. 'He is not at home—'

'Oh, no!' What was she to do? 'I am supposed to give the note to him.'

The man froze for a moment, then collected himself. 'Please come in, Miss Jenkins.'

She entered into a small foyer that led directly to a sitting room. The room had nice chairs and sofas and tables—nicer than she'd grown up with—but it did not have any decorations, except a mantel clock.

'Do be seated.' Mr Walker extended his hand towards the sitting room.

She did not know if she should or not. 'Will Mr Fitzmanning return soon?'

'I do not know.' His face had that sad look again. 'You may wait for him if you wish.'

She nodded and sat in one of the chairs as if she were the gentleman's invited guest. She patted her pocket, re-assuring herself that her precious note was still there. 'I did not expect you to open the door.'

His forehead creased. 'You did not?'

'Mr Covendale's valet would think it beneath him to open the door.'

He glanced away.

She feared she had injured his feelings. 'He is a very snooty man, though.'

He almost smiled and it made her heart skip beats. He stared at her as he had the day before and she fixed her gaze on her hands.

Just when she thought she would die from her dis-comfort, he asked, 'May I bring you some refreshment? Tea…or something?'

'Me?' She glanced up. 'Wouldn't Mr Fitzmanning think it improper?'

He laughed. 'Fitz would not care.'

'You call your gentleman Fitz? He's your employer!'

He shrugged. 'It is an unusual situation.'

She scrutinised him. 'Where are you from, Mr Walker? You do not talk like you look.'

He lowered his head. 'I owe that to Fitzmanning. He taught me to read and made me desire to improve myself in all ways.'

She did not know what to say to that. It was to his credit, surely.

He glanced away again and was silent. Penny examined the walls, as if there was something to see hung on them.

Finally Mr Walker spoke again. 'Is the note about a meeting with Kellford?'

She nodded. 'I must give it to Mr Fitzmanning today, because it says the meeting time is tomorrow morning.'

'Tomorrow morning?' His brows rose. 'Not much time.' He rubbed his chin, then quickly composed himself again as if the gesture had been too unseemly. 'You may leave the note with me, Miss Jenkins. I will make certain Fitz sees it.'

There was a knock on the door.

'Has he come?' She jumped to her feet.

Mr Walker rose more slowly. 'He would not knock.'

He crossed the room to the foyer and opened the door.

Penny heard a woman's voice say, 'Good day, Mr Walker. Is Leo at home? We have brought him something.' The woman did not wait for a reply but walked straight in, followed by a gentleman carrying two large, flat packages.

The woman—a very pretty lady—stopped suddenly when she spied Penny. Her brows rose.

Mr Walker closed the door. 'Mr Fitzmanning is not at home.'

The lady's eyes remained fixed on Penny. 'Oh?' She turned to Mr Walker. 'Do you remember me, Walker? I am Leo's sister, Mrs Milford.' She gestured to the gentleman toting the packages. 'Mr Milford.' She turned back to Penny. 'Who is this?'

Penny executed a quick curtsy. 'I am nobody, ma'am. Merely delivering a note from…someone.'

Walker approached. 'I was about to take the note from the miss, ma'am.'

Penny gave it to him and looked up into his eyes. 'You will see to it?'

'I will indeed.' His voice lowered just a bit and his eyes—very nice eyes, actually—were quite reassuring.

'Well.' Mrs Milford untied the string around the brown-paper wrapping. 'Let me leave these with you for my brother.'

The packages were about four feet wide and three feet high and Mr Milford rested one edge of them on the floor while his wife unwrapped them.

'Oh, they are paintings!' Penny exclaimed, then clamped her mouth shut.

Mr Milford smiled. 'My wife's paintings.'

The first one was of a grand house on a river. It was made of white stone that shimmered in sunlight. The second was a portrait of a man.

'It is Mr Fitzmanning!' Penny cried.

Mrs Milford did not seem to resent her outburst. 'I have long wished to give it to him.'

She removed the rest of the paper and her husband rested the paintings against the wall.

She gazed at them with an assessing eye, before turning to Mr Walker again. 'Would you please tell Leo how sorry we are to have missed him?'

'I will indeed, ma'am.' Mr Walker bowed.

'I must go.' Penny rushed to the door before she spoke out of turn again.

Mr Walker went after her and opened the door.

Before she walked out, she turned back to him. 'Thank you, Mr Walker,' she murmured.

He bowed slightly as if she were a lady. As if she were somebody important.

She curtsied in return and stepped out to the pavement. A carriage was outside, its driver holding the horses. Mr Milford's carriage, she supposed. A soft rain started to fall and she had forgotten to carry an umbrella. Surely her bonnet would be ruined and her dress would not be fit to wear to the servants' table for dinner.

She walked quickly to Piccadilly where she hoped to find a line of hackney coaches. A carriage stopped and blocked the way for her to cross the street.

Mrs Milford leaned out the carriage window. 'Miss Jenkins, may we take you to your destination?'

'Oh, no, ma'am,' Penny responded. 'I couldn't accept.'

'Of course you can,' the lady insisted.

She opened the door and Mr Milford extended his hand to assist her inside.

She did not know how to refuse. She climbed in and sat on the rear-facing seat.

'Where shall we drop you?' Mr Milford asked.

She thought before responding. 'Oxford Street.' It was better this lady did not know she was bound for Hereford Street.

Mr Milford leaned across her and opened the little window to tell the driver.

The carriage started and Mrs Milford looked at her so hard Penny squirmed in her seat.

'Your hair, your complexion, are lovely, Miss Jenkins. I wonder if you would allow me to paint you?' the lady asked.

Penny felt her cheeks burn. 'Oh, I could not do that, ma'am.'

She was relieved when the carriage reached Oxford Street. 'I can get out here.'

Penny ducked into a shop until their carriage drove out of sight.

The morning was thick with mist as Leo and Walker, dressed in workmen's clothes with masks at the ready, concealed themselves in the shrubbery near the spot where Mariel was to meet Kellford.

Leo still could not like placing her in this situation. Kellford was a dangerous man. He was bound to be angered by Mariel confronting him. If the man lashed out at her here, Leo and Walker would make short work of him, but what if Kellford saved his retaliation for a later time?

Mist crept through the trees, lending the scene an eerie quality which did nothing to allay Leo's foreboding. The day did not promise to be a fine one. Leo only hoped the rain would hold off until Mariel was back safe in her house.

A footfall sounded on the gravel path. Mariel appeared through the mist, wearing the same dark green hooded cape that she'd worn at Vauxhall. Her step was determined, her posture courageously erect. His heart swelled with pride for her.

Mariel had once been a daring little girl, the first to respond to a challenge or propose an adventure. Charlotte was her willing follower, Annalise more likely to impose good sense on the two of them. Even as a boy Leo had had a grudging respect for Mariel's pluck. Two years ago he'd fallen in love with it. Their courtship had been a daring adventure, as swathed in secrecy as Mariel was now swathed in her cloak.

She did not pace, merely stood still as a statue, waiting. The mist melted away from her skirts as if she'd willed it to disappear. Sunlight broke through the trees to illuminate her, standing strong and determined. Leo wanted to signal her that she was not alone, but if Kellford was near, he might hear.

The crunch of gravel signalled the man's approach. Mariel turned towards the sound, and, a moment later, Kellford appeared, swinging a walking stick.

'Mariel, my dear.' He spoke as if this was a friendly tryst.

'Sir,' Mariel replied curtly. 'Do you have the paper?'

Kellford laughed with apparent good humour. 'Come, come, my dear. Is that any way to greet your betrothed?'

Mariel's spine stiffened. 'No nonsense, if you please, Kellford. No one is here but you and I. There is no need to act out this farce. If you have the paper, show it to me. If you do not, I'll bid you goodbye and you may consider yourself a free man.'

Kellford's smile grew stony.

Leo glanced at Walker. Both men were poised to spring to Mariel's aid.

'I have the paper.' Kellford stepped closer to her. 'But what is your hurry?'

She stood her ground and Leo imagined her eyes flashing in anger. 'I dislike being in your presence, as you well know. And I do not relish spending a great deal of time alone in the park.'

He moved even closer, his walking stick tapping ominously on the ground. 'Now, now, my dear. You must become accustomed to my company. We will be together often after we are married. Allow me to show you how pleasant it will be.'

Leo's muscles tensed.

'Do not be tiresome, Kellford.' Mariel's voice was impatient. 'Show me the paper.'

'The paper...' He paused as if calculating his next move. 'My dear, you must believe that I am as eager to protect your father as you are. Otherwise I would do my duty and report his crime, would I not?'

'And lose the chance to gain my fortune?' Mariel folded her arms across her chest.

'Well, a favour such as mine towards your father cannot go unrewarded, can it?' He chuckled. 'Surely you see the logic in this.'

She tilted her head. 'Perhaps my suspicions were correct. You are simply bluffing. This paper is a mere figment of your imagination.'

His smile turned cold. 'Are you prepared to see your father hanged if you are wrong?'

She looked him directly in the eye. 'Are you prepared to lose my fortune?'

To Leo's amazement, Kellford backed away, laughing as if she'd said something very amusing.

Kellford stuck his stick under his arm and reached into a pocket inside his coat. 'When we are married, I shall have to teach you how to honour and obey.' He drew out a folded paper.

Mariel reached for it.

'No, no.' Kellford wagged a finger. 'Not so fast, my dear. Let me unfold it.'

He unfolded it and gazed at it himself before turning it towards Mariel.

Again she reached for it.

He snatched it away. 'You may read and not touch.'

'I wish to hold it in my own hands to examine it,' she insisted.

'Why?' His voice turned hard. 'So you can rip it up? Now who is being tiresome?' His smile vanished. 'Come closer and examine it. You may even touch it with one finger, if you must.'

She did as he said, bringing her eyes close to the paper.

Kellford went on, 'You will see, of course, that it is a bank draft signed over to your father. You will also see that it appears to be signed by his wealthy cousin. The signature is only an approximation of Doring's signature, as is very evident when compared to other documents he has signed.'

She examined the paper in an unhurried manner. Leo admired her steadfastness. Surely it must be unnerving to peruse the object of her father's ruin, but she gave no sign of it. If her hands came too close to the document, Kellford moved it away. If she had indeed planned to rip it up, he gave her no opportunity.

'Are you satisfied now, my dear?' Kellford changed his tone to a patient one.

She straightened, facing him with a direct look. 'We are done here, Kellford.'

Without another word she turned and walked quickly away. Kellford leaned on his stick, watching her with an amused expression. Leo glanced at Walker to ensure his readiness. Simultaneously they donned their masks.

Kellford let out an exultant laugh as he refolded the paper and put it back into his pocket. As if he had not a care in the world, he strolled on to the path leading out of the park, jubilantly swinging his walking stick.

Leo and Walker had already scouted the area, finding the best place to make their move. From the shelter of the shrubbery they beat a parallel course to the appointed spot, reaching it ahead of Kellford. He made it easy for them to anticipate his approach by whistling as he walked.

As he took a step past them, Leo sprang from the bushes and seized him from behind, pulling his upper arms behind his back so tightly he could not move them. Walker jumped in front of Kellford, snatching the walking stick out of his hand and tossing it aside.

'See here!' Kellford cried, but Walker stuffed a handkerchief in the man's mouth, muffling further sounds.

In a swift economy of movement, Walker emptied the contents of Kellford's pockets, finding his coin purse and, of course, the incriminating paper. Just as swiftly, Walker placed them in his own pockets. Last of all he ripped Kellford's watch fob from its chain, the timepiece with it.

While Leo continued to hold Kellford tight, Walker produced a cord with which he quickly tied Kellford's feet. Leo forced Kellford's hands together and Walker bound them with another cord.

Then they fled, hearing Kellford's enraged but muffled cries behind them as they ran.

The entire attack, made to appear like an ordinary robbery, took less than two minutes.

As soon as they were out of Kellford's sight, they removed their masks and stuffed them in their pockets. Their escape took a zigzag route, eventually re-entering the park and crossing it to exit at Hyde Park corner. From there it was a short walk back to Leo's rooms.

On their way they passed a one-armed, one-legged beggar in a tattered soldier's uniform. He held out his hat and pleaded, 'A ha'penny for a poor old soldier. Surely you gentlemen can spare a ha'penny.'

Leo grinned at Walker. 'Surely we can spare *something* for an old soldier.'

Walker threw Kellford's coin purse, his watch and fob into the beggar's hat.

Leo leaned down to the man and said, 'Take care in fencing the watch.'

Leo and Walker quickly walked away, hearing the beggar's astonished cry as they turned the corner.

Chapter Nine

After Mariel rushed away from Kellford, Penny helped her sneak back into the town house.

'Your parents are still sleeping,' Penny whispered as they climbed the stairs to Mariel's bedchamber.

As soon as they closed the door, Penny asked, 'What happened, miss? Did he meet you? Did he bring the paper?'

Mariel nodded, breathless more from belated nerves than from running back to her house. 'He showed me the paper.'

Penny clapped her hands. 'And did Mr Fitzmanning and Mr Walker steal it from him?'

Mariel pulled off her gloves and her hat. Penny skipped forwards and took them from her.

Mariel wrapped her arms around herself, trying to quiet her skittering heart. 'I do not know. I did not see any sign of them and I left the area quickly.'

She'd stood as quietly as possible at the meeting place, hoping Leo would somehow let her know he was near, but she heard nothing, saw nothing. Not knowing for certain that they were there was the hardest part.

She'd started wondering if they'd come to their senses and decided it was foolish to risk their necks.

Surely Leo would not have allowed her to be alone in the park with a man who relished hurting women, but a single sound, a whisper, a whistle, anything would have reassured her.

'How will Mr Fitzmanning tell you he stole the paper? Is he to meet you somewhere?' Penny apparently did not question whether he had come.

But she was still young, much younger than Mariel had been when her ill-fated romance with Leo took place—and ended with so much pain.

How could Mariel believe in any man after Leo had abandoned her, her father had lied to her—so many times she'd lost count—and Kellford wished to exploit her? She hoped she was finished with Kellford.

She wanted desperately to believe in Leo this time, to believe he'd done as they'd planned together.

He'd once broken the most important promise he'd made to her. He had said he would marry her, but had so easily believed her father's lies. She did not know if she could ever trust again after that.

She swallowed the pain. 'I do not know when I will see him.'

'Should I deliver another note to him?' Penny placed Mariel's hat in its box.

Mariel ought not impose on Penny again, merely to appease her anxieties. 'No, we must believe he will contact me.'

How long would she have before she knew for certain what he'd done, before she knew for certain that he had not abandoned her again?

What would she do if Leo had not risen early and come to the park to act like a common thief? She'd played the best card she'd had, but success all depended upon Leo. Nothing was left but to simply refuse to marry Kellford and to hope he did not report her father's crime.

She pursed her lips. Likely he would derive pleasure from seeing her father hang and seeing the lives of her mother and sisters ruined.

To think her sisters were at the country house, blithely under the care of their governess, a dear woman whom her father probably neglected to pay. Her sisters were like she had once been. Carefree. Happy. Anticipating one excitement after another. Augusta would probably be chattering on about her come-out, hoping it would take place next year, although it would probably be delayed until she was eighteen, or never happen unless Mariel gained access to her inheritance. Isabel was probably thinking of little else but her horses, too expensive to keep if they were plunged into poverty. Poor Isabel. She was as horse-mad as Leo had been—

Must her mind always wander back to Leo?

She lowered herself into a chair and looked up at Penny. 'We will wait for him.'

That was exactly what she'd told herself to do two years ago. Wait for him.

Mariel was too restless to stay at home all day, simply waiting. After she had breakfasted with her mother and father as if she'd just risen from bed, she took Penny out to the shops.

They did more walking than shopping. Mariel treated Penny to an ice at Gunter's Tea Shop, to make up for dragging her up and down Old Bond Street.

When they returned from the shops later in the afternoon, Mariel had no choice but to sit with her mother and receive callers. Several of her mother's friends visited, asking countless questions about Mariel's wedding preparations and gossiping incessantly, especially about that scandalous Leo Fitzmanning who had attended the Ashworth ball the other night.

There was another ball this night at Lord and Lady Sendale's, a society entertainment promising to be more lavish, more fashionable than all that had come before. Mariel had not been looking forward to it.

At least not until Kellford sent a note to say he was unable to escort her. This had not happened before. Her first thought was that something had happened to Leo. Was it possible that Kellford had thwarted him? Or was Kellford's note a sign that Leo and Walker had succeeded? How would she find out?

Her heart suddenly beat in excitement. The ball! That was where Leo intended to contact her. At the ball.

When Penny helped dress her for the ball, Mariel found herself taking more care in her appearance than usual, choosing her prettiest white-silk gown, one Penny had altered to show off Mariel's bare shoulders as was the latest fashion. For a belt she tied a long scarf bordered in deep scarlet flowers. Its fringed ends nearly reached her hemline. Her headdress was also deep scarlet and adorned with one curling white feather.

When the ensemble was complete, both Mariel and Penny stepped back to examine it in the full-length mirror.

'You have outdone yourself, Penny,' Mariel said. 'I cannot think I've ever looked so well.'

'No credit to me, miss,' Penny responded, although she stood like an artist surveying her work. 'You chose the gown and the smaller articles of dress.'

'I felt like fussing a bit tonight.' Mariel smiled at her. 'You see, Lord Kellford is not attending. I do not mind looking my best.'

Penny's eyes grew large. 'He is not attending the ball? Do you suppose Mr Fitzmanning and Mr Walker gave him a black eye or some such thing?'

Mariel grinned. 'We can only wish.'

Penny nodded with surety. 'We will find out when Mr Fitzmanning contacts you.'

Mariel examined her image again, fussing with the belt and smoothing the skirt. It had been a long time since she had really cared about how she looked.

Since Leo had left her, she realised with sudden surprise.

When she and her parents arrived at the ball, Mariel's father lost no time in retiring to the card room. Mariel remained at her mother's side as her mother promenaded around the ballroom, greeting friends as if she'd not seen them in a millennium, although some had been her callers that very day.

Mariel engaged in the required social niceties, but mostly she anxiously scanned the room for one tall gentleman with dark, unruly hair and changeable hazel eyes.

Her mother interrupted this quest by insisting she tell one of her bosom beaux all about the wedding plans, as if she had any real plans. A church ceremony. A wedding breakfast. She cared about none of it.

The butler's voice rang out, 'The Duke of Manning and Mr Leo Fitzmanning.'

Mariel swivelled around, her heart pounding like a schoolgirl with her first infatuation.

His black formal coat and trousers contrasted with

the brilliant white of his neckcloth. While other men embraced the nipped-in waist and puffed-out coat sleeves that were the fashion, Leo's coat had an understated cut that somehow made him stand out from the others.

After he and his brother greeted the host and hostess, Leo turned and, as if he'd known exactly where to find her, their eyes met and the ghost of a smile appeared on his face.

Her heart leaped and her spirits soared to the ceiling. He'd succeeded! He was safe. She was free. She felt like running to him and throwing her arms around him. What gossip that would generate!

Slowly his gaze slipped away, reluctantly, she thought. She dampened the enthusiasm bursting inside her and watched him melt into the crush of guests. It did not matter that she lost sight of him. She knew he would seek her out again.

The moment brought back the days of their secret courtship—meeting without anyone knowing, dancing together without anyone guessing the emotions that blossomed between them. She almost felt as if those exciting, breathless days had returned.

Mariel heard a laugh she recognised as Charlotte's. A scan of the room located her one-time best friend on the other side of the ballroom.

She touched her mother's arm. 'Mama, I see Charlotte. Would you mind terribly if I went and spoke to her?'

Her mother waved her away. 'Amuse yourself as best you can without dear Kellford here.'

Mariel would be delighted to amuse herself forever without *dear* Kellford.

She wended her way through the crowd while the musicians tuned their instruments, the notes blending with the discordant buzz of conversation. She heard Wellington's name mentioned several times, but then he was the new Prime Minister and everyone delighted in speculating upon whether he would succeed or fail in his endeavours. Ireland was spoken of, as well. So much discord in Ireland; Mariel hated to think about it, tonight of all nights, when she was determined to be happy.

Finally she neared Charlotte, whose eyes lit up at the sight of her and who walked towards her with arms outstretched.

'Mariel!' Charlotte exclaimed. 'How lovely to see you.'

They clasped hands.

'It has only been a few days, hasn't it?' Mariel smiled.

Charlotte laughed and the sound lifted above all the other din. 'At Vauxhall! I am so happy to see you this evening.' She tensed and suspiciously searched the room. 'Where is Kellford?'

Mariel tried not to display her disgust of the man. 'Not attending tonight.'

Charlotte relaxed noticeably. 'Well, come join us. You may be part of our party tonight, if you like.'

'I would enjoy that above all things.' Especially if the party included Leo.

Charlotte took her arm, and together they walked to a group of more familiar faces.

'Mariel!' Charlotte's husband Drew kissed her on her cheek and turned to the gentleman standing at his side. 'Say hello to Amesby.'

Amesby squeezed her hand. 'How are you, Mariel?'

Amesby had been one of Leo's old friends, another horse-mad fellow.

His wife Mary stepped forwards. 'May I also say hello?'

'Mary!' Mariel was genuinely happy to see them all. 'My goodness, I feel as if we are at one of Welbourne Manor's house parties.'

Charlotte fanned herself. 'Except we would have more space in the manor's ballroom.'

Drew put his arm around his wife. 'We should plan a party there.'

Charlotte grinned. 'Yes! And get Nicholas to pay for it.'

As the group chatted together, Mariel searched for Leo again, glimpsing him at his brother's side. Everyone wished to talk to a duke. It took an age for them to work their way to her side of the room. She kept track of their progress.

'Nick! Leo!' Charlotte called to them as soon as they were close enough.

Leo walked directly over. Nicholas was detained.

Charlotte took Leo's arm and he leaned down to give her a kiss on the cheek. Mariel well remembered how his lips felt against her skin. She touched her cheek in memory.

'Look at us!' Charlotte exclaimed to him. 'We just said this might be a house party at Welbourne Manor.'

Leo's gaze lingered a moment longer on Mariel than on the others. 'Indeed. Good to see all of you.' He shook hands with Drew and Amesby.

Amesby's handshake was enthusiastic. 'It has been an age, Leo. It is a happy thing to see you back among us. I'd relish an opportunity to make up lost ground.'

'We must do so,' Leo replied.

He greeted Mary and, finally, Mariel.

'Good to see you again, Mariel.' His tone hinted at nothing.

'Leo,' Mariel managed, not quite erasing the expectation in her voice.

The orchestra quieted and the first dance, a quadrille, was announced, to be led by the host and hostess.

Amesby turned to his wife, a loving look on his face. 'Shall we dance, Mary?'

Her smile was his response. He took her hand and led her to the dance floor.

Drew turned to Charlotte. 'Shall we join them?'

Charlotte glanced uncertainly at Mariel. 'Are you engaged for this dance, Mariel? I cannot just leave you.'

'Of course you can!' Mariel shooed her off, but Charlotte was reluctant to go.

Leo stepped forwards. 'I will keep Mariel company.'

Charlotte and Drew hurried to join Mary and Amesby.

Mariel turned to Leo, knowing her complexion was bright. She told herself her anticipation had only to do with the banknote. 'Did you get it?'

Leo grinned. 'We did. It went without a hitch.'

She felt dizzy. 'I want to hear all the details. And we have to plan a way for you to give it to me. And I must have a safe place for it, as well—'

Leo took her hand. 'Time enough for that later. Will you dance with me?'

Mariel was ready to dance for joy—with Leo.

He closed his fingers around hers and led her to the gathering dancers, joining three other couples looking for a fourth. The other couples were as young as she and Leo had been when they'd fallen in love. The young people exchanged dismayed glances.

Leo laughed. 'Do not fear. We shall keep up.'

The music started and the figures were called. Mariel and Leo danced as if they, too, were young and full of gaiety. Twirling, skipping, performing the figures with as much enthusiasm as their younger partners.

They spoke little. What could they say where others could overhear? It did not matter. Mariel was almost too happy to speak. Leo had rescued her. She'd thought she was doomed to marry Kellford, but she was free! Leo had set her free.

They came together for a moment, and Leo asked, 'Where is Kellford?'

The dance parted them for a moment, before she could answer. 'He begged off. He did not say why. I wondered if he had become ill…or something.'

They parted again.

When they joined hands, Leo answered, his voice a monotone. 'He was well enough last I saw him.'

Mariel understood. They'd not injured him.

When Leo came close again, his eyes smiled. 'Of course, he was a bit tied up at the time.'

She laughed and put even more energy into the dance.

At its end she was out of breath.

'Shall I get you something to drink?' Leo asked.

'Please.' It felt marvellous to be on easy terms with him.

He walked her back to Charlotte, who seemed to take no special notice of her dancing with Leo.

His brother joined them and greeted Mariel warmly. 'You look lovely tonight, Mariel.'

She flushed with the compliment. 'Thank you, Your Grace.'

He made a face. 'I remember pulling your pigtails. It feels silly for you to call me your Grace. Nicholas will do.'

The Fitzmanning Miscellany, as others called them, always made her feel as if she were one of them, an honour few experienced. When Leo left for the Continent, she let herself grow distant from them, rarely seeing even Charlotte, who'd been her very best friend. The reminders of Leo had been too painful. Now being among them again felt like being with family, a feeling she did not have when she was with her own parents.

She could not be more content.

Leo handed Mariel a glass of champagne and sipped one for himself. A moment later Brenner and Justine joined them, along with Mary and Amesby. The Miscellany and their friends were together again, all except Annalise and her husband Ned, but they rarely attended functions like this.

It seemed wholly familiar to Leo to be with them all again, talking and laughing. Mariel's presence reminded him of earlier days, when he and she would pass each other secret glances across ballroom floors and eventually contrive to be alone.

Other guests were tossing less-than-approving looks at them, and more than once Leo heard the word *miscellany* spoken. This, too, was familiar. He knew how these conversations went. *Scandalous family,* someone would say. Another would gesture his way. *The bastard son.*

Not the duke. Not the duke's brother. Not the earl. *The bastard son.* Soon the whispers would be about all the scandalous things he was said to have done. His flight to the Continent merely fuelled what they wished to believe of a bastard—the worst.

They did not know the worst, however. They did not know how many times Leo had been tested in the last two years, how much violence he'd been engaged in, how hard he'd fought to stand on his own and succeed.

He was no longer a mere member of the Fitzmanning

Miscellany, no longer merely the bastard son. He had changed. He was separate from this privileged ballroom set. He was his own man.

But he danced and talked with the others as if time had not altered a thing. He watched Mariel smile and laugh, the cares lifted off her shoulders. She looked as if she were in her element. At ease with all these people who scorned him.

He had danced only one dance with her. Society dictated no more than two dances with the same partner. Break that rule and tongues would wag. In the past she'd always insisted they behave with utmost propriety. She had always been careful not to blemish her family name. In private, though, they'd shared many kisses, many embraces.

Today Leo cared nothing about what these toplofty people would think of him, but he'd play their game for Mariel's sake.

And he'd have his second dance with her. He'd make certain it was a waltz.

Eventually the two of them were left standing alone while the others had paired up for a mazurka, a new, fast, Russian dance brought to England by the Duke of Devonshire.

Leo seized the opportunity. 'Would you like to get some air?' he asked her.

The ballroom was stifling. No one would look askance if he escorted her to the open doors leading to the veranda, an unusual feature in a Mayfair town house.

Her gaze lifted to his. 'I would like that.'

She took Leo's arm and he led her through the open doors. Once they would have contrived to find the darkest spot in the garden where Leo could hold her in his arms and kiss her beautiful lips. This time he led her to a place on the veranda out of earshot of the other strolling couples.

'We can speak freely here,' he said.

She grasped his arm. 'Tell me what happened? I am perishing from curiosity.'

Her touch inflamed him, but he remained controlled. 'We trailed him until we had the opportunity to seize him and steal the paper.'

'Did he see who you were?'

He shook his head. 'We were disguised and masked. We didn't speak. There was no way he could identify us. The whole business was over in an instant.'

She released a pent-up breath. 'I do not know how I can ever thank you, Leo. It was a brave and foolhardy thing to do.'

This was more foolhardy.

The night breeze loosened a lock of her hair. He reached over and brushed the wayward curl off her forehead. 'I owed you that...and more.'

Looking into her eyes was like diving into a warm, sensuous pool, plunging deeper and deeper to the yearning in his soul. His hands slid to her arms, holding her in place, not an embrace, but tethering himself to her. She licked her lips and his grip tightened, bringing her inches closer, so close he could feel her breath on his face.

She sighed. 'I am so grateful to you.'

His fingers tightened around her arms.

'So grateful,' she repeated.

He wished time could be erased, that two years could vanish, that all he had done in that time period would not stand like a wall between them. All he wanted now was to take possession of her lips, to taste her sweetness once again.

'Mariel,' he murmured.

She rose on tiptoe.

Slowly, as if desire alone controlled him, he bowed his head and touched his lips to hers. Sheer will restrained him lest the violence of his emotions erupt, the grief for all the kisses lost in two years. She quivered in his grasp and wound her arms around his neck, pressing her lips to his with a hunger that matched his own.

With a low moan, he responded, parting her lips, tasting her tongue, pressing against her.

His entire body was afire, like the gas lamps in the trees at Vauxhall. Before, he'd been in darkness; now all was light. They were again among the stars.

Laughter sounded nearby. Another couple ascended the steps from the garden to the veranda and would soon pass near them.

He pulled away, his body still throbbing for her. They moved even deeper into the shadows.

'Forgive me for that.' He still held her arm.

'Forgive you?' her voice was breathless.

'So much has changed,' he managed to say. 'I should not have done that.'

A line creased her forehead. 'Why did you, then?'

Why? Because it had been impossible to resist her. 'I was caught up in…remembering.' The ache of still wanting her pierced his insides.

'Has so much changed?' she whispered.

'I have changed.' He'd turned away from everything that was familiar to her and entered a world of which she could not be part. 'I am not the same man. I've… I've lived a very different life these last two years and I cannot go back to what once was.'

'I see.' All expression fled her face. 'Well. I should be glad, then, that you thought to come to my aid.' Her tone was biting. 'We must plan a time for you to give me the paper, though.' She pulled away from his grasp. 'After that your job will be done.'

He set his jaw, detesting the loss of camaraderie between them and battling a need to possess her lips once more.

'I do not wish to meet in the park again,' she went on. Was she afraid to be alone with him, afraid of another moment like this one? 'Meet me at Hatchards Bookshop at eleven o'clock tomorrow. I will be browsing through the novels.'

'Hatchards at eleven,' he repeated.

'And take me back to my mother, please.'

He nodded. It was for the best he not mislead her. The life he had chosen, exciting to him, would certainly be censured by her world. He might be willing to take risks to achieve what he wanted, but he refused to place her in any more jeopardy.

He still wanted her, though.

But it was too late.

Lord Kellford stepped out from where he'd concealed himself near the door and watched Mariel and Fitzmanning leave the veranda.

He had decided to attend the ball after all. No sooner had he arrived than he'd seen Mariel walking through the doors to the veranda with Fitzmanning. He'd followed them, but was unable to move close enough to make out more than a word or two of what they said to each other, not enough to glean what had transpired between them.

Was the chit cuckolding him with the likes of

Fitzmanning? A mere bastard son? She'd soon regret it if she were. He'd be no man's laughingstock.

Then the word *paper* had wafted over the wind and it all became clear.

The chit had humbugged him.

Kellford could see it all in his mind's eye. She'd convinced Fitzmanning to steal the paper, Kellford was certain of it. *That* was why she contrived the meeting in the park. Everyone knew she was a great friend of the Fitzmanning Miscellany; she'd chosen its most disreputable member to do her dirty work. One of his brothers had probably been the cohort.

Fitzmanning. The bloody prig. Sticking up his nose about a mere frisk with a serving girl, as if anyone cared a whit about what happened to a tavern maid. Fitzmanning had taken a dislike to him ever since that time. A tavern maid, for devil's sake! Where did that compare to the robbery of a peer? The man's hypocrisy was not to be outdone.

Nor was Mariel's deceit. One thing was certain. She would not be allowed any contact with the Fitzmannings after the wedding.

And he would show her what happened to chits who aspired to outwit him. She thought she could stop this wedding? Deprive him of his fortune? Let her try.

She did not know the lengths he was willing to go to ensure she would never dare to thwart him again.

Kellford glanced through the doorway. Making certain no one saw him, he made his way to the hall, collected his hat from the footman and departed.

Chapter Ten

Near the time the ball would end, a waltz was announced. Leo crossed the ballroom to where Mariel sat at her mother's side.

He extended his hand to her. 'This dance, Miss Covendale?'

Her mother waved her on. 'Oh, do dance, Mariel. Try to have some enjoyment even though dear Kellford is not here.'

Mariel flashed him a wounded look, increasing his guilt for kissing her.

But he could not resist dancing with her one more time, sharing again with her that unspoken passion, that undeniable and impossible kinship between them.

They joined the circle of dancers. He bowed to her curtsy and placed his hands at her waist. She hesitated before resting her hands on his shoulders. As at Vauxhall they twirled through the dance, the circle turning like a colourful wheel on its axle.

His gaze remained steadily on her, but it took several turns around the ballroom before she met his eye. So many emotions were visible in her ginger eyes. Anger.

Confusion. Wariness. Need. He ought to be ashamed at himself for putting her through such discomfort.

One last time.

In many ways he had become the man he'd thought she had rejected, but it had freed him to become a man he could respect. They could not find their way back to each other.

When the dance was over they stood a moment longer, still caught in each other's eyes. It was Leo who moved his hands first. Mariel blinked rapidly before dropping hers off his shoulders. He walked her back to her mother and bowed. They'd not spoken a word the whole time.

After one more dance, which Leo sat out, the ball was over. A few moments later he was out on the pavement, waiting for the Duke of Manning's carriage, still several carriages behind in the queue. The cool evening air was welcome. Leo needed cooling off after his waltz with Mariel.

He still felt the light pressure of her fingers on his shoulders, still saw the struggle of emotion in her eyes. She was not unaffected by him. Her response to his kiss proved that. He could seduce her, he supposed, if he wished it, but seduction would be unconscionable. One thing was certain: he needed to keep control of himself whenever near her.

Like tomorrow at Hatchards.

While his brother engaged in conversation with other gentlemen, Leo paced the pavement, thinking of Mariel.

She'd fallen in love with a man who wanted to raise horses on his family estate and rear his children in his family home. Now he'd cast off the chains that bound him to the past and carved out his own future through daring and risky investment. The riskier the better.

He mixed with tradesmen who were little more than smugglers. He befriended men who defied government barriers to find ways to increase a profit. Many of his dealings were clandestine. This was not a life for her.

In only two years she would be wealthy and would be able to assume control of her life. He did not wish to jeopardise that for her, not when independence was what he most wanted for his own life.

His brother walked up to him and placed a hand on his shoulder. 'What troubles you, Leo?'

Nicholas gazed at him with intense concern. Would his brother never stop being protective?

'Nothing troubles me,' he responded. 'Why do you ask?'

'You were pacing.' Nicholas leaned forwards for emphasis. 'What happened at the ball? Your whole demeanour changed. At the beginning you seemed almost happy. Then something changed.'

Had Leo been that transparent? He must be more careful.

'I merely grew bored,' he lied.

Nicholas did not look reassured.

Their carriage arrived and both climbed in.

Leo took advantage of the distraction. 'You were in demand tonight. What was of such importance that everyone needed to speak to *the duke* about it?'

Nicholas hesitated a moment before answering, as if he knew Leo was merely changing the subject. 'There is a great controversy afoot. Ireland's in an uproar with riots and other discord. Wellington favours concessions to the Irish and Lords is divided on whether to grant the concessions or to oppose anything to do with Catholic Emancipation.'

Leo well understood why the Irish would despise another country controlling them.

He asked Nicholas more questions about the matter. They managed to travel the entire distance without his brother turning the topic back to Leo's behaviour at the ball.

The next morning after breakfast Mariel dressed to go out, but this time a plain brown walking dress would do, one she'd worn countless times. She had Penny merely pin up her hair and cover it with a lace cap. A simple bonnet would go over the cap.

Leo's kiss had unsettled her. Or rather her response to it had done so. It was so clear that she remained as vulnerable to him as ever. It had been devastating to her when he pulled away and apologised for it, calling it a mistake.

For a brief moment it had seemed like two years had vanished, but she'd misread him. He no longer wanted her.

She steeled herself. She'd survived the two years without Leo; she could survive another two years, inherit her money and be free of any man's influence.

That was her plan. No more kisses. No more giddy schoolgirl infatuation. No more pretending happiness lay in partnership with a man, or comfort in a man's arms.

Even if those arms were Leo's.

There was a knock at her bedchamber door. 'A caller, miss,' Edward, the footman, announced from the hallway.

A caller? So early? 'Who is it, Edward?'

'Lord Kellford.'

Mariel exchanged an alarmed glance with Penny.

'What shall I tell him, miss?' Edward asked through the door.

'Tell him... Tell him to wait in the drawing room. I'll be down directly.' She listened to the footman's footsteps recede before speaking to Penny. 'Wait for me in the hall, Penny. I will try to dispatch him quickly and still make the appointment with Mr Fitzmanning.'

Penny nodded.

Mariel's parents were still abed, which was fortunate. She preferred they not walk in on her hopefully short conversation with Kellford. What could he possibly want? She'd thought he'd simply disappear.

The two women descended the stairs and Mariel strode straight to the drawing room.

Kellford swung around when she entered.

She closed the door behind her. 'What reason do you have, sir, to call upon me at this early hour?' It was half-past ten.

He sauntered towards her, a grin on his face. 'Good morning, my dear.'

'You must know I am not pleased to see you, Kellford. Did you come to explain why you begged off from the ball last night?'

He advanced on her and drew a finger down the length of her arm. 'Did you miss me?' He held his lips close to her ear.

Involuntarily she inhaled his cologne, the scent sickening her. She stepped back. 'You know I did not.'

His eyes flicked over her, the smile still fixed on his face.

She shivered. 'I thought you would insist upon taking me to the ball. To gloat.'

The smile faltered, but he soon recovered it. 'Do not

take me for a fool, Mariel, *my dear*. I know what you did. What you had Fitzmanning do for you.'

A stab of fear shot through her. 'I am certain I do not know what you mean. Are you talking about Charlotte Bassington's brother?' Was he guessing or did he know?

He laughed. 'Did you think I would not remember she was your friend? Although I do not think her a very proper friend for the wife of a baron.'

'You cannot control whom I choose to make my friends.' Where was this leading?

He suddenly came so close she could see where his razor had cut his chin. 'A wife must honour and obey.'

She pushed against his chest. 'Stay a proper distance, sir!'

He grinned again and moved only a step away. 'I am all that is proper, my dear.'

She crossed her arms over her chest. 'And you are tiresome, as well. With your hints and threats.'

He lifted his hands in mock surprise. 'My hints?'

'You obviously wish me to beg you to tell what Fitzmanning is supposed to have done for me. Or do you just wish to contrive a way to threaten to spoil my friendship with Charlotte?' She tossed her head. 'I would simply prefer you leave.'

Instead he seized her and pulled her closer.

'Let me go or I shall scream for a footman!' His grip hurt.

'You will not.' He pressed his body against hers as Leo had done the previous night, but the sensations were so different. 'What did you promise Fitzmanning as payment? Money? A kiss?'

He placed his lips on hers with a violence that spoke nothing of love. She feared she would retch.

She tried to twist away, but his fingers were like a

vise. She struggled against him and managed to bring her leg down hard on his foot.

'You cursed wench!' He released her and staggered backwards.

'Do not touch me again.' She backed towards the door. 'I do not know what you are talking about. Payment? For what?'

He advanced on her again, but remained an arm's length away. 'Did you think I would not discover who stole the paper for you?'

Her insides churned. He could not know it had been Leo. He and Walker were masked, Leo had said.

'What paper?' she stalled.

'Idiot!' he snarled. 'The forged banknote.'

She made herself laugh. 'You are trying to make me believe you no longer have the paper? Why would you say such a thing? Surely you know I would be delighted if that were true...'

On the other side of the drawing-room door, Penny stood with her ear pressed against the wood. From the sounds inside the room, she thought Lord Kellford had attacked Miss Covendale in some way.

But then *he* cried out and her voice became stronger. Even if he was not hurting her any more, this was still very, very bad. Kellford knew Mr Fitzmanning had stolen the paper!

Penny felt she must do something. She could not open the door, Miss Covendale would not like that, but she also could not stand by and let that horrible man hurt her lady again. She must do *something*.

Penny ran back to the hall. 'Edward! Edward! Are you here?' He was supposed to be attending the door.

He emerged from the dining room. He had probably pilfered a piece of ham. 'What is it?'

'Come with me.' She dragged him by the arm to the door of the drawing room. 'You stand here and if you hear something that sounds like Miss Covendale is… is hurt or…or frightened, you open the door and help her. Do you understand?'

He looked baffled. 'But she is in there with Lord Kellford.'

'I know.' Penny tapped her foot impatiently. 'But do it just the same. If she comes out and asks for me, tell her I've gone to Hatchards.'

'To Hatchards?' His brows rose. 'The bookshop?'

She slammed her bonnet on her head. 'Yes. She will understand. Just do as I say, will you, Edward?'

'If you like,' he mumbled. 'Seems rummish to me, though.'

'Just do it.' She hurried back to the hall.

Penny departed through the front door because it was faster than the servants' entrance. As soon as she reached the pavement, she lifted her skirts and ran, stopping only for carriages and horses to pass so she could cross Oxford Street.

She ran to the hack stand and yelled up at the first jarvey. 'Take me to Hatchards and hurry.'

The jarvey chuckled. 'First time anyone wanted me to hurry to a bookshop.'

Once inside the coach, she stuck her hand in her pocket and breathed a sigh of relief. She had two shillings for the fare.

The mile-and-a-half ride seemed much too long. When the coach finally stopped in front of the bookshop's bowed windows, Penny jumped out and handed the driver his fare.

Standing in front of the shop's door, she took a deep breath and smoothed her skirt before walking in. The clerk behind the counter eyed her suspiciously. He had probably worked out she did not shop in Hatchards very often.

She wandered around the shop until she saw Mr Fitzmanning gazing into one of the books.

She hurried up to him. 'Mr Fitzmanning, sir!'

He looked up. 'Penny, isn't it? Where is Miss Covendale?'

'Oh, sir, she could not come, because Lord Kellford came to call and I heard them arguing and I heard him say he knew you sto—' She stopped and lowered her voice to a whisper. 'He knew you stole the paper.'

'He could not!' He stiffened.

'I heard him say so…and…and I heard him do something to Miss Covendale. I think he hurt her.' She tried to talk quietly, but her voice kept rising on its own.

'Hurt her?' His eyes flashed.

'Well, she hurt him, too, I think,' Penny went on. 'He cried out awful bad. But I thought you should know right away, because she could not come to this meeting.'

He took her by the arm. 'I'm going to her.'

'Oh, no, sir, I do not think you ought—' But she could not finish because he rushed her out of the shop, to the surprised stares of the other shoppers—including Mr Fitzmanning's sister, Mrs Milford.

Leo had difficulty tolerating the slow pace of the hackney coach. When it reached Hereford Street, he opened the door and climbed out before the vehicle fully came to a stop. After helping Mariel's maid from the coach, he dropped several coins in the jarvey's hand.

If Kellford had hurt her, he'd kill the man and his

conscience would not bother him any more than the first time, the only time, he'd taken a life.

'I'll not knock,' he said to the maid. 'You admit me.'

She reached the door and opened it. He followed her inside.

A footman stood in the hall. 'There you are, Penny.' He gaped at Leo. 'What is this?'

'Never mind, Edward.' Penny waved an impatient hand at him. 'Why are you not standing at the drawing-room door?'

'His lordship left a few minutes ago,' Edward said defensively.

'Where is Miss Covendale?' Leo demanded.

The footman's eyes grew wide. 'In the drawing room.'

Leo rushed directly there, opening the door without knocking.

Mariel sat on a sofa, her head in her hands. She sat up. 'Leo!'

Penny entered the room behind him. 'He was set on coming, Miss—'

Mariel turned to her. 'Thank you, Penny. You may leave us alone.'

Penny curtsied. 'Yes, miss.' She walked to the door.

'Oh, Penny?' Mariel called her back. 'Warn us if my parents are about.'

'Yes, miss.' She left and closed the door behind her.

Leo crouched down to meet her at eye level. 'Are you injured, Mariel? Did he hurt you? If he did, I'll—'

'He didn't hurt me.' She rubbed her arms.

He moved her hand away.

Red marks, the shape of fingers, ringed her upper arms. By day's end they'd be purple bruises.

'That cur!' His blood boiled.

'It is of no consequence, Leo. I did worse injury to him.' She squeezed his hand. 'I must tell you. He has discovered you stole the paper.'

'He could not. It is a bluff.' Their disguises had been complete. 'You did not admit to the theft?'

'No, of course I did not.' She released him. 'I acted as if I believed he made it all up. But, Leo, he says he does not need the paper. He says he has the bank clerk. He's hidden the bank clerk away somewhere.'

The bank clerk. The only witness to Covendale's theft. What arrangement had Kellford made with this clerk? Had he promised the man money? Or was Kellford threatening him, as well?

It was not finished after all. 'I must find this man, Mariel.' Whatever Kellford had offered the man, Leo would offer more. 'Leave it to me.'

'There are only two weeks left.' She covered her face with her hands.

Leo moved to sit beside her on the couch. He put his arm around her.

She allowed him to hold her close and, for a moment, he cared about nothing but comforting her.

'He frightened me, Leo,' she said. 'He is a monster. I cannot bear to marry him, but I also cannot bear what will happen to my mother and sisters if I do not.'

The clock on the mantel struck the half-hour. Half-past eleven. Surely her father or mother would be up and about soon.

'Let me talk to your father, Mariel.' This time Leo would make the man heed him. 'I'll offer to help him.'

She sat up and wiped her eyes with her fingers. 'It would be no use. My father is convinced his cousin will see him hanged.'

He lifted her chin. 'Do not lose courage. Let me try to convince him otherwise.'

Leo and Walker would find the bank clerk. Leo wanted Mariel's father to be on their side when they did.

'Stay out of it, Leo. Kellford will exact revenge on you as well as on me and my whole family. He was so angry. Who can tell what he will do?' Her voice trembled.

He stood. 'I can take care of the likes of Kellford.' He touched her face. 'I'll send word to you.'

She nodded, tears forming again. She rose from her seat and wiped them away.

Even with nose and eyes red from crying, even in a simple lace cap, she looked beautiful. She had fended off Kellford by herself, brave girl. Leo admired her. No, not merely admired her.

He loved her.

He had never stopped loving her. He could run to the far reaches of the world—to China, Brazil, Africa—and it would not be far enough to change the fact that he loved her and would do anything for her.

Especially rid her of Kellford.

She walked with him to the drawing-room door.

When he placed his hand on the doorknob, she covered it with her own. 'Promise me you will not speak with my father,' she insisted.

Leo had no fear of meeting her father. In fact, there was much he wished to say to the man. Such as, how dare he come between them two years ago with his lies? And, now, how dare he sacrifice his daughter to save his own skin? 'Why should I not speak to him?'

'It will make it worse for me.' She looked so weary he did not have the heart to pursue the matter. 'Promise me, Leo.'

He blew out a breath. 'Very well. I promise.'

He opened the door, but turned back to her. 'The paper. I almost forgot.' He pulled the bank draft from his pocket and handed it to her. 'Hide it somewhere safe.'

She rolled it in her hand. 'I will.'

He gazed into her tear-reddened eyes and was tempted to draw her closer and share his strength with her. For a moment she moved nearer to him, but just as quickly moved away again.

He opened the door and walked out, not looking back.

He hurried to the hall, placing his hat on his head as he went. The footman, who had been standing with Penny in the hall, rushed to do his duty at the door. As the man opened the door for Leo, a voice from behind called after him, 'You, sir! Wait. Who are you?'

As Mariel had requested, Leo paid Covendale no heed. He exited the house and walked swiftly away.

Mariel had followed Leo to the hall to watch him leave, her head spinning in confusion. When they were together she felt powerfully attracted to him and it was so easy to melt into his arms.

It also seemed more and more impossible that he would be able to keep his promise to her.

Her father's voice sounded from the top of the staircase. Quickly she folded the bank draft and tucked it down the bodice of her dress.

He reached the bottom of the staircase. 'Who was that gentleman?' he demanded of Edward.

The footman kept his eyes averted. 'I do not know, sir. He left no card.'

Penny slipped behind Edward and hurried up the stairs.

'What was he doing here?' Mariel's father demanded.

Edward looked as if he was about to faint. 'I do not know, sir.'

Mariel stepped into her father's view. 'He called upon me, Papa.'

'You?' Her father turned to her. 'Who was he?'

'None of your concern, Papa.' She trusted he would not notice she'd been weeping. He never examined her that closely.

'See here, Mariel—' He seized her by the arm and led her away from the footman's hearing. 'I'll not have you speak to me in that tone, especially in front of the servants.'

She winced. His hand pressed into her bruises. 'You are hurting me, Papa.'

He released her.

She pointed to her arm, already turning blue. 'See this?'

'I didn't do that!' he cried. 'How did that happen? Did that man—?'

'No, not *that* man,' she retorted. 'Lord Kellford.'

'Kellford?' He squinted. 'He called, too?'

She nodded. 'He is fond of cruelty—or did you forget?'

His nostrils flared. 'Enough impertinence, girl. What mischief are you about having men call at all hours?'

She glared at him. 'You may be able to force me into this marriage for the sake of Mama, Isabel and Augusta, but I have something that will ensure you behave from hereafter.'

'I do not know what you are talking about,' her father huffed.

She looked him in the eye. 'I have the incriminating banknote in my possession. It will not be enough to stop Kellford, to my deep regret, but it will stop you from placing your family in such peril again.'

She pushed him aside and walked up to her bedchamber to find some place to hide the paper, a hiding place her father would never discover.

Chapter Eleven

Over a week passed and Mariel had heard nothing from Leo. She'd attended two breakfasts, a musicale and another ball and he'd been at none of them.

She'd assumed he would keep her informed, but again she was caught in the agony of not knowing where he was, what he was doing.

She thought she'd go mad.

Desperate for information about him, she decided to call upon Charlotte, something she had not done more than once or twice since Leo had disappeared the first time. The day promised rain, like the previous several rainy days, but that would not stop her.

When she was announced, both Charlotte and her sister Annalise were in the sitting room. Both women jumped up from their chairs and, squealing with delight, ran to her and exchanged hugs. Charlotte's dogs yapped excitedly at their feet.

'It is so delightful you have come,' Charlotte exclaimed.

Annalise squeezed her tightly. 'I have not seen you in an age. I've missed you so.'

'Let us sit.' Annalise sat with Mariel on the sofa. Charlotte pulled the chair closer to them. The two pugs leaped into her lap as soon as she lowered herself into the chair.

Mariel asked after their children and felt a pang of envy as the sisters caught her up on the children's ages and their latest antics. She'd once pined to have children.

With Leo.

'And you, Mariel,' Annalise said, her cheerful tone sounding forced. 'You are to be married, I hear.'

Charlotte's smile became wooden.

'In less than a week,' Mariel managed.

'How lovely,' Annalise said too brightly.

Charlotte stood. 'Come up to my bedchamber and see these new gowns I had made. They were delivered this morning.'

The two dogs ran along with them. Two gowns were draped across the bed—one a pale aqua, the other, rose.

'This V-shaped waist is to be all the rage, the modiste said.' Charlotte ran her finger over the seam. 'As well as the flounces on the skirt.'

'They are lovely.' Annalise laughed. 'I cannot believe my tree-climbing sister is prosing on about dresses!'

Charlotte poked her. 'I like to look pretty for Drew.'

As Mariel had once wanted to look for Leo. She had been right to stay away from Charlotte and Annalise. In their presence all she could think of was Leo.

'Where do you plan to wear the gowns?' she asked.

'I thought I'd wear one to dinner at Nick's tonight.' Charlotte fingered the cloth of one, then the other. 'If I can decide which one.'

'The rose,' her sister said. 'It will enhance your complexion.'

'Nicholas is hosting a dinner tonight?' Mariel asked.

Charlotte moved the dresses to a *chaise longue* in the room and climbed on the bed.

Annalise climbed up beside her. 'For the family. His wife is expecting, you know. She is due any day now and goes nowhere. She is starved for company.'

The pugs made several efforts to jump on the bed, to no avail.

Mariel picked up the dogs and handed them to Charlotte before joining her friends. 'Is everyone attending?'

'The whole Fitzmanning Miscellany.' Charlotte turned to Annalise. 'You should have been at Lady Sendale's ball. It was like old times, wasn't it, Mariel?'

Too much like old times, Mariel thought. 'Almost.' Her voice wobbled.

'Even Leo attended,' Charlotte went on. 'Although he was vexed about something at the end. Before that we were dancing like we were back at Welbourne Manor. Weren't we, Mariel?'

She'd danced joyfully with Leo at first. It was painful to think on their waltz together, though. 'Is Leo attending Nicholas's dinner?'

Charlotte threw up her hands. 'Who knows! None of us can make any sense out of what Leo does. I tell you, he's been quite erratic since the fire. We cannot talk any sense into him, and, believe me, we've tried.'

'I know what is wrong with him.' Annalise turned smug.

Charlotte squirmed to attention. 'What? Do tell us.'

'A woman.'

'A woman?' Charlotte laughed. 'It is about time. Drew and I have often said Leo needs to settle down.'

Mariel sat very still, as if even moving a finger would betray her pounding heart. 'Who?' she asked.

Annalise shrugged. 'I do not know precisely, but it

makes sense, does it not? A man involved with a woman always behaves oddly.'

Had Annalise seen her with Leo? Where? In the park? Impossible.

But Annalise must be speaking of her. Mariel might not know what progress or lack of it Leo was making in finding the bank clerk, but she was certain there was no other woman.

Not the way he had kissed her. Not how he had held her. Something else caused him to pull away.

'A mistress?' Charlotte cried. 'Leo? I should have known. It goes with his gambling and drinking and who knows what else he's been engaged in.'

Theft and burglary, Mariel thought. All terrible risks. For her sake.

Was he engaging in even more serious risks? Was that why she had not heard from him? The idea caused knots of fear to twist inside her. She had the right to know what he was doing. She needed to know. This was her problem and he should not shut her out. She was of a mind to march right up to his door and demand to know what he was doing for her.

Demand to see he was unharmed.

She could not call upon a gentleman herself, of course. She would send Penny with a note insisting that Leo meet her tomorrow. The park might not be a good idea. Rain was likely. Besides, who knew how tempted she would be if alone with him again?

Hatchards would do. Hatchards it would be.

Later that afternoon, between rain showers, Penny stepped from a hackney coach and knocked upon the door to Mr Fitzmanning's rooms, her insides fluttering, not from nerves but from expectation.

Maybe Mr Walker would open the door.

It was silly of her to be so excited about seeing him again. Even sillier that her thoughts so often wandered to him. While she was brushing out Miss Covendale's dresses or putting hairpins back into their silver box, he popped into her mind and refused to go away again. She'd never been a dreamy girl, not with losing her parents and having to go into service so young.

She did not know what to do with all these feelings about Mr Walker. How was she to stop thinking of him and start paying attention to her work again? She could not tell the housekeeper about this man. She would merely ring a peal over her head because she wasn't working hard enough. The other maids were likely to gossip about her and make it into something that would get her in trouble.

And it would not be at all proper to ask Miss Covendale what to do.

She knocked at the door again. Perhaps he was not even inside. She rocked on her heels, waiting, and lifted her hand to knock again.

He opened the door.

She gasped. His coat was unbuttoned and he wore no neckcloth. She could see his bare chest through the slit in his shirt, dark hair peppering it. His hair was dishevelled and his chin unshaved. He looked quite magnificent.

'Miss Jenkins!' He quickly buttoned his coat and moved aside for her to enter.

She stepped just across the threshold. 'I have a note from Miss Covendale.'

'Is anything amiss?' He ran a hand through his thick brown hair, only slightly taming it.

'I do not think so.' She looked up at him.

He gazed down at her, his expression confusing to her. She could not tell if it was admiring or disapproving.

He still grasped the doorknob. 'Fitz—Mr Fitzmanning—is not at home.'

He remembered their conversation about calling his employer Fitz. Who else thought her prattle worthy enough to remember? Except Miss Covendale, of course.

'I will give the note to you, then.' She fished it from her pocket and placed it in his bare hand.

His fingers brushed her glove as he accepted it. It made her feel all warm inside.

That confused her. She started to chatter, 'Miss Covendale wondered why she has not heard from Mr Fitzmanning for so long. There isn't much time left, you know, and she is worried.'

Mr Walker averted his gaze. 'We have been working on it. Fitz—Mr Fitzmanning—has been to Coutts Bank where the teller worked and he's spent a great deal of time in gaming hells trying to get information.'

'Are you helping him?' she asked. He said *we,* after all.

He nodded. 'My part has been to befriend Kellford's servants, particularly his valet. You can tell your lady that we believe we are getting close to locating the clerk.'

'Are you?' How very clever of them! 'She will like hearing it. I should tell her straight away.'

She took a step backwards as if to leave.

'Wait!' He cleared his throat. 'Will you wait for me to…to make myself more presentable? I will walk you back to your lady's house.'

She glanced outside. The rain looked as if it would

hold off long enough, and, if it did not, she carried an umbrella this time. She would much rather walk the mile and a half with Mr Walker than ride in a coach. Perhaps Miss Covendale would not mind if it took her a little longer to get back.

'I need the air and I would enjoy the walk…' he paused '…and the company.'

She turned back to him and smiled. 'I would like that very much, Mr Walker.'

That evening Leo planned to visit two or three gaming hells to see if any new talk about Kellford was circulating. Word was he was 'up to something,' but no one knew what. Tonight he hoped someone had discovered what it was. Walker was already out. Kellford's valet had arranged to meet Walker at the tavern where they had met before. Between the two of them they might be able to discover precisely where Kellford was hiding the bank clerk.

Leo crossed the room to leave when there was a knock at the door. He cursed. Who would call upon him at this hour?

He opened the door and the answer was obvious.

Brenner.

His eldest half-brother, his mother's legitimate son, stood in the doorway. 'Good evening, Leo. I've come to collect you for Nicholas's dinner party.'

Good God. It had slipped his mind completely.

He made a dismissive gesture. 'I cannot attend, Brenner. I have an important meeting.'

Brenner pushed past him and entered his rooms. 'You cannot mean that, Leo.'

He did mean it. Finding the bank clerk could be a matter of life and death for Mariel.

Brenner's gaze slid to Annalise's paintings still leaning against the bare walls. 'The family is already gathered at the Manning town house.' He glanced back to Leo. 'We are waiting dinner for you.'

They were waiting for him? How like them to be stubborn enough to wait until the food was unfit to eat and would be wasted and then blame him for it.

'That is ridiculous, Brenner. Surely one person should not hold up an entire dinner party.'

Brenner gave him a steady look. 'I agree. Come with me now.'

Leo threw up his hands. 'This is precisely the sort of pressure I despise. And you all excel at it. I have important matters to attend to, but that means nothing to you.'

Brenner's gaze remained steady. 'What important matters, Leo? We know something is troubling you. Tell us what it is.'

Could Brenner not conceive that there might be something he preferred not to share with his siblings?

Brenner's voice turned low. 'Perhaps we can help you. We all want to help you.'

Leo bit down on an angry retort. His siblings always assumed he could not handle his own problems without their advice and assistance. If he did talk with them about Mariel, they would merely explain to him all that he'd done wrong—as if he did not know—and then they'd get busy fixing it.

There was nothing they could do that Leo could not do himself.

He made himself return Brenner's gaze. 'Some things a man must do on his own.'

Brenner did not look away. 'A man also recognises when he needs help.'

Leo rubbed his temples, which had begun to ache.

'I'll attend the dinner with you.' He had no wish to hurt them. He'd go to the gaming hells afterward. They'd be open all night. 'But don't tease me further about this.'

The next morning Mariel waited by a shelf of novels at Hatchards Bookshop, paging through one volume of *Armance* as if she were considering the purchase of it.

She could not even see the words.

What if he did not come?

She steeled herself. If he did not come, would it mean he was hurt? Or in danger? Or—or imprisoned in New-gate? Penny had reported no such thing yesterday, but much could happen overnight.

How like two years ago that she had not heard a word from him.

She took a breath. What was she to do if—if Leo failed—what could she do to escape Kellford? She was going to be a wealthy woman in two years. Surely some-one would lend her the money to support her mother and sisters for two years.

But paying back what her father had stolen would mean revealing the theft and that meant her father's life.

If theft meant her father's life, it could mean Leo's, as well. What if he'd been caught in another theft or some such thing on her behalf?

'Mariel?'

His voice startled her. She snapped the book shut and turned, weak with relief.

His tall frame filled the space between the shelves and charged the air, making her senses tingle. He was definitely very fit, very uninjured.

'Is anything amiss?' His gaze was intense, his pos-ture taut, as if he were ready to march into battle for her. When he looked upon her that way, she could almost believe in him again.

She mentally donned armour. 'I meant to ask you the same thing. Is there anything amiss? I have heard nothing from you and it has been an age.'

He stepped closer. 'I told you to leave it to me. Walker and I have been working day and night to learn the whereabouts of the bank clerk.'

Penny had reported as much from Walker.

Mariel lifted a brow. 'And?'

His mouth slowly widened into a smile. 'And... We know where he is.'

They'd found the man? Mariel placed her hand on his arm. 'Where is he? Have you spoken to him? What does he want for his silence?'

He covered her hand with his own. 'We only know where he is. It will take some travel to reach him.'

'Where is he?' she cried.

'We must keep our voices down.' He glanced around, but there was no one in earshot. 'Kellford has a hunting lodge near Maidstone, not far from Marden Thorn. A day's ride by coach.'

She was still touching him and he, her, she realised. She pulled her hand away. 'When do we leave?'

'We?' He shook his head. 'You are not going, Mariel. Walker and I will go.'

Oh, no. She would not be left behind this time. They were in this together.

She opened her mouth to argue, but quickly shut it again. She knew him well enough—or thought she did—to predict he would merely dig in his heels if she pressed the matter.

'Very well.' She must be craftier than he. 'Will you ride? That would be fastest, would it not?'

'We will engage a coach. We'll have to bring the bank clerk back to London. A coach seems the most secure way. We should reach Maidstone in five or six hours on good roads.'

'You will have to leave very early.' She used a cautionary tone.

'The coach and driver will fetch us at six,' he assured her. 'We will have time if we need it, never fear. We'll find the clerk and be back with days to spare. You will see.'

He took her hand and squeezed it gently.

An ache grew inside her.

She believed he would do as he said, precisely as he had done since he first learned of her problem. But that episode in her drawing room had convinced her Kellford could be very dangerous. If Leo became imperilled, she was determined to be there to assist him.

She dropped her voice to a whisper. 'I am worried.'

He moved closer and leaned down as if he were going to kiss her. Nothing impeded her moving away from him. Except she could not.

His lips hovered inches from hers, but he retreated again. 'I will not fail you, Mariel. Trust me. Leave it to me.'

The word *trust* made her flinch. It was not Leo she mistrusted. It was Kellford.

Leo smiled again. 'I had better leave now. There is still much to do.'

Unable to speak, she merely nodded.

He hesitated a moment, as if reluctant, but then turned and walked away.

Mariel leaned her forehead against the bookshelf, trembling inside, wishing his mere presence would not affect her this way.

She straightened her spine and made her decision. When she walked out of the shop, it had begun to drizzle. She hurried to find a hackney coach and gave the driver the address.

A short ride had brought her to Charlotte's house. A few minutes later a footman escorted her to Charlotte's sitting room.

The two pugs ran to her as she entered. Charlotte, still in a morning dress, greeted her with outstretched arms.

'Mariel! I am surprised to see you again so soon.' She clasped both of Mariel's hands and was too kind to mention that it was unfashionably early for callers.

'I have come on an urgent matter, I'm afraid,' Mariel told her.

'Urgent?' Charlotte gestured for her to sit. 'What is it?'

The dogs jumped up and settled beside her.

Mariel swallowed. 'I need a favour and I could think of no one else to ask.'

Charlotte laughed. 'Well, I should hope you would think of me. What do you need?'

She faced her friend. 'I need you to lie for me.'

Charlotte's brows rose.

How to tell her? How much to tell her? 'I need to tell my parents that I am visiting with you for a few days. I—I need to go some place and I do not want to tell them where.'

Her friend's expression of concern looked so much like Leo's that it took Mariel aback. 'What is this about, Mariel?'

Mariel stood and paced. 'I—I do not wish to marry Lord Kellford, but, for reasons I cannot explain, I cannot merely cry off. I must contrive it so he no longer wishes to marry me. To do that I must go away.'

Charlotte leaned forwards. 'You do not wish to marry Kellford?' She breathed a relieved sigh. 'I am so delighted. I confess, I could not like him at all. Oh, I know he is charming, but—I cannot put it in words. He is not at all the husband for you. I will do whatever you need for me to do.'

Lord Kellford looked up as the man entered his library. 'Well? What information do you have for me?'

After witnessing Fitzmanning and Mariel together, Kellford hired a man to keep watch on Fitzmanning. Fitzmanning was up to something, Kellford was certain. He'd had it in for Kellford for a long time.

Hughes, an average-size, nondescript man, faced him. 'I have good information.' His posture was not at all deferential. 'But it will cost extra.'

'Extra?' Kellford fumed. 'I am paying enough already.'

Hughes shrugged. 'I had to add some men to follow Fitzmanning's servant.'

'A servant?' This was too much. 'What has a servant to do with a gentleman's business?'

'Pay more and I'll explain.' Hughes folded his arms across his chest.

Why not? In a less than a week he'd be a wealthy man—if he prevented Fitzmanning's interference. 'Ten pounds more.'

Hughes scoffed. 'One hundred.'

Ridiculous! 'Thirty.'

'Fifty,' Hughes persisted.

'Fifty,' Kellford conceded. He lifted a finger. 'But only if the marriage takes place. If you do not succeed in that, you will be paid nothing more.' He'd already secured the man's work with twenty pounds.

'That is the agreement.'

Kellford waved his hand impatiently. 'Well, get on with it. What information do you have?'

Hughes wore a smug expression. 'Seems that Fitzmanning's man has befriended your valet, who has told him that you are hiding someone at your hunting lodge in Kent. There is a carriage hired to take Fitzmanning there tomorrow.'

'My valet.'

That was good information, indeed. Worth fifty pounds and more.

Of course, his valet would regret having big ears and a loose tongue. He had no doubt eavesdropped on an early conversation with Hughes. Well, he'd be dealt with. Turned out within the hour and given no references. In fact, Kellford would pass the word that the man had stolen from him—which he had by stealing information—he'd never work again.

Kellford turned his attention back to Hughes. 'Leave today and remove our friend from Marsden Thorn.'

He wanted the bank clerk to be in London for the wedding anyway. Hughes would merely bring the man back a few days early.

Kellford leaned forwards. 'Then deal with Fitzmanning. Hire as many men as you need. I'll pay. I want you to stop his interference once and for all.'

Hughes gave an acquiescing bow.

Kellford went on. 'I do not care how you do it, but you must stop him. Do I make myself clear?'

'Fifty quid more and I'll guarantee it,' Hughes said.

Kellford took no time deliberating that offer. 'Agreed.'

Chapter Twelve

The next morning dawned fair, warm and clear, a perfect day for travel after the rains of recent weeks. Leo was glad of it. He'd promised Mariel to return in mere days, and he wanted to fulfil that goal, to stand before her and tell her the ordeal was finally over.

He and Walker had packed quickly, well practised in doing so after their travels throughout the Continent. Each had only a small bag, now resting by the door ready to grab as they went out.

Leo paced, trying to think of anything he might have missed that would affect their success. He worried a bit about leaving Mariel alone. Who knew what Kellford would do? Although the man would be a fool to do anything to ruin his chances with only days left before the wedding.

Walker sat by the window, his nose in a book.

'What are you reading this time?' Leo asked.

Walker did not look up. 'Plutarch's *Lives*.'

'Good God. You are reading that for enjoyment?' Leo remembered it from his school days.

'It is fascinating,' Walker said. 'All these brave, ancient men either overcame their flaws or perished because of them.'

Ah, that was it. Overcome or perish. Walker had made the choice to overcome his past, to leave his criminal days behind him. He'd merely required a little help in eliminating the shackles that imprisoned him in that life.

Now that he was out of it, there was no limit to what Walker could do, what he might become. He would not be a servant forever. Leo counted himself fortunate to have Walker as a friend and companion. He wondered how long before Walker needed to strike out on his own as Leo had done.

There was a knock on the door.

'The coach?' Leo glanced at the hall clock. 'It is early.'

'Must be. I heard it outside.' Walker closed his book and rose to cross the room to the door. He opened it.

'My God!'

Leo turned.

Mariel crossed the threshold, her maid behind her. Each carried a portmanteau. 'Good morning, Leo.'

'Mariel, what the devil?'

'We are accompanying you.' She placed her bag on the floor.

'The devil you are,' he said sharply. 'You cannot want this, Mariel. Your reputation will be ruined.' Her ruin was not his biggest fear. He and Walker were heading into danger. The clerk would be guarded, certainly. Kellford was no fool.

She laughed. 'Leo. My reputation is the least of my worries, as you should realise; however, to my parents and the world, I am visiting your sister Charlotte. No one will know I am with you.'

Damned Charlotte. Still ready to be talked into folly.

Walker approached the maid and took her bag. He nodded a greeting. 'Miss Jenkins.'

The maid lowered her lashes. 'Mr Walker.'

Leo glanced back to Mariel. 'You will hamper us.'

She waved a dismissive hand. 'Trust me to know when to stay out of your way.' She faced him, looking defiant. 'I'll not wait here in London without a word from you. I endured that two years ago when I did not know where you were, what you were doing—'

'Did you think I would leave again? Is that what you thought?' She ought to know by now he would not again desert her.

She narrowed her eyes. 'Have you not shown me already that you have no wish to be with me? I do, however, believe you will keep your word about helping me. But I intend to accompany you.'

Walker and the maid watched their conversation with raised brows.

'I refuse to allow you to accompany me,' he said tersely.

'Well.' She took a breath. 'I refuse to stay behind.'

'It might become dangerous, Mariel.' This was the crux of it.

'It cannot be worse than marriage to Kellford,' she countered.

Another carriage rolled to a noisy stop in the street outside.

She glanced out the open door at it. 'Enough talk. Let us go.'

She reached down to pick up her bag, but Leo grabbed it first. 'I could force you to stay.'

'You will not!' She tried to pull the bag from his grip.

He wrenched her bag away from her and carried it out to the carriage.

Walker picked up the other bags, including the maid's, and followed him. Mariel and Penny trailed behind.

The carriage was attended by a coachman and post boy. Leo handed Mariel's bag to the coachman who threw it up to the carriage's roof.

'Thank you, Leo,' Mariel murmured.

The post boy took the other bags from Walker.

Walker turned to Leo. 'I will ride outside. It will give you more room.'

'Miss Covendale,' the maid broke in. 'May I ride outside, too? It is such a fine day.'

'If you like, Penny,' Mariel responded.

Walker looked uncommonly grim as he climbed up to the carriage's roof and reached down to pull the maid up beside him on a seat behind the coachman. Leo assisted Mariel inside the carriage.

There would have been barely enough room for all four of them inside, Leo realised. As it was, he and Mariel could not fail to touch if seated side by side. He chose the back-facing seat, which meant gazing at her and brushing his legs against hers.

The carriage started and, as it made its way through the Mayfair streets to the Strand, Mariel stared out the window. She did not move even as they reached the Waterloo Bridge.

'Do we spend this whole trip in silence, Mariel? It will be five hours or more.' Leo asked. 'We once had more to say to each other.'

She slowly turned to face him. 'We did, once.'

'How many ways must I say I am sorry?' He knew

she would understand he was speaking about two years ago, nothing else.

The corners of her eyes etched in pain. 'You cannot know what you put me through.'

'I did not know at the time.' He'd thought she'd found a better man to marry. 'Even if I had gone to you, your father would never have approved our marriage. You would have lost your inheritance.'

'You knew that did not matter to me.' Her voice cracked.

'You would have lost respectability, as well, and that did matter to you,' he reminded her. 'Defying your father and losing your money would have created a scandal.'

'I did not care about scandal,' she insisted. 'Except for its effect on my mother and sisters. Besides, my father would have given in. I certainly know now that he would not have given up any potential source of money.'

But neither of them had known it two years ago.

He leaned forwards. 'You must understand. I had nothing to offer you. After the fire, I had nothing.'

Her eyes flashed. 'I did not know of the fire on that day. You thought I would marry someone else even before I could learn of it. I read of the fire in the newspapers. The newspapers, Leo!'

He sat back, averting his gaze.

She spat out her words. 'Why did you not let me share in the tragedy of your stables burning down? Did you not know how sad I was for what happened to you? How much I would have wanted to help?'

'There was nothing you could have done.' His muscles tensed. Ashworth had everything and he'd had nothing.

'You just went off,' she went on. 'You didn't allow

your family to help you. You never allow anyone to help you.'

He felt a knot tighten inside him. 'My family helped me. They bought Welbourne Manor from me.'

Her voice cracked. 'You know what I mean! Could you not have shared your pain with me? I thought we were to share everything.'

The desolation he'd felt two years ago returned now.

Her lip quivered. 'I do not blame only you. My father is the real villain. He decided what I should want and what I should do. You merely agreed with him.' She lifted her eyes to his. 'How could you have believed him?'

Leo shrugged. 'He was very convincing. He had the special licence with your name and Ashworth's on it. He said you and your mother were visiting Ashworth's estate.' He met her gaze. 'And he showed me your note.'

'My note?' She looked surprised.

'The one that said "Father will explain it all."'

Her face paled. 'I did not mean…'

He reached out to touch her hand, but caught himself in time.

'In any event,' he managed. 'Neither of us can change what happened.'

They fell into silence again.

Matters between them were so complicated, he did not know what to say to her. He had not meant to put any blame on her for what happened. She'd been wounded deeply. Not only by him but by her father. Leo accepted his responsibility. After the fire—after his failure—he'd been primed to believe she could not love him.

But he did not want this depressive gloom to remain

with them the whole trip. He tried changing the subject. 'How did you get Charlotte to agree to your scheme?'

She gave him a direct look. 'I asked for her help.'

That took him right back to her accusation—that he never asked for help.

He could inform her that he sought Walker's help all the time, but he suspected she would say that was different because Walker was in his employ. And he'd asked for Nicholas's help, hadn't he? Of course, he'd lied to his brother about why he wanted to attend society events. He suspected Mariel would have something to say about that, as well. Truth was, the last thing he and Mariel needed was his family taking over and making matters worse.

Although Leo had to admit, at the dinner two nights ago, his brothers and sisters made an effort to restrain their intrusive questions and offers of assistance. Their restraint caused nearly as much tension as if they'd plied him with litanies of what he should be doing and how they could assist him. Nothing was worse than people treading on eggshells around him, holding back all they wished to say and do for him. It was clear they thought he would make a mess of things if left on his own.

Mariel turned back to the window and Leo lowered his hat to shade his eyes. Did she view him in the same light? he wondered. Certain he would fail unless she kept watch?

He stretched his legs as far as possible. He'd had no more than a couple of hours of sleep the past two nights—that must be why he was thinking like a schoolboy instead of the man he'd become, a man who could handle himself very nicely.

He opened his eyes a slit, just able to see she'd turned back and was staring at him.

It was not likely he could sleep.

Walker lifted his face up to the sun beaming from the cloudless sky. They'd travelled out of the city into the countryside with its green fields and rolling hills that never ceased to awe him. When he'd been a child, he'd had no idea such places existed outside of heaven.

His gaze slipped to Miss Jenkins. If the Kent countryside was heaven, then she surely was an angel.

Had she chosen to sit with him or had it been the fresh air she was craving? He did not know, but he was glad to be at her side.

The carriage hit a rut in the road and dipped suddenly. Walker threw his arm around her, holding her securely in place. She turned to him, her eyes wide, her mouth forming an O.

He released her. 'I beg pardon, miss. I feared you would fall.'

'I did not mind. I was frightened is all.' She threaded her arm through his. 'Do you mind if I hold on to you, in case it happens again?'

Her touch aroused him, surprising him and making him feel ashamed. She was a respectable young woman, not the sort he usually lusted after.

She looked around her. 'Is not the country beautiful? I remember being so surprised at all the green hills and the trees and all in the country the first time I saw it.'

His eyes widened. It was as if she'd read his thoughts—or at least his non-carnal ones. 'When did you first see the country, miss?'

Her brow creased in thought. 'It was about a year

and a half ago when I was sent from London to be Miss Covendale's maid.'

'You grew up in London, then?' As he had. He'd guess, though, that she'd not known the Rookerie. He'd also wager that he'd lived almost half his life before she was even born.

She nodded. 'My parents had a glove shop in Chelsea.' Her voice cracked ever so slightly as she spoke.

'Your parents?' he asked, wanting her to say more, always hungry to hear of what it was like to have parents.

She put on a brave smile. 'They are dead now and the shop gone. That is why I went into service.'

He took her hand. 'I am sorry for it.'

She covered his hand with her other hand. 'And your family?'

The pain of losing his mother still scraped at Walker's insides. He did not even know how old he'd been, only that he'd been very young and on his own ever since.

'Dead, as well.' He could not tell her his mother made her meagre living on her back and his father could be any one of countless men. She'd died from disease given to her by one of those men.

She held on to him tighter. 'We are lucky, then, are we not, to have such good employment?'

'Indeed,' he answered. He'd be dead without it.

'My lady worries that you will not find this man you are looking for, but I believe you will.'

When had anyone shown such blind faith in him— besides Fitz, that is?

'We will find him.'

The carriage pulled into a posting inn to change horses.

Leo broke their silence. 'You should stretch your legs a bit, Mariel.'

She nodded in agreement and he exited first before turning to help her out, putting his hands on her waist and lifting her down. From the roof of the carriage, Walker helped the maid down to the ground.

'Do you need me, miss?' her maid asked.

Mariel glanced at Leo. 'I do not believe so.'

Leo pulled some coins from his pocket and handed them to Walker. 'Would you purchase some food for all of us?'

'I'll help you,' Penny offered.

Leo turned to Mariel. 'We might have time for a quick cup of tea. Would you like that?'

'Very well,' she responded.

They entered the public room of the inn and Leo asked for tea to be served right away. A pot and two cups were quickly placed on a table. Mariel poured, remembering exactly how he took his tea. She did not seem to notice anything remarkable in that knowledge.

As soon as she put the cup to her lips, she set it down again.

'Oh, look!' She rose and walked over to the hearth.

A mother cat lay on a blanket, nursing her kittens. A yellow tabby kit toddled its uncertain way off the blanket.

Mariel scooped it up and held it against her cheek. 'Look at you, you sweet little thing.'

The other kittens became curious and left their meal to look up at her. She lowered herself to the floor and gathered them into her skirts, where they climbed and fell as if encountering some strange new land.

Leo's heart ached at the sight. He forced himself to smile. 'I remember when you and Charlotte and Annalise found kittens in the barn at Welbourne Manor. You looked much like you do right now.'

She made a face. 'I must have been all of eleven years old.'

But still a beauty. He hadn't realised it then, but he'd known that day had been a moment to cherish.

As was this moment.

Their gazes caught and held.

He spoke quietly, 'We've known each other a long time.'

A horn sounded to call them back to the carriage. He rose from the chair and offered her his hand. She scooped the kittens back onto their blanket and put her hand in his, letting him pull her up.

They came close, inches from each other, and neither moved as their gazes caught and held. He inhaled her scent, felt the warmth of her body.

The horn sounded again and they hurried to the yard.

Walker met them. 'There is a basket of food in the carriage.'

Leo asked the maid, 'Would you like to sit inside the carriage now? I can sit on the roof.'

She looked stricken. 'I—I like being outside.' Her glance darted to Mariel. 'Unless you would prefer I ride with you, miss.'

Leo watched Mariel look from Penny to Walker and back again. 'You may ride outside, if you like.'

Her maid beamed. 'Thank you, miss!'

Once Leo and Mariel were back inside the carriage, Mariel remarked, 'I believe there is romance afoot.'

'Romance?' He was puzzled.

She gestured to the outside. 'Penny and Mr Walker.'

His brows rose. 'No?'

'I am fairly convinced.' She peered at him intently. 'Must I worry for her sake?'

'Worry about Walker?' Leo laughed. Walker, for all

his rough past, would never trifle with an innocent such as Mariel's maid. 'He's a fine man.'

'Good.' She averted her gaze. 'I would not wish Penny to be ill used.'

'Neither would I.' True, he and Walker had engaged in encounters Mariel must never learn about, but all was different now—although their business was not entirely on the up and up.

She plucked cat hairs off her skirt. 'You? With your reputation?'

He frowned. 'Gossip, Mariel.' He'd not been a saint, but he didn't debauch innocent women. 'Do you believe the tales told of me?'

She cast him a long look before finally saying, 'Your sister Annalise believes you have a mistress. Shall I not believe her?'

'A mistress?' He shook his head. 'What mistress?'

She held her gaze steady. 'You must ask her.'

He could not tell if she was teasing him or not. 'Mariel.' He spoke firmly. 'I do not have a mistress. I do not have any idea what Annalise was talking about.'

Mariel lifted one eyebrow.

The carriage rolled through the village to the open country again. Pristine green hills passed by, and the rain-swollen Medway River. None of it provided enough distraction for him.

Where the devil had Annalise got the idea he had a mistress? She wouldn't have seen him with a woman. Good God, he'd not been with any woman besides Mariel, had he?

The entire next hour was consumed with reviewing in his mind everywhere he had been and whom he had spoken to. The only woman he'd been with had been Mariel.

He suddenly sat up straight. 'That's it!'

She started.

He laughed. 'Penny!'

She blinked. 'What about Penny?'

'It was driving me mad.' He leaned towards her. 'The mistress was Penny. Annalise saw me with Penny. At Hatchards. And Annalise called at my rooms the afternoon Penny delivered your note. It was Penny.'

She cocked her head. 'Well, that explains it, doesn't it?'

He could not tell if she believed him. 'I have never kept a mistress. My reputation might suggest otherwise, but the truth is I—'

She reached across and put her gloved fingers on his lips. 'I never believed you did. At least not at present. I knew Annalise was mistaken.'

He captured her hand in his. 'I will not say I've been a saint, but, Mariel, you are the only woman I ever truly desired.'

Yearning filled her eyes. 'Oh, Leo! Then why can we not forget these past two years? We could start over.'

He felt himself grow cold. 'I told you. I am not the same man as I was then—'

'I do not care if you lost your wealth,' she broke in.

He gave a dry laugh. 'It is not that. I have plenty of money.' And a small fortune coming soon by ship, God willing.

'Then, why, Leo?' Her voice cracked.

Some things were best unspoken. 'I no longer belong in polite society. As for why? It is best you do not know.'

She pulled her hand away and turned from him.

Chapter Thirteen

Hughes stood in the centre of the road watching for the carriage. How fortunate he and his men had spied Fitzmanning when the carriage stopped to change teams at an inn. They'd ridden ahead to this spot.

This perfect spot.

All was going according to plan.

The rumble of an approaching carriage reached his ears. Was their luck still holding?

'Make ready!' he called. His men were hidden from the road, obscured by shrubbery.

Hughes's excitement grew. This task was almost too easy. He wanted to shout in triumph, but first he needed to make certain this was the correct carriage.

It came into view. He kept his eyes peeled on the post boy, the coachman, the passengers seated on top. This was it!

'On my signal!' he cried, stepping out of view.

He waited until the horses reached his mark in the road.

'Now!'

His men pulled on a rope they'd strung across the road.

The rope caught the back legs of the wheelers. The

horses stumbled and the rope caught in the carriage's wheels. There was a loud snap—the shaft breaking, perhaps?—and the horses broke free of the vehicle, the post boy frantically trying to get them under control as they galloped away.

The carriage jolted and rocked and tilted on its side. Finally it fell, tossing the outside passengers and the coachman like rag dolls. Its momentum thrust it towards an embankment at the side of the road.

Hughes let out a laugh.

He glimpsed Fitzmanning inside as the carriage slid down the embankment and landed with a splash in the river.

Hughes had counted on this scheme impeding Fitzmanning's progress. If Fitzmanning were injured, so much the better. But having him lost completely in a rain-swollen river was the best of all possible outcomes. Kellford would be pleased.

Hughes watched the fast-moving current sweep the carriage away, pulling it deeper and deeper into the water.

'Off!' he shouted to his men. They retrieved the rope and scurried away, before the coachman, holding his head in his hands, gathered his wits about him. The passengers were nowhere to be seen, but they were of no consequence to Hughes. The post boy was probably a mile away by now, still fighting the horses.

The event would be written off as another unfortunate coaching accident. Its cause would remain unknown. And, for it, he and his men would be paid handsomely.

It had all happened so fast. The shout of the coachman. Mariel's screams. The snap of something breaking.

The carriage suddenly crashing on its side and sliding into the water, the cold water.

Leo could only think to grab hold of Mariel, to shield her with his body. At first, the carriage floated like a boat, but quickly water poured in through the windows.

'We have to get out of here.' He scrambled for the door, but could not push it open. The windows were too small to crawl through.

Mariel pushed at the door along with him, but the water pressed on it with a force too great for them to counter. In no time the water was up to their necks. Remnants of their food basket floated around them.

'Take a deep breath,' Leo told her. 'Get as much air into your lungs as you can.'

She nodded and her gasp for air was the last sound he heard before the water covered her and reached his ears. He took his breath and joined her underwater.

They pushed at the door again and this time it opened. Leo gripped her arm and pulled them both out, kicking hard to bring them up to the surface. He could feel the weight of her skirts trying to drag them down and the current sweeping them away from the carriage, but he kicked towards the daylight shining above the river water.

He broke through to the surface and pulled her up with him, lifting her so that she could fill her lungs with air. The river dragged them under again. Leo kicked to the surface once more and they were able to grab another lungful of air before going under again.

Leo had only one thought. To save Mariel. He'd fight to reach the shore, because he refused to allow Mariel to die this horrible death, unable to breathe, knowing life was ending.

He clasped hold of the front of her dress, gripping it

tight. He would die before he released her. One of his arms was free to fight the water like the enemy it had become. Mariel gamely did her part, kicking and adding her own strokes to the effort.

A memory flashed through his mind. Swimming in the pond behind Welbourne Manor, the boys and the girls together in their underclothes, unsupervised as usual, but innocent in their play. He remembered dunking Mariel and laughing when she came up sputtering.

In the rushing river, though, he fought to keep her head out of the water. He increased his effort, though his muscles ached and fatigue threatened. No matter. He must save Mariel's life.

The shore came closer and closer by inches. Suddenly the river pushed them towards the trunk of a fallen tree jutting out into the water. With all his strength Leo lunged for the tree's branches and grasped one at the last second. The river continued to try to sweep Mariel away, but he hung on to her and pulled her towards him until she, too, could grab hold of the tree.

He lifted her onto the fallen tree, although it took several tries. She made it finally and straddled the trunk. Leo lost his grip and the water tried to capture him again, but Mariel grabbed his coat and held on until he could fight his way back and again catch hold. Finally he, too, straddled the trunk.

Leo's muscles felt like jelly as he rested his cheek against the wet wood, savouring its solid surface. He had no idea how long they'd battled the water or how far the current had taken them. They were alive.

Mariel was alive.

'Are you hurt?' he called to her.

She turned her head to look back at him. 'No.'

His muscles relaxed in relief.

But relief was short-lived. He remembered Walker and Penny, the coachman and the post boy. What had happened to them? The coachman, Penny and Walker must have been thrown from the vehicle. Had they been thrown clear of it? Were they alive?

And what had caused the accident in the first place?

He raised his head to look at Mariel. 'We need to get on land. Can you move?'

She nodded. 'I'll try.'

She inched her way down the tree trunk to where the river became quieter. Tips of shrubs peeked up through water that had overflowed the river's banks. A breeze rippled the surface of the water and chilled his skin. She must be cold as well, he thought. Cold and weary.

But she kept on, crawling to where dry land beckoned.

The tree acted as a bridge to the dry shore. When close, Mariel stood and navigated the rest of the way on foot, until she dropped to ground that was muddy but firm.

Leo came right behind her. When his feet touched the ground, he reached for her, holding her in his arms, pressing her against him. Her life was the solid earth beneath his feet.

'Mariel.' He seized her lips in a kiss.

All his terror for her, all his relief, were poured into the kiss, as if this alone would affirm that she was alive and safe and not lost to him forever. His embrace was almost violent in its intensity, but she matched him. Her arms encircled his neck, holding fast. She returned his kiss with equal fervour, clinging to him as hard as he was clinging to her.

When they broke apart, both were trembling. He

could not release her. At this moment it would have felt as if she would be swept away from him.

He embraced her again, more gently, holding her against him, while his heartbeat and breathing gradually slowed to normal.

'Thank you,' she whispered against his chest. 'Thank you for saving me.'

Mariel wanted never to leave the safety and security of Leo's strong arms. Death had come so close and he battled it away. Emotions that she'd kept at bay during the danger now threatened to engulf her like the river water that had tried to sweep her into oblivion.

Leo had saved her. He'd held on to her and saved her.

'Come.' He pulled her away, but kept his strong arm around her shoulders. 'We need to move away from the edge.'

She needed no further coaxing.

The shore at this spot was thick with shrubbery and they had to push their way through, feet slipping on wet ground underneath. Finally they came into the open.

The clear day that greeted them at the beginning of their journey had vanished. The sky was grey. Dark rain-clouds gathered in the distance. Nothing was in view but green fields. No houses. No road. Not even a church spire poking into the sky.

Where were they?

She seized his arm. 'Leo! What happened to Penny? And Walker and the coachmen? Did they fall in the water, too?'

He faced her and looked directly into her eyes. 'They must have been thrown from the carriage when it tipped over. The horses broke free, I think, the post boy with them.'

Thrown from the carriage? How could Penny survive such a horrible event? She could have been smashed against a tree or tumbled onto rocks or—or—crushed under the carriage.

'We need to get dry. Find shelter.' Leo was changing the subject and she did not like that. 'Would you like to remain here while I look for help?'

'Do not leave me!' she cried. 'I want to go back and find Penny. They might need us.'

His expression was sympathetic. 'We do not know how far the river carried us. It might be miles.'

'I do not care,' she insisted. 'I want to find them.'

He held her again. 'I think it a better plan to find you a safe place to recuperate. Then I can go back to the site of the accident.'

'No. I'm going with you.' She could not bear it if he left her to worry and wonder about where he was and what he might find.

It took a moment for him to respond. 'Very well. We'll look for them together. There is a chance that they are safe. As horrific as our part of the accident was, we came out unharmed. Walker knows how to keep his wits about him. After all he has been through, it will take more than a carriage accident to undo him.'

'Kill him, you mean,' she said.

'Yes, that is what I mean.' He released her.

He was trying to give her hope, but she'd already steeled herself for the worst. She could bear discovering the worst better than waiting and knowing nothing.

He took a breath. 'If we walk upstream we'll eventually find the road and the site of the accident. Perhaps it is closer than I think.' He peered at her. 'But if I find someplace where you can be cared for, I will insist that comes first.'

She would cross that bridge when she came to it. 'Thank you, Leo.' She gave him a swift embrace.

Mariel pulled out the few pins left in her hair and wrung it as best she could before trying to pin it into a knot at the nape of her neck. Her bonnet had been lost in the river. Her clothes were still dripping wet and there was no sun to warm them.

'I'm ready,' she said.

Leo took her hand and they started walking.

It was hard going. Mariel's skirts were heavy and her muscles weary. Her half-boots were soaked and her feet chafed from her wet stockings. Worse, she kept reliving the carriage falling on its side, sliding into the river, filling with water. Worse still, she pictured Penny lying broken and still by the road.

'I should never have brought Penny with me,' she said as she put one foot in front of the other.

'You could not have known what would happen,' Leo responded. 'Try not to think about it.'

'What did happen, Leo? All of a sudden the coach just lurched and fell on its side.' She felt it again. The jolt of the carriage. The crash of the fall.

He shrugged. 'It felt as if we hit something in the road.'

She tried to think of other things, as he suggested.

She thought of his kiss. It spoke of loving her. She could not deny that. And of her loving him. She had never stopped loving him, she realised. No matter that he had left her two years ago. He was back and he'd fought the river to keep them alive.

She glanced at him. His face revealed the effort it took to keep walking, as did hers, she supposed. His was a strong face. The sight of it still made her breath catch.

Her mind flashed with the image of the water trying to sweep him away from the tree, right before she'd grabbed his coat. The thought that he might die had been so much worse than his leaving her two years ago had been.

Tears stung her eyes, but she blinked them away and glanced up at the sky. 'It is going to rain.'

Leo nodded. 'Yes, it is.'

Rain would only make matters worse for Penny, Walker and the coachman. 'I hope we find them before the rainfalls.'

Surely they'd walked at least three miles by now. You'd think they would have spied a village or a farmhouse, someplace where they could get help for Penny and Walker. They'd seen no buildings at all. They'd not even found the road. Mariel's feet ached. She was tired and hungry and cold.

Just when she thought she could not feel any worse, the rain started. Fat drops, falling here and there, quickly thickened into teeming sheets of water and sent them running for the shelter of a tree.

'Stay here,' Leo said to her. 'I'm going to run over the ridge to see if I can find shelter.

He sprinted away, not giving her an opportunity to stop him.

She started after him. 'Leo! Wait!'

He acted as if he didn't hear her, which was certainly possible in the roaring rain. He quickly disappeared from view. She abandoned the chase and made her way back to the tree to face the agony of not knowing where he was or if he would make it back to her.

The minutes seemed like hours and all her doubts and worries flooded her like the rains flooded the river. She wept for poor Penny, convinced the fall from the carriage had killed her. She also wept for Walker, and for the fledgling love budding between them.

Mariel also grieved the loss of all the hopes and dreams and delights that had accompanied her first romance—her only romance. She again let herself feel her love for Leo, her need of him.

She slid to the ground and buried her face in her hands, trying to stop herself weeping, trying to make herself strong and determined and self-reliant.

'Mariel!'

She looked up. Leo emerged through the grey curtain of rain and strode towards her from the crest of the hill.

She wiped her face as she stood, then hurried to meet him.

He caught her in his arms. 'I've found shelter!'

Pulling her arm through his, he led her up the hill and over another until she saw below them a small house. No signs of life around it, no smoke from its chimney, but it had a roof and, at the moment, that was more than enough.

They ran towards it, their feet slipping on the wet grass.

When they reached the door, though, it was padlocked.

'I don't suppose you have Walker's keys with you?' Mariel said, her voice catching on Walker's name.

He smiled at her. 'No, but I'm game to try one of your hairpins.'

She pulled one out and her hair tumbled down. She handed the hairpin to him. He inserted it in the lock and moved it carefully until, finally, the lock opened.

'See, a hairpin can undo a lock,' she commented. 'I was not so foolish at Lord Kellford's.'

His gaze pierced into her as he opened the door. 'You were foolishly brave.'

They walked in.

The little house was dark and consisted of one large room with a table, three chairs, a fireplace and a cot. It smelled of dust and disuse, but it was dry.

'It looks like a groundskeeper's cottage,' Leo said.

'How long before the rain stops?' she asked.

He glanced towards the window, rattling from the force of the rain. 'I have no idea, but while we wait we should try to get warm.'

She could not argue. There was no use to keep going in the rain.

He walked over to the fireplace. 'There is a stack of wood and a pail of coal.' He immediately set about laying a fire.

Mariel spied a pump and went over to examine it. 'It looks like there is water.' She sighed. 'Not that I wish to see any more water today.' She tested the pump, but its pipe must have been filled with air.

She was suddenly thirsty, even after swallowing all that river water. She found a large jug and carried it to the door. 'We'll need water to prime the pump.' She opened the door again and set the jug out in the rain. At the rate the rain was falling, it would be filled in no time at all.

Leo started a fire in the fireplace, no more than tinder burning at the moment, but a fire nonetheless.

Mariel walked towards it. 'It will be lovely to be warm again.'

He stood and, suddenly, she felt the intimacy of being in this small space, in the darkness with him. The rain pattered on the cottage roof, but she fancied the sound of her beating heart rose above its din.

He glanced from the cot in the corner back to her, moving closer to her. His hazel eyes seemed to glow in the flame's reflection. He touched her hair, a wet, tangled mass heavy on her shoulders.

Gently he combed it back with his fingers, his eyes on hers. 'Mariel, you need to remove your clothes.'

Chapter Fourteen

'Remove my clothes?' Mariel pulled back.

He reached for her again, but withdrew his hands. 'You are shivering. You'll never get warm unless you get out of your clothes. Turn around. I'll untie your laces.'

'But...' she protested.

'You must. You'll become ill if you don't.' He twirled his finger.

She knew he was right and did as she was told.

The knots had undoubtedly been made tighter by being wet. He struggled to undo them and she could smell the river on him. It brought back the terror of being pulled under the water over and over, fearing she would drown or, worse, she would watch Leo drown.

She trembled.

'I will hurry,' he said.

He finally undid the knot and loosened the lacings. Once she had dreamed of undressing for him on her wedding night. Never had she supposed the circumstances would be like this. She let her gown drop to the floor and she stepped out of it.

As soon as her dress was off, he started to work on the laces of her corset, a task Penny so often performed for her. Dear Penny, who took such pride in Mariel's clothing and her appearance. Was she lying dead or injured in the cold rain? Mariel shook her head. She must not think about it.

Leo loosened her corset, which, like her dress, she let slip to the floor. He walked over to the cot and picked up one of the blankets that had been folded at its foot.

Holding it like a curtain around her, he said, 'Take off your shift. You can wrap this around you.'

When her shift joined the other sodden clothing on the floor, he wrapped the blanket around her naked body like a cloak.

He dragged the cot close to the fire. 'Sit here and I'll take off your shoes and stockings.'

This seemed even more intimate than removing her corset. He rubbed her red and blistered feet to warm them, sending sensation shooting throughout her body. She forgot her chill, aroused now by his touch.

But as soon as he stopped she shivered, even under the blanket.

'Lie down, Mariel. The fire will soon warm the place.'

She lowered her head onto the pillow and he stepped out of her sight. The sounds of his undressing made her wish to turn and watch him. He took a second blanket from the bed and she heard him wrap it around himself.

He climbed onto the cot and held her close against him. 'Forgive me this liberty. It is the fastest way to take away your chill.'

This liberty? Her senses craved more than *this* liberty. She was not so green a girl that she did not know what she craved was the intimacy of a husband and wife. It immediately felt right to be enfolded in his arms, to feel his breath on her neck and the strength of his body next to hers.

'I was thinking,' he spoke quietly. 'Chances are the post boy was unhurt. Surely he would have ridden to get help. Or likely another carriage came by and found them. Perhaps at this very moment Penny and Walker and the coachman are warm and dry and well tended.'

It was the nicest thing he could have said to her. His words made perfect sense and, for the first time, gave her real hope. There were other people who would help Penny and Walker and the coachman. She could relieve herself of that responsibility and the guilt of failing at it. She could think of Penny, well fed and in clean nightclothes, safely tucked into a clean bed at a comfortable inn.

It helped her relax enough to close her eyes. She was so tired that even lying naked next to Leo, a mere blanket between them, was not enough to keep her awake.

It was enough that he held her, that they were together, that they were alive.

The surgeon stepped away from the bed and lowered his voice. 'Nothing is broken. She has a nasty cut on her forehead, but that is all. I suspect tomorrow she'll be right as rain.' He glanced to the window where rain poured down as if from buckets. 'Pardon the expression.'

Walker accompanied him to the bedchamber door and pressed a coin into his hand. 'Thank you, sir.'

The post boy and the coachman, his head wrapped in a bandage, hovered in the inn's hallway.

'She will recover,' Walker told them. 'It is only a cut. Thank you both for your help.' He shook their hands.

The post boy had ridden the team of horses to the next inn and sounded the alarm. They'd not had long to wait for help to arrive, but even that short period of time had been agony for Walker.

Miss Jenkins had been bleeding severely.

The accident had happened so fast. Suddenly the horses stumbled and the carriage lurched. With only a split second for decision, Walker grabbed hold of Miss Jenkins and jumped from the carriage at the moment it fell on its side. They landed in some bushes, barely escaping being crushed under the vehicle. They fell hard. Miss Jenkins's head struck a rock and instantly blood poured down her beautiful face. He had gathered her into his arms as the carriage slid into the river and disappeared beneath the water, Fitz and Miss Covendale trapped inside.

Walker's jaw flexed with emotion, but there was no time to grieve. Miss Jenkins needed him.

He bid good day to the two men who had shared the tragic experience and closed the door, returning to the bed where Miss Jenkins was propped up by pillows, tears rolling down her cheeks.

He sat in the chair next to her bed. 'Did you hear that, miss? The surgeon says you will be well tomorrow. It is only a cut.'

'I keep seeing the carriage.' She wiped her eyes with her fingers. 'My poor lady! What will I do without her?'

Walker glanced away. What would he do, as well? Fitz had given him his new life.

'I don't want to think of myself.' Miss Jenkins sobbed. 'It is so bad of me, but, without Miss Covendale, how will I ever get another position? There is no one to recommend me.'

Walker took her hand, still damp from her tears. 'Do not upset yourself,' he murmured. 'These things have ways of coming to rights.'

If truth be told, he shared her worries. He'd depended upon Fitz to keep him from needing to return to his former life. He could not go back to that existence.

She looked up, her eyes glistening. 'I should have stopped her from coming on this trip. She'd be alive if I did. I wish I had. She'd be alive then.'

He squeezed her hand. 'That kind of thinking gets you nowhere. None of us possesses second sight. We could not know the coach would have an accident.'

Was it an accident? He'd seen nothing amiss on the road, but something elusive had caught the corner of his eye after they'd hit the ground. A man in the wood? He could not say for certain.

He turned his thoughts back to Miss Jenkins. 'We were all merely trying to do something worthy. To help Miss Covendale.' He'd thought Miss Covendale's plight worthy of an Ann Radcliffe novel…if not for its tragic end.

Miss Jenkins nodded. 'I did think I was helping her. That's all I ever wanted to do.'

A bruise had formed beneath one of her eyes and a bandage was wrapped around her head, but she still was the loveliest woman Walker had ever seen.

He resisted the impulse to bring her hand to his lips. 'You were devoted to her.' As he'd been to Fitz. 'Think. Would she want you to worry so? Do not worry over the future. You have me to help you.'

He would see that no harm came to her. He'd devote his life to the task if she'd allow him.

Her eyes widened, but he could say no more at this moment, at least about his feelings for her.

He swallowed. 'You must think of what she would wish you to do. We must both think of what they would wish us to do.'

She blinked, but looked into his eyes again. 'Do you think Lord Kellford will still ruin her father?'

He preferred this topic. 'He might. Such men are spiteful.' Kellford would certainly be enraged that his hopes for Miss Covendale's fortune were dashed.

'My lady would not like to see her family suffer. She is very devoted to her sisters.' She broke down again. 'I mean, she *was* devoted....'

Without thinking, he moved to sit beside her on the bed, wrapping his arms around her. 'There, there,' he soothed.

A dim memory glimmered. His long-lost mother had once held him in the same way. He shuddered. When was the last time he allowed himself such a memory of his mother? If grief over Fitz was nearly undoing him, what would happen if he gave in to his grief over his mother?

He forced his thoughts back to Miss Jenkins. 'Would you like for us to still find this bank clerk? We might at least save Miss Covendale's family from ruin.'

Her face glowed. 'Could we? I would like that above all things.'

He could not help but smile. 'That is what we will do, then. In the morning. If the rain ends, that is.'

She hugged him. 'As soon as the rain ends!'

The trusting warmth of her arms almost loosed the tenuous hold he had on his emotions. His eyes stung with tears he refused to shed, but his heart wept in grief for the only two people in his life who had ever cared about him.

Leo had not intended to sleep, but the comforting sound of Mariel's even breathing had lulled him. When he finally opened his eyes he had no idea how long he'd dozed. Rain still sounded on the roof and windowpanes, but it was dark outside. The only light in the room came from the fire in the grate, now burning low. It had done its task, though. The room was warm; his bone-cold chill had vanished.

Sometime during the night, Mariel had rolled over to face him. He gently tucked her blanket around her and simply gazed at her lovely face.

She looked relaxed and peaceful in sleep. Rather than a woman who'd nearly drowned, she resembled that little girl he'd once teased and taunted at Welbourne Manor. How he wished he could recapture those innocent days.

So much had happened in the meantime, so much disappointment and heartache. He'd hoped to atone for all she'd suffered by finding the bank clerk and freeing her of Kellford. Now he feared they would run out of time.

Tomorrow they must find a village and he must discover what happened to Walker and Penny. Would they have time to hire a new carriage to take them to Kellford's hunting lodge, secure the bank clerk's cooperation, and still return to London by the day Mariel was to be married? It was cutting it close to the quick.

What would happen then? Kellford would no doubt enact his revenge. Mariel's father would be arrested and her family would be awash in scandal made even worse by Leo's name being attached to it.

In that case, Leo would marry her, although he suspected that, like his parents' own scandalbroth, the damage to Mariel's reputation and that of her mother and sisters would be long-lasting.

Leo could at least try to help Covendale fight the charges. If he failed at that and the man was hanged, he could, at least, support Mariel's mother and sisters, make sure they wanted for nothing.

Two things he could not guarantee for them: preserving Covendale's life and preserving the family's reputation. Those two things were the very reasons Mariel had agreed to marry Kellford in the first place. Would she feel any better being forced to marry him instead and still suffer the consequences she so wished to avoid?

He took a deep breath. Under no circumstances would he force her to marry him.

He sat up abruptly.

What he could do was give her the best of his efforts without requiring anything of her. No matter what, he would fight for Covendale's life. No matter what, he would support Mariel and her family. No one would have to know the money came from him. And in two years' time she would become an heiress and need no one's help.

Mariel opened her eyes and rose on one elbow. 'Leo? Is something amiss?'

His heart pounded in his chest. Even if he failed to stop Kellford, he could help her.

'Nothing,' he replied. 'A thought. That is all.'

She gathered her blanket around her. His had slipped down to his waist.

'About the accident?' She rubbed her eyes.

'No.' He waved a hand. 'It was nothing.' It was everything to him, but nothing he need speak of right away.

She turned towards the window. 'It's dark and still raining.'

'Indeed,' he managed.

He stood, wrapping the blanket around his waist as

he did so. He went to the fireplace and put more coal on the fire.

'Are you thirsty?' she asked. 'I am very thirsty.'

He'd not thought about it, but he was both thirsty and hungry. 'We could get the pump working.'

She rose from the cot. 'I'll go outside and fetch the jug I left out there. It should be full by now. Plenty of water to prime the pump.'

He intercepted her, touching her arm. 'I'll go. No need for you to get wet again.' He crossed the room to the door, but turned back to her. 'Look away, Mariel. I'm going to take off my blanket. To keep it dry.'

He could not tell in the dark whether she turned away or not, but he dropped his blanket, opened the door and walked outside. The rain felt good on his bare skin, clean, compared to the river water. He stood in the open and let it pour over him, lifted his face to it and tasted it in his mouth. He did not know how long he stood there, but it felt wonderful to wash the river out of his hair, off his skin.

'Leo?'

He turned and saw Mariel silhouetted in the doorway. 'Mariel! What are you doing?'

'I—I—you took so long. I thought something had happened to you.' She averted her gaze.

'I'm letting the rain rinse me off.' He must look deranged, standing in the pouring rain, stark naked. 'Go back inside.'

The silhouette disappeared.

He picked up the jug of water and carried it into the hut. As soon as he crossed the threshold, there she was, right inside the doorway.

'What the devil, Mariel?' He put the jug down and snatched up his blanket.

'I want to rinse off, too,' she said.

She didn't wait for him to answer, but walked past him, dropping her blanket right before stepping outside.

To not look was impossible for him, but he remained far enough inside that he would not be visible to her.

She was a mere shape in the rain, but still took his breath away. She lifted her arms to the sky and twirled around, graceful and sinuous. Her innocent abandon reminded him of their childhood days.

Her perfect beauty, though, was that of a woman and his body responded.

He could not turn his eyes away. His hands begged to slide down the curves that were merely suggested in the rainy night. His lips yearned to taste her again. His loins throbbed to possess her.

He must have moved forwards. She turned to face the doorway and she stilled. Slowly she moved towards him.

He remembered how powerfully he'd wanted her when they'd escaped the river; he wanted her even more now. He stepped outside and the rain cooled his fevered skin.

But did nothing to dampen his desire.

She walked directly into his arms and he captured her lips. Passion coursed through his veins, heightening his yearning for her. The kiss sent him back to when he'd so nearly lost her. The danger they'd endured fuelled his ardour once more.

His hands slipped down her back and rested on her derrière, so satisfyingly round and feminine. He pressed her against him, against his arousal, wanting more. Needing more.

She gasped beneath his lips.

He loosened his hold on her and looked down at her, unable to speak the question in his mind. Did she want this?

'Let us go inside,' she murmured.

Chapter Fifteen

They were standing in the rain, naked, on a chilly rainy night. He ought to feel the chill, but he was aflame.

He lifted her into his arms and carried her inside, stepping over the blankets that had once covered them. It seemed more natural that no barriers existed between them.

He carried her to the cot and lowered her onto it. She pulled him down atop her, kissing him again, sharing her tongue with him as if she, too, could not get enough.

He forced himself back to his senses. 'Mariel, are you sure you want this? There are consequences…' They could create a life by their lovemaking. He would stop if that was what she desired.

'I don't care. I don't care,' she rasped. 'We almost died yesterday. We might die tomorrow. I will not die without making love with you.'

And I cannot live without it, Leo thought.

Her hands explored him, kneaded at his flesh, urged him on. He became too fevered to think clearly. He knew he should go slow, prepare her, be gentle, but his need was too powerful and she was too tempting, too willing.

His wonderful Mariel, never one to balk, always game to do what needed to be done, fearless in forging ahead. He loved her for it.

Loved her.

'I love you, Mariel,' he whispered. 'I have never stopped loving you.'

Her legs parted for him and he rose above her, wanting to plunge into her and hasten his release. He fought for the control to slow down, to enter her slowly, letting her body adapt to him.

She gasped and stiffened when he filled her completely.

He stopped. 'Did I hurt you?'

She shook her head and raised her hips, her hands pressing on his back.

He tried to hold back, but she writhed beneath him, impatient sounds escaping her lips. The rhythm of lovemaking drove him to move faster inside her.

Sensation grew, that exquisite hunger that demanded to be slaked, but other feelings, too, because this was his valiant Mariel beneath him, surrounding him, joined to him.

She moved with him, her need intensifying, as well. He wanted to give her the pleasure he knew he would experience at the end. Nothing was more important than giving himself totally to her.

But his need took over, becoming more intense, building higher, until his release exploded within him. At the same moment his seed spilled inside her, she cried out, convulsing around him in the culmination of her own passion. Together they writhed in pleasure until sensation ebbed and languor took over.

He slid to her side and held her close.

'I did not know it would be like that,' she murmured. 'Is it always like that?'

He kissed the top of her head, her hair still wet from the rain. 'Only with you.'

She sighed. 'Promise me you will not be sorry for this in the morning.'

Be sorry for it? He would never be sorry for making love to her. The risks were all hers. 'I should ask that of you, Mariel.'

Her body was humming with pleasure from joining with him. It might have been wrong of her to seize the moment, to act without thought to propriety, without heed to the consequences. But was not propriety meaningless after facing the prospect of death? And if Leo's child grew inside her, could anything be more wonderful?

She sat up to gaze at him steadily. 'I have no regrets.'

He made love to her one more time before retrieving their blankets and filling cups with water, which they sipped as if it were the finest wine. As the new day dawned, they sat together on the cot, wrapped in the blankets, the fireplace warming them in a cocoon of their own creation. It seemed to Leo as if nothing in the world existed except the two of them.

He embraced the illusion. It was preferable to imagine these walls as the confines of the world than to think about the complications that faced them outside.

She turned to place a kiss on his bare chest, warmed by the fireplace and their lovemaking. Her fingers traced one of the scars that were reminders of the worst he could do. Or had it been his finest act? He could never be certain.

Her touch was gentle, such a contrast to the wound

that created the scar. 'What happened, Leo? How did you get these?'

What would she think if he told her? 'It is best you not know.'

She shifted and looked him straight in the eye. 'Do not say that to me. Do not put secrets between us. Not now.' Not after making love, she meant.

'I was in a fight,' he finally said. 'In Paris.'

'A fight?' she repeated.

She wanted more, he was certain, but it was not an episode he wanted to share. He did not want to place it in her memory, giving her images he did not wish her to have.

He knew too well how impossible it was to shed those images.

It involved his meeting with Walker. Walker had grown up in an East End rookery and had belonged to a gang of thieves virtually his whole life. Like Leo, though, Walker had not belonged in the world where he was born. Like Leo, Walker wanted more. He'd dared to leave the gang and the rookery and made his way to Paris, where Leo happened upon him in a three-against-one street fight. Knives were pulled and the fighting became life or death. One cut-throat slashed at Leo, causing the wounds whose scars Mariel so tenderly touched. Leo managed to wrest the knife away, but the man lunged at him and the knife plunged into the man's chest.

Leo could still see the look of surprise on the man's face before he fell, never to rise again.

The others scattered and Walker pulled him away from the body before the gendarmes could be summoned. It was only later Leo could reflect on what he'd done. He'd taken a man's life, and even though he'd do it again to save Walker and himself, it disturbed him.

He faced Mariel and tried to adopt a light tone. 'It happened to be a very a nasty fight.'

Mariel searched Leo's face. She sensed there was a great deal more to Leo's story than he had disclosed to her, something that caused him great emotional pain as well as physical injury. She waited for him to go on, but he added nothing.

'Tell me more,' she pressed. 'Why were you fighting?'

'Who recalls?' He shrugged. 'I found myself in many scrapes while I was on the Continent.'

He knew the reason, she realised.

She stared at him and finally said, 'You will not tell me, will you?'

His gaze remained steady and his voice turned low. 'The less anyone knows about those days, the better.'

His words created a leap of anxiety inside her. What had happened to him in the past two years? The rumours made it sound as if he'd turned into some sort of dissolute rake. Each contact she had with him left a different impression. He was still like the Leo she'd fallen in love with, except there was a darkness inside him, a darkness he would not share with her.

Perhaps she could learn more from Walker—she swallowed—if Walker was alive.

An image of Walker and Penny being flung off the carriage assaulted her, but she pushed it away. She could not think of Walker and Penny. Not yet. She wanted to remain cocooned here with Leo and keep all the ugliness that surrounded them at bay. If only they could do so forever.

Perhaps she and Leo should just run away to Switzerland, like the poet Shelley had done years ago with his lover, Mary Godwin. That flight had caused heartache for those they left behind, especially Shelley's children and his wife, who later killed herself.

By drowning, Mariel remembered. She shuddered, knowing precisely what Harriet Shelley experienced before her death.

A knot formed in Mariel's stomach. Think what running away would do to her family. Her father would hang and who would look after her mother and sisters?

She quickly changed the course of her thoughts once more.

'What woke you so suddenly before?' she asked Leo.

He frowned.

Would he leave this question unanswered, as well? What did he hide this time?

Finally his gaze rose to meet hers. 'I'd been thinking of the reason we came on this trip.'

'Oh.'

Most of all Mariel did not wish to think about Kellford.

But Leo continued. 'With luck we should still have time to find the bank clerk.'

She held up a hand. 'Must we speak of this? While we are here we are powerless, are we not? Let us not even talk about it.'

Their time together would soon enough come to an end. When the day cleared and their clothing dried, they would walk out this door and whatever reality they faced would cause great pain.

Leo placed his cup of water on the floor and took her hand. 'There is something I must say. We need to plan for what to do if we do not find the clerk.

At least he was saying 'we,' including her in making plans, but what was there to do if they did not find the bank clerk? All would be lost.

She pulled her hand away and used her fingers to comb the tangled mess that was her hair. 'Very well. Say what you must.'

He positioned himself behind her, pulling her between his legs, resting her back against his chest.

'In the event we run out of time…' he seemed to choose his words carefully '…I want you to know I will do whatever I can for you and your family. I will support you and your family and help your father in any way I can. I will pay back what your father stole from his cousin.' He paused. 'If you wish it, I will marry you.'

His offer was incredibly generous. He also made it sound like an obligation.

'You do not have to do such a thing,' she said.

He spoke near to her ear, his breath warming her skin. 'I owe it to you.'

She moved out of his arms and wrapped the blanket around her. 'Because we made love? I was equally responsible for that.'

He faced her. 'Not because of that.'

It was hard to look at him. 'I have no wish to be an obligation.'

His eyes creased as if in pain. 'I know it would not be a respectable marriage for you. I am aware of my reputation. If we are discovered to have been together, it will make the scandal even worse. The burden would be yours—you'd be the one with a bastard husband with a disreputable past.'

A past he kept secret. 'And you would endure the shame of marriage to the daughter of a thief.' She lowered her eyes. 'Once we did not care what anyone thought of our romance.'

His eyes pierced into hers. 'You cared enough to keep it secret. You worried about scandal even then.'

'Not for my sake!' she cried. She'd never cared about such nonsense. 'I worried that if we eloped it would reflect badly on my family, that it would hurt my sisters' chances for good marriages. I had to think of them.'

He held her by the shoulders and held her gaze. 'That is the one thing I cannot prevent. If we fail to find the bank clerk on time, I cannot prevent the scandal or gossip or the damage to your family's reputation. I cannot promise to save your father from the hangman's noose.'

She stopped breathing. Could reality be any uglier? The marriage she once dreamed of would cost her father's life, her family's reputation.

She wished she could collapse under the enormity of it all.

As if he sensed her despair, his blanket slipped off his shoulders and he wrapped his arms around her, giving the comfort she so desperately needed. She leaned her head against him, her ear against his bare chest filled with the sound of his beating heart.

He held her until her heartbeat matched his. He sought her lips and kissed her as hungrily as if they'd just escaped the river again. They lay back on the cot, she atop him, prolonging the kiss, feeding her own need along with his. Their tongues touched and explored, their breath mingled.

Flames shot through her body and she burned with desire for him once more. She needed to be joined to him. Needed the pleasure they created together. Breaking free of his kiss, she savoured him, rubbing her hands over his muscled chest, over the scars from wounds that might have cost him his life.

He slid his hands up to her breasts, his touch hot and erotic. Sensation flashed through her, consuming every inch of her. She never knew a man's touch could be so glorious.

Leo's touch.

He filled his hands with her breasts, tenderly kneading and scraping her nipples with his palms. When she thought she could not endure this exquisite thrill a moment longer, his hands moved to cup her derriére. She straddled him and rubbed herself along his erect manhood, trying to ease the aching that grew inside her.

A part of her stepped outside herself to wonder at the experience. She'd always known she wanted to make love with Leo, but she had understood nothing of the glory of it, of how freeing it would be to abandon herself to sensation, to cast off worries of the past and future and simply relish the intimacy of bare skin and secret places. In a moment she would take him inside her and be filled by him. The pleasure they would create together was unlike anything she could have imagined.

Perhaps she should be selfish and marry him, obligation or not, family or not.

She gasped. Pleasure fled as swiftly as the river's water had whisked them away.

'What is it?' His body tensed.

Tears filled her eyes. 'If I marry you, it will mean my father will die and my family will be ruined. If I have you, it means I destroy them.'

'It is not you who would destroy them,' he murmured. 'Your father and Kellford bear that responsibility.'

'But I could change it.' By marrying Kellford, she added silently.

He stroked her tangled hair. '*We* may yet change it and prevent those dire results.' He gestured to the window. 'The sun is rising and the rain has stopped. We'll be able to leave here soon. We'll find Penny and Walker and then we will find the bank clerk. We will only be a little delayed.'

His fingers and his words calmed her. Lying next to him made anything seem possible.

Her arms encircled him and she placed her lips on his. Together they lay down on the cot and she took sustenance from his kiss, as if he were breathing his strength into her. He ran his hands over her body as if she were his most cherished possession, as if he might never have another chance to touch her. She explored the contours of his muscles, so firm and thrilling. At this moment she could sweep past and future aside and relish this passion between them.

She said a prayer of thanks for his strength and his will and for the joy of touching him so intimately. Nothing separated them now. They were mouth to mouth, skin to skin, body to body, as they were meant to be. Her senses flared with desire for the pleasure they could create together.

His hand covered her breast and the need for him intensified again. His mouth covered her nipple and his tongue created new delights. She nearly cried aloud at the rapture of it.

Her fingers dug into his back. Her hips rose as his hand slid down to her feminine place. She suddenly needed for him to touch her there. How could she have guessed such a need existed? At the moment she wanted nothing more.

She pushed his hand lower and his fingers gently circled the area. She felt herself become wet under his touch. The excitation he created pushed her somewhere between ecstasy and agony, the agony of craving more.

She could bear the waiting no longer and he obliged her as if her feelings were his own. He moved over her and she opened for him. He entered her quickly and she knew, like her, he could not wait an instant longer. His strokes soothed her at first, but quickly made her desire even more acute.

This was a moment to savour, she realised, as her need was rapidly growing too strong for thought. This was a moment she would possess forever. Perfect joining. Perfect accord.

Perfect man.

He moved faster and faster and she moved with him, certain nothing could be wrong as long as she was with him, joined to him.

He drove her to her peak and she cried out with the glory of it. His muscles tensed and she felt him spill his seed inside her.

As her climax ebbed, a calmness washed over her, along with a fledgling feeling of hope. There was still time. They would succeed and she would be together with him for all the days of their lives and all their nights.

She sighed in contentment and he lay next to her, snuggling her against him.

'We'll succeed, Mariel,' he murmured, his voice deep with emotion. 'I'll make it right if it is the last thing I do.'

Chapter Sixteen

Mariel hated donning the clothing that reeked of the river, especially putting on her damp half-boots over her sore feet, but the sun was high in the sky and it was time to leave the cabin.

For one, they were hungry. The last food they'd eaten had been in the carriage before its accident, a lifetime ago, it seemed.

They tidied the cabin, doused the fire in the fireplace and put the place back to rights as best they could. Leo left a note and a few coins as payment for the coal and wood they'd used to keep warm.

Their last act was to lock the padlock.

In daylight, without rain pouring down, a path leading away from the cabin was clearly visible.

'It is bound to lead us somewhere,' Leo said.

They could reasonably expect to find a village within a day's walk, especially if the path led to a road. Neither wished to return to the river.

It was not an easy walk. Although the ground had dried somewhat, the path was riddled with puddles and their boots still sank into mud. The sky was grey and smelled of more rain. Mariel did not relish the idea of becoming soaked again.

With each step her hunger grew; she started thinking of meat pies and lamb roasts, tureens of oxtail soup, of bread warm from the oven, butter melting on a slice, jam piled atop it.

It did not take long for the path to lead to a road. There was a choice to make. North or south?

'Would you like to choose this one, Mariel?' Leo asked. 'Which way should we head?'

'I do not know how to choose.' Which would lead her to Penny? 'I have no idea where we are.'

'Neither do I.' Leo looked from one direction to the other. 'It doesn't matter overmuch. We will know how to proceed no matter what village we reach.'

He chose south.

This road led to another. East or west.

He chose east.

They'd been walking almost three hours and Mariel's feet hurt her more and more. The sky clouded over and there was a chill in the air made worse by her still-damp dress. If she had not been with Leo, she would have succumbed to a fit of weeping, but, even with sore feet, damp clothes and hunger, she preferred being with him than alone in comfort.

They'd walked this new road only a short distance before hearing the welcome sound of a wagon approaching behind them. It was a farmer's wagon making slow progress pulled by one sturdy-looking horse.

Leo stood in the road to halt it.

'Can you assist us, sir?' He asked the driver, who was dressed in the clothing of a farm worker, an unlit pipe between his teeth. 'We were in a carriage accident yesterday and we need to get to a village.'

'Carriage accident?' the man's bushy eyebrows rose. 'Out this way?'

'I'm afraid we were carried some distance by the river.' Leo put his hand on the wagon. 'May we ride with you?'

The man shrugged. 'I'm bound for Aylesford, if that will do.'

'That will do nicely.' Leo turned to Mariel, who hurried to the wagon.

'Good day, ma'am,' the driver said, tipping his hat.

'Thank you so much for helping us,' she replied. With Leo's help, she climbed into the wagon.

They were its only cargo. The driver explained he was headed to Aylesford for supplies. Mariel fancied she could smell produce from the wood of the wagon. Kale and asparagus and rhubarb, although it could very well have been her imagination.

The ride to Aylesford provided welcome comfort, even with every bump and rut in the road intensified by the hard wooden floor of the wagon. Anything was preferable to walking. Mariel began to long for the slippers she'd had Penny pack in her bag at the last minute. Her slippers—and maybe Penny—were long gone, however.

Any chance she had for happiness was gone, as well.

Leo caught the gloom that settled on Mariel's face and he feared she was giving in to worry. He put his arm around her. If only he alone could carry this burden.

She rested her head on his shoulder and he tried to savour the simple pleasure of having her next to him, but fears of how to find Walker and Mariel's maid and then seek out the bank clerk plagued him.

He tapped on her head. 'Are you worrying about your maid?'

She shifted, but remained nestled next to him. 'I force myself not to think of Penny—too much, anyway. I was thinking about the future.'

His insides twisted. 'I will take care of you and your family no matter what, Mariel.'

She nodded. 'I did not say before how generous of you that would be.'

She did not know the half of it. It meant giving up the excitement of his less-than-legal, but highly profitable trade. It placed him at the fringe of society again, at a time when he was happy to simply turn his back on it.

She sighed. 'I just wish we could run away and stay away forever and pretend none of this ever happened.'

Why not? His heart beat faster. They could live well in Belgium or France or Italy. 'Is that what you wish, Mariel? Because I suspect everyone will think us dead. We could catch a coach to Dover, change our names and set up housekeeping anywhere we like.'

She took his hand in hers. 'I had that fantasy, but I could not abandon my family. Besides, one cannot truly run away. Your past must always catch up to you.'

'It can be done,' Leo insisted. 'I did it. I succeeded.'

She squeezed his fingers. 'But I am the past that has caught up to you. And look how awful it is.'

He could not regret this time with her, even in its grim circumstances. How could he ever regret making love to her? It was a memory to cherish for as long as he lived.

The wagon rolled along for half a mile before she spoke again. 'I was thinking that I should take the first coach I can find back to London. After we discover what happened to Penny, that is. I—I should like to make arrangements for her.'

'We will find her, but do not give up hope that she will have survived the accident.' He was trying not to give up on Walker, either.

She smiled sadly. 'I have resigned myself to her loss. And to the fact that I must hurry back to London in time to marry Kellford.'

He could not believe his ears. 'No. No matter what, you must not marry Kellford. I cannot permit it.'

'It is the only way,' she insisted.

He frowned. 'Do you fear the taint of being connected to me? Because of the past? Because of my reputation? Do not tell me Kellford is preferable to that.'

'Never think that, Leo!' she cried. 'I love you. I have never stopped loving you. Did not our time in the cabin prove that to you? I cannot be with you, though. Not at the cost of my father's life and my family's reputation.'

His hand curled into a fist. 'Your father does not deserve this sacrifice of you. Your life with Kellford will be hell on earth.'

'I agree my father is undeserving of any mercy.' She uncurled his fingers and gently rubbed his hand. 'But, still, I cannot cause him to die. Most of all, I must look after my two sisters. They are innocent of any wrongdoing, surely.' She paused. 'We are back where we started about Kellford, are we not? I do want you to know that I will cherish this time we have had together. I will hold the memory of making love with you in a special place in my heart. It will be with me always.'

'Mariel—' He did not know what to say. He did not like her giving up.

He must find the bank clerk. It was more important than ever now.

They fell silent, but held hands as the vibrant green of the countryside passed before their eyes. The fields were

dotted with buttercup and cowslip, daisies and dande-
lion. In more innocent days, he and his brothers used to
chase Mariel and his sisters over fields much like these.

Soon a stone tower of a church came into view, then
a peek of red rooftops.

'Aylesford.' The driver gestured.

Leo watched the village come closer and closer. More
traffic filled the road. People walked by carrying huge
bundles. Men rode on horses. Simple wagons, like the
one in which they rode, rumbled behind finer vehicles.
He ought to feel relief. Instead his tension grew. How
long would it take to discover what had happened to
Walker and Penny? Would they be alive? Would he have
enough time to find the bank clerk?

He glanced at Mariel and saw tension pinching her
lovely features. Let them at least discover good news
about Walker and Penny.

The closer they came to the town's centre, the greater
his trepidation. At every turn bad luck had dogged them.
Would good luck never come? He tried to appear reassuring for her sake.

'Can you drop us at a coaching inn?' he called to
the driver.

'Yes, sir,' the man replied.

The man stopped at an inn bearing a sign of St
George slaying the dragon. Leo fished inside a pocket
and handed the man some coins.

The farmer stared at the money in his palm. 'Thank
you, sir!'

Leo helped Mariel out of the wagon and she winced
when he placed her on her feet again.

He frowned, but she waved away his concern. 'It is
not so bad. My feet do not hurt overmuch.'

They entered the inn, where the innkeeper, a round, balding man, met them.

'Good day!' the innkeeper said cheerfully, though he eyed them with more than curiosity. 'What may I do for you? Do you want a room?'

'A meal to start,' Leo said. 'In a private parlour, if that is possible.'

The man looked askance. 'Begging your pardon, sir, but do you have the ready to pay?'

They must look a sight and smell worse, with their dank and dirty clothing, caked with the dust of the road.

'I do.' Leo pulled out his still-damp purse and opened it to show the coins. 'We are in urgent need of food.'

'Come this way.' The innkeeper led them to a small parlour at the back of a public room. 'Hungry, are you?'

Leo answered, 'Very hungry. Bring us whatever is easily prepared. Some ale, as well.' He looked questioningly at Mariel and she nodded approval.

'Very good, sir.' The innkeeper left, closing the door behind him.

Mariel immediately lowered herself in a chair and removed her shoes and stockings. She rose again to put the shoes and stockings near the window, hoping they would dry.

She glanced out the window. 'Oh, no.' She turned to him. 'This inn is right on the river.'

He crossed the room to the window. The river was swollen enough that some of the inn's garden was under water. It was as if the river were reaching out to snatch them back.

He put an arm around her. 'Try not to think about it.'

She leaned on him a moment before swivelling away and choosing a chair that faced the door. 'I want to ask about Penny.'

'We can ask when he brings the food.' He sat down, as well, and unbuttoned his coat. 'I confess I could think of nothing but food.'

She reached across the table and took his hand again. 'I have been thinking about it for the past three hours. Right now I think I can tell by scent alone every dish and drink the public room serves.'

The innkeeper brought food right away. A mutton-and-oyster stew, thick-crusted bread and cheese. A tavern maid carried in ale.

While the tavern maid placed the tankards on the table, the man lingered, still eyeing them curiously. 'Anything else, sir?'

Leo held up a finger while he took a quick gulp of ale. 'We have not eaten in a day. We were in a carriage accident yesterday—'

The innkeeper's brows rose. 'That's odd. Yours is the second carriage accident in two days.'

Leo straightened. 'You know of a carriage accident?'

The man nodded. 'Heard about it yesterday.'

Mariel looked as if she might leap from her seat. 'What did you hear, sir? How do you know of it?'

He shook his head. 'A tragic thing. Two people died, they said.'

Two people died? Were their worst fears coming true?

'Tell us what you know.' Leo pressed.

The man shrugged. 'Don't know much. One of the coachmen who passes through here talked about it. Said he heard about it at the Swan.'

'The Swan?' Leo's voice rose. 'Where is the Swan?'

'West Malling,' the man replied. 'Not far from here. Two or three miles on the London Road. That's where this accident happened, supposedly. On the London Road.'

'How did the man hear of it?' Mariel asked.

The tavern maid spoke up. 'He heard it from someone who was in the accident.'

The innkeeper looked at her in surprise. 'How do you know that?'

She shrugged. 'He was a talkative sort.'

'Sir,' Leo broke in. 'We need fresh clothing. And someone who can drive us to West Malling. I'll make it worth your while if you find both by the time we finish eating.'

'A carriage to take you to West Malling?' He rubbed his chin. 'I cannot think who—'

'Charlie will do it,' the tavern maid piped up.

'Charlie.' The man nodded. 'That's right. He should be willing to do it. What kind of clothing do you want? We don't have much choice in that, I fear.'

'Any clothing will do as long as it is clean.' Leo added, 'And dry.'

'And shoes for me,' Mariel added. 'Shoes and dry stockings.'

An hour later the small carriage that carried them from Aylesford pulled up at the Swan in West Malling. Leo and Mariel lost no time in climbing out of the vehicle and entering the inn. No one was in the hall, so they made their way to the tavern. Most of the booths were empty, but conversation buzzed and tavern maids bustled back and forth.

Leo spied a man behind a bar. 'Sir! Sir!' he called from the doorway and strode quickly toward the man.

The publican continued to wipe glasses with a white cloth. 'Yes?'

'There was a carriage accident yesterday. Do you know anything of it?'

'Heard people talk of it,' the man said.

Leo turned towards the room and raised his voice. 'If anyone has information about a carriage accident yesterday, will he please come to me now. I will give you a handsome reward for good information.'

He heard someone shuffling in his seat, but he could only see the tops of heads over the high sides of the booths. One man moved out of a booth and into the light.

'By God, Walker.' Leo hurried towards him. 'You are alive.'

Leo shook Walker's hand, but relief overtook him and he hugged his friend.

'What of Penny?' Mariel cried.

'I am here!' Penny ran into her lady's arms. 'Oh, miss!'

The two women burst into tears and fussed over each other. The maid had a black eye, which Mariel tenderly touched. Her head was also bandaged.

Walker turned back to Leo. 'We had no hope you had survived. No hope at all.'

'How fared the coachman and the post boy?' Leo asked.

'The coachman hit his head, but otherwise was unhurt. The post boy suffered no harm. He rode the horses here and brought us help.' Walker blinked, half expecting his friend to disappear. 'How did you manage it?'

Leo caught the eye of the publican. 'Is there a private parlour?'

'Of course, sir.' The man ushered them to a private room and they ordered more refreshment.

Penny clung to Mariel while Leo told the story of their survival.

'My poor lady!' Penny exclaimed. 'It must have been horrible!'

'It was at that,' Mariel admitted. 'I would have drowned if not for Leo.'

'And I would have drowned if you hadn't caught me when my hand slipped from the tree,' Leo responded.

'It is sufficient that you both survived.' Walker beamed at them.

Leo and Mariel asked more questions about what happened to Walker and Penny and received more explanations of their ordeal. Walker asked where they had spent the night and Leo told about finding a cabin for shelter. Walker's brows rose, as if he suspected what had transpired between them.

'What is the story of your clothes?' Walker asked.

Leo laughed. 'Does my attire offend my valet's sensibilities?'

Walker grimaced. 'You know I never truly acquired a valet's sensibilities.'

Penny piped up. 'We have your bags! They were thrown from the carriage when it fell.' She turned to Mariel. 'There is a fresh dress for you, and we still have your brush and comb and hairpins.'

'I have been very grateful for the dress I am wearing. If you could have seen my other one...' She made a face.

Leo sat up straighter. 'Now that we know you are safe, we must attend to other matters.' He looked towards Mariel.' 'We must be close to this hunting lodge. Let us find the bank clerk. We have time.'

Walker exchanged a glance with Penny. 'The bank clerk is gone.'

Chapter Seventeen

'Gone?' Leo could not believe his ears.

'Miss Jenkins and I went in search of him today.' Walker explained. 'We just returned a short while ago.'

'You did not find him?' Mariel's voice rose in distress.

Leo drummed his fingers on the wooden table, waiting for Walker to explain.

'We found the hunting lodge with no problem, but the bank clerk was not there.' Walker's expression was grim. 'The housekeeper told us that some men called upon him yesterday morning and that the clerk left with them in some haste.'

'Did she say where they took him?' Perhaps they could still find him in time.

'She heard the men say they would take him back to London, but she did not know more than that.'

'London…' Leo curled his fingers into a fist. 'To Kellford, I'll wager. He'll use the man to ensure Mariel goes through with the wedding.'

Mariel's eyes turned solemn. 'Leo, it is as I feared.'

'It changes nothing,' he insisted. 'We still have four days. We can find him in London.'

'Three days, Leo,' Mariel corrected. 'It is too late to do anything today.'

Leo glanced to the window. 'There's still daylight left.'

But it would soon be evening. Already the sun was low in the sky. Even if they found a carriage to take them to London, there would not be enough daylight left to reach the city.

'There is something else, Fitz,' Walker broke in. 'I am not so certain that the carriage mishap was an accident.'

Leo looked at him. 'Why do you say so?'

Walker rubbed his chin. 'Well, it is nothing so clear, but after we jumped from the carriage, I saw something. I took no heed of it then, as there were other matters more important.' His glance slid to Penny and back to Leo. 'But afterwards I remembered. I saw a man in the wood, running from the accident. Why would he run from it unless he caused it?'

'Why would he cause it?' It made no sense.

'To stop us on our errand.'

'But no one knew we were going after the bank clerk.' Had Leo missed something?

Walker shrugged. 'Kellford's valet might have guessed.' He glanced away. 'Although I swear I never gave him any reason to think I considered what he told me anything more than gossip. Even so, he never showed any inclination to help his employer in any way. But it is a possibility....'

'Or someone in the gaming hells might have told Kellford I was asking about him.' A sick feeling lodged in Leo's stomach. 'Kellford would have wanted to stop me.'

Leo had made a mistake. He'd underestimated Kellford and the lengths the man would go to in order to achieve his ends.

Mariel touched his arm. 'But he would not have wanted to hurt me. What would that serve?'

'He did not know you would be in the carriage.' Leo himself had not known she would come.

Kellford could not have conceived Mariel would be in the carriage, too.

Her eyes widened. 'Leo, he tried to kill you for helping me.'

'He wanted to stop us, not kill us,' Leo said. 'No one could have planned for the carriage to fall in the river.'

'They took the bank clerk away the same day,' Walker added. 'So they could have been on the road the same time as we were.'

'Kellford must have known our plan.' There was no other explanation.

'He also must have known you could die,' Mariel insisted. 'People die from carriage accidents.'

Penny nodded vigorously.

'Likely he did not care,' Leo mused. 'He has long held me in ill favour.'

Mariel shook her head. 'But there was also Walker and the coachman. Surely he could not have had a dislike for a coachman!'

The world abounded with men who cared only for their own gratification and nothing for another's life. Kellford was but one of them.

She lowered her head into her hands. 'He is a monster.'

Leo regarded her intently. 'That is why you must not marry him.'

'It is too late,' she whispered.

Once again happiness had been within Leo's grasp,

but luck had failed him, as it had failed him before when it came to being with Mariel.

No. He refused to give up. Stone-hard determination grew inside him. He refused to give up.

He stood. 'It might be too late to reach London to-night, but we can get a great deal closer. I am going to find a carriage to take us as far as possible tonight. We might still be able to find the bank clerk in time.'

'I'll go with you,' Walker said.

'I will, too.' Mariel rose from her seat.

Leo put a stilling hand on her arm. 'No, Mariel. Rest your feet. We can move faster without you.' He assured her, 'It is only to procure the carriage. We will return very soon.'

Penny extended a hand. 'Come with me, miss. All our things are here in the room Walker got for me. You and I can pack and have our bags brought to this parlour so we will be all ready to go. We can wait for them here.'

Mariel nodded.

Leo embraced her quickly.

His resolution was strong. He'd not fought for Mariel two years ago. This time he'd fight to the bitter end.

For an hour Mariel paced the length of the private parlour, ignoring the pain in her feet. Penny sat by the window, busying herself with some mending.

The situation was worse than ever. Now her choices were to marry Kellford or risk *Leo's* death—and the death of anyone else who got in the way.

She paced faster.

Finally there was a knock on the door. Before she could say, 'Enter,' it opened and Leo appeared.

Mariel clasped her hands together expectantly. 'Leo?'

He avoided her eye, instead looked towards Penny. 'Miss Jenkins, would you mind leaving us alone for a moment?'

Penny rose and curtsied. She hurried to where Walker waited just outside the doorway.

Mariel faced Leo and instantly knew they'd not had success. 'You did not find a coachman to drive us.'

He met her gaze steadily. 'We enquired everywhere. No one was willing to transport us anywhere before tomorrow.'

She turned away. Leo would be safe tonight. If only he would never go back—

She swung around to him. 'Leo! You do not need to return to London at all. You can simply disappear.' She strode over to him, curling her fingers around his arms. 'Penny and Walker could go with you. I can hire a coach tomorrow and still return to London in time. No one would know I was with you. Once I am married to Kellford, you'll be safe.'

'No. That would never do.' He held her face in his hands. 'I have hired a horse. I will ride to London tonight and start the search for the bank clerk.'

She moved away from his grasp. 'No, Leo.'

'The horse is already saddled and waiting for me.' His voice was firm.

She could not allow him to go to London. 'Kellford will discover you. He will try to kill you again.'

His eyes hardened. 'I can handle myself.'

She gripped his coat. 'I cannot let you do this, Leo. It is too dangerous.'

He remained steady. 'My brothers used to tell me what I could and could not do, what was too dangerous. I have faced danger before, Mariel. I can conquer it.'

'Not alone, then,' she persisted. 'Take Walker with you.'

'I need Walker to stay here with you and Penny.' His voice turned low. 'I will not leave you unprotected.' He leaned down and touched his lips to her forehead. 'Do not worry over me.'

His kiss only increased her pain.

She pulled away. 'Do not leave,' she begged. 'I fear all kinds of frightful things. You put me through this once before, I cannot bear it again. This time I know you will be in danger. We may all travel back tomorrow, then. But I want you to give up trying prevent my marriage. Kellford has won.'

He stroked her cheek. 'I am not ready to give up. I'll have more time if I reach London tonight. Trust me that I can take care of myself.'

Helpless tears stung her eyes, but she refused to stop. 'This is the worst thing you could do, leaving me to worry over you.'

He swept fingers over her hair, a soothing gesture. 'I will be in touch with you as soon as possible.'

When he'd left her two years before, her imagination had gone wild with fear that some danger had befallen him. This time she knew precisely what the danger would be—Kellford. She remained unbending, even when he embraced her and touched her cheek. She was already afraid that this might be the last time she saw him.

She watched him say a quick goodbye to Walker and Penny. He glanced back at her.

Her gaze met his as she stood in the doorway, her fears abounding. She watched him until he disappeared from the public room. Despair threatened. Despair and utter helplessness.

She could see no good outcome. She could only see losing him again.

Penny approached her and put an arm around her. 'Mr Walker is ordering us some food. You should sit now.'

She let Penny lead her to a chair. What difference did it make what she did now?

When Walker entered, she looked at him accusingly. 'You should have stopped him, Walker.'

His brows rose. 'I do not tell him what to do, miss.'

'You should have told him this time,' she insisted. 'He is riding into danger; I am sure of it.'

Walker looked towards the door as if still watching his employer leave. 'He is accustomed to danger.' He turned back to Mariel. 'Do you know how he met me?'

She crossed her arms. What difference could it make?

Walker regarded her intently. 'In Paris I encountered some vicious men intent on stealing my purse. I had but a few coins to my name, so I fought them. It was three against one, but I was raised on the streets and knew how to fight. Turns out Paris street fighters fight with their legs—*savate,* it is called—and a kick has a longer reach than a punch. They were kicking me to a fair pulp, when suddenly this fellow I never saw before jumps in to help me. The other men pulled out knives, but this stranger still fought hard. We beat them off.'

The fight where Leo suffered the wounds that scarred his chest? He'd been heroic. He'd saved Walker. Despair threatened again. He would attempt to be heroic again.

Walker went on. 'Fitz and I have been in other dangerous situations. He handled himself well then, too.'

Mariel closed her eyes; all she could see was men beating Leo and no one to come to his aid.

She regarded Walker again. 'You are not there to help him now, are you?'

'Now he knows someone is after him, he'll take care. Do not worry.' Walker sounded confident.

Mariel tried to be reassured, but she knew when she lay in her bed to try to sleep this night, her fears for Leo would return.

Leo made the most of what was left of the daylight, changing horses frequently at the posting inns along the way, resting little himself. He had ridden through another bout of rain and, in the last two hours, near pitch-black darkness, hardly able to see past the horse's head. The roads were muddy and full of ruts from the day's earlier traffic. For many moments he held his breath against the chance that the horse would stumble or, worse, break a leg.

He rarely rode these days but found little pleasure in returning to horseback for such a difficult journey. Each horse he mounted showed a distinct personality. Some were adequate to the task of getting him back to London as fast as possible. Others were not.

He needed to concentrate on the road. His nerves were strained to breaking point and the darkness ahead was an oppressive void.

Dark and oppressive were his fears of failing Mariel. He simply could not fail. He must find a way to stop Kellford before Kellford married Mariel. Each mile convinced him that finding the bank clerk would be impossible. The man would be well hidden. There was no time for him to discover where. He needed another plan.

His horse stepped into a rut, stumbled and faltered

before regaining its gait. Leo drew his concentration back to the road.

Suddenly hoofbeats sounded from behind. In front of him a man on horseback emerged from the blackness and blocked the road.

'Stand and deliver!' the man shouted.

No bloody way, Leo thought. He urged his horse into a gallop and rode directly for the man.

A shot rang out, its explosion illuminating the darkness for an instant. It missed its mark. Leo continued straight for the man.

The highwayman's horse jumped away at the last minute. Its rump brushed against Leo's leg as he sped past. He heard more than one man riding after him, but Leo did not slow down until their hoofbeats faded into the night.

His heart continued to race and the exhilaration of thwarting danger pumped through his veins. From surviving the river to escaping highwaymen, Leo felt like a soldier who'd run a gauntlet and emerged triumphant.

Only one more trial to endure.

After a final change of horses at the next posting inn, the glow of London's gas lamps soon shone in the distance.

The closer Leo came to London, the more he could turn his thoughts to planning a confrontation with Kellford. If there was no time to find the bank clerk, all that was left was to face Kellford directly and convince him to withdraw from marrying Mariel.

Leo returned his horse to a posting inn at the edge of town and hired a hack to take him to Jermyn Street. Once back in his rooms he built a fire in the grate, took off his clothes and washed himself from top to toe, finally feeling clean of the river. He climbed into bed and fell into an exhausted sleep.

Lord Kellford, seated at the desk in his library, looked up from his papers. 'What news have you for me, Mr Hughes?'

He disliked having this common ruffian come to his house, but it was the lesser of two evils. It would be vastly more unpleasant to meet Hughes in whatever hovel he might dwell.

'Your clerk is safely tucked away in Covent Garden.' Hughes smiled an ingratiating smile. 'And the other… matter…will not trouble you again.'

Kellford's brows rose. 'Not trouble me again? Do not say you have eliminated the problem completely?'

Could he be so fortunate? To be rid of Fitzmanning, that self-righteous prig?

Hughes's grin turned more genuine. 'There was an unfortunate carriage accident. The carriage fell into the Medway River. I saw it disappear under the water and be swept away.'

'And he was inside?' Could this be true?

'He was indeed.'

'Ha! Ha!' Kellford clapped his hands. 'Who could have imagined it? I thought you were merely going to stop him.'

Hughes withdrew a piece of paper from a pocket. 'Here is an accounting of my expenses and the fees we agreed upon.' He handed the paper across the desk.

Ah, yes. An accounting. No doubt Hughes would charge as much as possible.

He took the paper from Hughes's hands and peered at the figures.

He gaze shot up. 'This sum is astronomical! It is twice as much as we agreed upon.'

Hughes shrugged. 'Carriage accidents come at a high price.'

How he detested dealing with these low lifes. As soon as he had his fortune, he'd pay this creature and be done with him. From then on he'd move only in the most esteemed circles, precisely where he belonged.

Kellford glared. 'Your task is not completed yet. You still have to produce the clerk at the church Saturday morning. I want my new wife to see him seated in a pew. Not too close to my guests, mind you, but where she can see him.'

'I'll tend to it personally and produce the final accounting afterwards.'

Kellford was sure putting the bank clerk in a pew at church would be quite an additional cost.

He favoured Hughes with a false smile. 'I am very certain you will.'

There was a knock at the door and Kellford's footman appeared. 'You have a caller, your lordship.'

It was much too early for reputable callers. That was why he'd scheduled Hughes at this hour. It would not do for his reputable visitors to catch him with such a man. Obviously his precautions had not worked perfectly.

'Well, who is it?' Kellford snapped.

The footman answered, 'Mr Leo Fitzmanning, sir.'

Kellford felt his face drain of colour.

'I saw him float away,' Hughes whispered. 'I swear it.'

Kellford signalled for him to be quiet. He turned to the footman. 'You may tell Fitzmanning I will see him here.'

The footman bowed and left.

Kellford, anger raging inside him, ripped up Hughes's tally of expenses. 'Unless a ghost walks in here, Mr Hughes. You failed to complete your task.' He waved him away. 'Hide yourself now while I hear what Fitzmanning has to say.'

Hughes walked to the other end of the room and concealed himself behind the curtains.

The footman appeared again. 'Mr Fitzmanning,' he announced.

Kellford fumed. It was not a ghost who walked in. Fitzmanning was very much alive.

'Surprised to see me, Kellford?' Leo's tone was sarcastic.

Surprised and acutely disappointed, Kellford thought, but he fussed with his papers and acted as if this visit was a mere annoyance.

'Nothing you do surprises me, Fitzmanning,' he drawled. 'Even calling upon me at this hour. To what purpose?'

'To discuss your wedding,' Leo growled. 'Call it off, Kellford. Before you carry this too far.'

'Come now.' Kellford made himself laugh. 'I cannot call it off. Happiness is within my grasp.' He peered at Leo. 'It astonishes me that you think this is any of your affair.'

Leo glared at him. 'I have made it my affair.'

Kellford raised a finger in the air. 'Ah, I recall. My lovely betrothed and your sisters have been friends from childhood. You are here at your sisters' behest. The famous Fitzmanning Miscellany coming to each other's aid.'

Leo looked threatening. 'Enough nonsense. I have an offer. I know you started this whole charade in order to pay your debts. I will pay the money lenders for you.

Release Miss Covendale from her engagement. Give up the ruin of her father. Stop now before you are the one taken to the gaol.'

Did Fitzmanning think *he* was behind the carriage accident? No, no, no, no. That was Hughes's idea.

Kellford raised his brows, pretending surprise. 'You are the one speaking nonsense. As to my betrothal…' he wagged his finger '…a gentleman does not cry off. Only the lady has that privilege. Miss Covendale has only to say she does not wish to marry me and I will properly withdraw.'

Not bad bluffing, thought Kellford smugly to himself.

Leo leaned across the desk. 'And then you will proceed to destroy her father and ruin her family. *That* is not the behaviour of a gentleman, sir.'

Kellford's knees started shaking, but he didn't dare show weakness. He lifted his chin. 'I hardly think one of your birth and reputation is a proper judge of gentlemanly behaviour.'

Leo's back stiffened. 'Never mind about me. This is about Miss Covendale. Release her.'

Kellford put on a charming smile, gratified that he'd got under the other man's skin. 'I shall tell you what I will do. I will forbid my wife to see you or any of your family. I must protect her from your corrupting influence.' He could not resist another barb. 'Your interference is unconscionable… But, then, what should I expect from the bastard children of a debauched duke?'

Leo's voice turned even more menacing. 'Murder, perhaps?'

Kellford could not breathe, but he managed to feign indignation. 'Are you threatening me? Oh, dear. That I cannot tolerate. I'm afraid you must leave now.' He waved the man away as if he were an annoying fly.

'Watch your back, Kellford. I mean to stop you.' Leo looked extremely lethal.

He turned on his heel and strode out of the room, slamming the door behind him.

Kellford drew in a breath. He fussed with his papers, trying to calm down.

Hughes stepped out of his hiding place.

Kellford looked up at him. 'What are you waiting for, Hughes? Follow him. Do not fail this time.'

Chapter Eighteen

Hughes hurried out of the town house onto Mayfair street. Fitzmanning was nearing the end of the street, walking at a fast pace.

Still angry, Hughes figured. Kellford had made the man spitting mad.

Hughes whistled for his men. Two of them had accompanied him in case Kellford gave them any trouble.

They emerged from where they were hiding.

'We have to nab that fellow.' Hughes pointed to Leo. 'Try to get ahead of him. He's probably going to Jermyn Street. When it is safe, we grab him.'

The men nodded and took off in different directions to get ahead of Leo without him knowing. Hughes followed behind, keeping him in sight.

His quarry strode towards Berkeley Street. It was busy with traffic. Not a good place to capture him. Not that there were any good places for it between here and the man's rooms on Jermyn Street. They might have to break into his rooms. Not good odds if his servant was in there, though.

Hughes did not see his men, but trusted they were

somewhere ahead. They'd better be. Too much money was at stake and Hughes was not about to lose out at this late date.

Leo strode into the crush of pedestrians on Berkeley Street, still angry. He'd come close to hauling Kellford out from behind his desk and killing him with his bare hands. It had been a huge gamble to try to get Kellford to listen to reason.

He was fresh out of options. He could go to Doring and beg him to accept the return of his money without prosecuting Mariel's father, but why should the man listen to him? What influence could he have?

He had no doubt he and Walker could find the bank clerk eventually, but in less than three days? It had taken them longer than that the first time and now Kellford knew he was looking for the man.

Leo resisted the impulse to push his way through the crowded street. What was he in a hurry for? It was merely anger propelling him forwards. The crowd thinned and he increased his pace again.

It had been a mistake to call upon Kellford, but what else was he to do? Where could he look in London for a man who was meant to be kept out of sight?

Leo crossed Piccadilly, wondering why he was headed back to his rooms. There must be something else he could do, something he'd not thought of yet.

When he started across Arlington Street two men sprang out. Before he could gather his wits, the men pushed him into an alley. Leo twisted out of one man's grip. He swung and landed a hard right to the other man's jaw, sending him sprawling. The first man pulled a knife and charged for him.

Leo grabbed the man's wrist and spun him around,

pulling up on the man's arm behind his back. The knife fell and Leo dived for it.

He picked it up and held it out in front of him. 'Get back!' he growled, slashing at the air, like Walker had once shown him. He inched towards the entrance of the alley.

He was about to step into the safety of busy Piccadilly Street when he was seized from behind, his arms immobilised. The first two men surged forwards. They punched him in the stomach and face. Again and again.

Leo was consumed with pain. If he did not do something, these thugs would beat him senseless.

Unless he became senseless first.

Leo made himself into dead weight, letting the knife fall from a hand gone slack. If he pretended to be knocked out, perhaps he'd have another chance to escape.

'Now we got him, do we kill him or what?' one of the men asked.

Leo felt a new surge of fear.

'Bloody good idea,' the man holding him said. He was lowered to his knees and his head jerked back to expose his throat.

He'd be damned if he'd let them get away with that.

Leo sprang to life, twisting the man, holding him into the path of the knife.

'Ahh!' cried the man who clutched his arm.

Leo ran.

'Don't stand there!' he heard behind him. 'After him!'

He didn't look back and didn't stop, even when he reached the street. He ran to St James's.

This had been no robbery attempt. He'd been the target for killing, just as he had been in the carriage accident. And how coincidental that he'd just left Kellford's.

He heard the pounding of feet behind him. He was the target, for certain. He was close to his rooms, but instinct told him it wouldn't be safe there. That's precisely where they expected him to run. He needed to fool them again.

Leo ran down Jermyn Street, letting them think they knew where he was bound, but, at the last minute, he turned into the churchyard and crossed through it to return to Piccadilly.

He entered the Burlington Arcade, surmising his pursuers would not try anything with the beadles guarding the place. Breathing hard, he ducked into a shop and received curious stares from the clerk and other shoppers. He pretended to look at the merchandise, but watched until his pursuers hurried by.

He walked out, melding into the Arcade's other visitors. He went back to the entrance, trying not to call attention to himself. He moved into Old Bond Street, disappearing from sight as quickly as he could, trying to decide where to go. Where to hide.

He'd succeeded in fighting off the three men, but he might not be so lucky if they caught him a second time. They'd underestimated him once and were not likely to do so again. Now he had a new problem—how to avoid capture and certain death and still save Mariel.

He crossed Berkeley Street again and lost himself in the labyrinth of Mayfair. He walked aimlessly, avoiding Charles Street, although he toyed with the idea of calling on Kellford again and giving him a taste of what he'd just been through.

He thought better of it.

Leo wandered to Park Lane, considering his options. Perhaps he should call upon Mariel's father, convince the man his neck was not worth the sacrifice of his daughter.

He laughed to himself. Covendale would never listen to him. If Covendale cared about his daughter, he would never have put her in this predicament. Indeed, if he cared about her, he would have accepted Leo's suit all those years ago. Besides, if Leo stood in front of the man, he'd more than likely say exactly what he thought of a father who sacrificed his daughter to a man like Kellford.

Leo had time to contemplate his next move. He walked slowly up Park Lane, glancing at Hyde Park on his left, remembering first telling Mariel about Kellford there, remembering how it felt to see her again, how unchanged his feelings had been towards her, how deeply it hurt to have lost her.

The pain of losing her again shot through him, worse than the recent blows to his gut and face. He closed his eyes until he could bear the agony. When he opened his eyes he was staring at Manning House.

His brother's house.

His throat tightened and his insides felt as shredded as if the knife had sliced into him.

Suddenly Mariel's voice came to him. *Ask for help.*

Leo sprinted up to the door and sounded the huge brass knocker with its ducal crest. This time the footman who answered the door was a man who had also been in his father's employ.

He immediately recognised Leo and ushered him in. 'Master Leo! What has happened to you?'

Leo was touched by the man's obvious concern. 'A minor mishap, Shaw. Is my brother at home?'

'I'll see, sir. Come wait in the drawing room.' Shaw moved as if to assist Leo.

Leo shook his head. 'Don't worry over me. I look worse than I feel. Just find my brother.'

It seemed a long time since Leo had been in this room although it had been mere days since his brothers and sisters gathered for the dinner party. So much had happened since then.

He heard footsteps running on the marble floor of the hall. The door flung open and his brother entered, hurrying up to him.

'Leo! Shaw said you were injured.' Nicholas examined him, then put an arm around his shoulders. 'Come sit, for God's sake. Why are you standing?'

Leo lifted a hand. 'I am not hurt, Nick. But I am in trouble. Big trouble. I just need for you to listen to me. Hear me out.'

Nicholas nodded, but sat Leo in one of the chairs. Holding up a finger, he signalled Leo to wait and went to a cabinet and produced a carafe of brandy and two glasses. As if he were a servant and not a duke, Nicholas poured one drink for Leo. Then he positioned a chair directly facing Leo and poured a glass for himself.

He didn't even speak after all that. He simply waited.

Leo took a long sip of the brandy. The warming liquid slid down his throat and calmed him. He took a breath and looked directly at his brother.

'Nick, I need your help....'

Hughes's men met him at the tavern in Covent Garden near where the bank clerk was comfortably housed. Hughes intended to be paid for all the work he'd done and that would not happen unless they found Fitzmanning.

'Well?' he addressed the men.

'We lost him,' one admitted.

'In the Burlington Arcade,' the other said.

Hughes's anger boiled. His arm ached from the gash that the surgeon had just stitched closed. He was in no mood for failure.

'You lost him? You incompetent curs!' He pounded the table with a fist. 'Go back out there and *find* him.' He summoned another man to the table. 'These dunderheads lost him. Round up as many men as you can and find him. Set some men to watch his rooms, Covendale's and Kellford's. While you are at it, have men watch the houses of his brothers and sisters. And the gaming hells, any place he might hide. I'll brook no failure in this. We find him and eliminate him or we do not get paid.'

'Yes, sir,' the man said.

Hughes drained his glass of gin. 'Do not fail me in this. I want him found.' He lowered his voice. 'I want him dead.'

Leo told Nicholas the whole story, and, for once, his brother did not interrupt.

When he finished, Nicholas poured him more brandy, and said, 'I think we should send for Brenner and Stephen.'

Leo nodded.

Within an hour Brenner and Stephen arrived, and, in the meantime, Nicholas had persuaded Leo to wash, don a fresh set of clothing and eat a generous meal. It was nearing noon. Mariel could be arriving in London any time now.

The brothers gathered in Nicholas's library under the watchful eyes of their father's portrait. Leo remembered how his father always made it seem possible to do anything he wanted to do. It was how his father had lived his life, whether what he wanted defied convention or not. It was a lesson Leo had only belatedly learned. Here with his brothers surrounding him, Leo could almost feel the optimism that had been his father's hallmark.

He repeated the story a second time for Brenner and Stephen. It was easier than before, with Nick sitting next to him, filling in details he'd forgotten.

'My God,' Stephen said after it was all over. 'Mariel Covendale? Now you say it, I can very well imagine the two of you together.'

'You are skipping over the little matter of Kellford,' Leo responded.

Stephen waved a dismissive hand. 'We'll fix that.'

Brenner leaned forwards. 'What do you want to do now, Leo?'

Leo could think of only one thing. 'I want to take away the problem once and for all.'

Stephen broke in, 'Kill Kellford, do you mean?'

'It is a thought.' Leo blew out a breath. 'Although I have no wish to hang for the likes of him. No, better to go to Doring. Compensate him for the money Covendale stole from him and convince him not to take any action against his cousin.'

'I agree,' Brenner said.

'I can put up the money.' Nicholas grinned. 'I'm good for it.'

Good for it? He was rich as Croesus.

'No, Nick. I need to pay,' Leo said sharply.

Nicholas peered at him. 'Are you certain, Leo? Because it is truly a trifle to me.'

'I know, but it is a matter of importance to me.' It was of vital importance to Leo. He owed it to Mariel.

'Very well.' Nicholas rose and poured them all more brandy.

Leo gaped at his brother. He'd expected a huge battle, with Brenner and Stephen joining in, insisting he should take Nicholas's offer.

'The problem is,' Leo went on. 'I am not even acquainted with Doring. Why would he allow me to convince him not to prosecute?'

'I have had some contact with him on a parliamentary matter,' Nicholas said.

'I know him slightly,' Brenner added.

'As do I,' Stephen said.

'We should all go to call upon him.' Brenner stood, as if they were leaving this very minute. 'Strength in numbers.'

'We may need strength in numbers if Kellford's men find us.' Stephen glanced out the window.

'Nick, you must not go,' Leo said. 'Not with Emily increasing.'

'She will understand,' Nicholas reassured him. 'Besides, a couple of days won't make a difference. She's not due that soon.'

Could they accomplish all this in time?

Leo glanced up at their father's portrait. He could almost hear his father bellow, 'Of course you can.'

Leo's brothers debated how they should travel to Doring and how to get Leo out of the house unnoticed, just in case Kellford's men were watching. Likewise they discussed how to get messages through to Walker and Mariel.

Leo watched them. He needed them, he realised. Never had he known that with such surety than at this moment.

He could be his own man and still not do it all alone.

When the brothers settled on a plan, Brenner turned to Leo. 'What do you think? Is this what you wish to do?'

Leo looked from one to the other. 'I am unused to my

brothers asking *my* wishes. I thought you would scold me for mucking up matters with Mariel in the first place and then go on to tell me precisely what I'd done wrong every step of the way.'

Nicholas touched his shoulder. 'Leo, this isn't merely some scrape you've gotten yourself into; this is your life at stake. Did you not think we could tell the difference?'

Stephen laughed. 'Yes, we never guessed it was about you and *Mariel Covendale*. Charlotte and Annalise are going to have apoplexy when they find out. They're the ones you should worry about.' He clapped Leo on the back. 'You must let me be there when you tell them. I want to see their faces.'

There was a knock on the door.

'Yes?' Nicholas said.

Shaw opened the door. 'Mrs Bassington, your Grace.'

'Seems I'll be granted part of my wish,' Stephen murmured.

Charlotte burst into the room. 'Nicky, I must speak with—' She came to a sudden halt as her brothers all rose. 'Oh, my!' She looked from one to the other. 'What are you all doing here?'

Nicholas walked over to her and gave her a peck on the cheek. 'What are *you* doing here, Charlotte? You are not even toting one of the pugs.'

She gave him an exasperated look. 'Do not jest. I am in such a pickle and Drew is off somewhere with Amesby. I could not think what to do.'

Nicholas put his arm around her shoulders and gave her a squeeze. 'Come, sit and tell us. With all of us here, we should be able to help you.'

Her expression turned wary. 'It is a rather private matter concerning someone else. I do not know if I should tell all of you.'

Brenner also approached her. 'Now, if you cannot tell your brothers, who can you trust? We have no secrets in this family.'

'Or not too many...' Stephen clarified.

Leo watched this with growing trepidation.

Her explanation came in a flood of words. 'I lied about Mariel...*for* Mariel actually—Mariel Covendale, you know—she asked me to say she was staying at my house, but her father discovered that it was not so, and now I am certain I have managed to get Mariel in terrible trouble, but I do not know what to do about it.'

'They know she was not at your house?' Leo cried. 'When did they discover it?'

Charlotte regarded him with a puzzled expression. 'This morning, apparently. Why?'

'Damnation!' He pounded his fist on Nicholas's desk. 'Could they not have waited a few more hours?'

Charlotte's brows rose so high they almost disappeared into her bonnet.

Stephen sat down next to her and took her hand. 'We have quite a tale to tell you, Charlotte.'

Chapter Nineteen

The hackney coach stopped in front of the Covendale town house. Mariel and Penny climbed out and retrieved their baggage. It was midafternoon. Would Leo have sent a message already? Mariel hoped so.

Ever since he had ridden off the day before, her nerves had not settled. Riding at night posed enough dangers, but how much worse it would be if Kellford discovered Leo was back in London and sent more men to kill him? During the long carriage ride from their inn in Kent her imagination had provided endless dire consequences for him.

She tried to block her fears, reminding herself that Leo said she must trust him, but the fears always broke through.

A message was all she desired.

The town-house door opened before she and Penny had a chance to knock.

'Ah, good day, Edward,' Mariel said to the footman. 'You must have seen us arrive.'

'Yes, miss.' His expression looked distressed.

'Is something amiss, Edward?' she asked.

'You father,' he said quietly. 'Towering rage.'

'Mariel!'

It was her father's voice, booming from the stairway. He descended, looking more than enraged. He looked panicked.

'You and your maid will attend me in the drawing room immediately,' her father ordered.

Penny looked as if she would faint. Mariel took her arm and walked her into the drawing room.

'Where have you been, Mariel?' her father demanded, his voice high-pitched.

'I left you a note. I visited Charlotte Bassington.' She kept her gaze steady.

Her father marched up to her and wagged a finger inches from her face. 'You did no such thing!'

She forced herself not to flinch. 'I assure you I did.'

His eyes looked wild and spittle formed at the corners of his mouth. 'I called there this morning to bring you back. You were not there!'

'I left early in the day,' she responded calmly.

'You are lying to me!' her father shouted.

'It is the truth.' She *had* left early, but not from Charlotte's house.

He put his fists on his hips. 'Then where have you been all day?'

This time she would lie. 'Shopping in Cheapside.'

They could have been shopping in Cheapside. A few days ago she would have shopped anywhere merely to avoid him.

Her father scoffed. 'I do not believe you.' Turning to Penny, he demanded, 'You were with her, girl? Where was she? If you value your employment, you will tell me now.'

Penny still clung to Mariel. 'Ch-Cheapside, sir.' Mariel felt her trembling. 'Shopping.'

Mariel's father pulled Penny away from Mariel and shook her by the shoulders. 'Tell me the truth. Or you are fired.'

'Cheapside!' Penny sounded terrified.

Mariel's father shoved Penny away so forcefully, the girl almost fell. 'One more chance, girl, or you will be discharged immediately.'

'No!' Mariel put a protective arm around Penny. 'Leave her alone!'

'Cheapside,' Penny rasped. 'Shopping.'

Mariel's father grabbed Penny by the front of her dress and pulled her from Mariel's grasp. 'Out!' He pushed her towards the door. 'You are discharged!'

Mariel ran to her. 'You cannot do that, Father.'

'I pay her wages. I most certainly can.' He pointed at Mariel. 'You tell me the truth and she may stay.'

'No, miss,' Penny pleaded.

'Very well, Father, I will tell you where I was.' Mariel stood between Penny and her father. 'I was with a lover!'

'A lover?' Her father turned so white she thought he would pass out. 'You fool! Who is this lover? What if Kellford gets wind of this? He'll not want damaged goods! You'll ruin everything. What will happen to me?'

'To you?' Mariel spoke in a low tone. 'Is it not time to consider me? Or if not me, my mother and sisters? You are responsible for this trouble, Father. Not I.'

'That is neither here nor there,' he said to no purpose. 'Everything was settled. Now you could ruin it!'

Mariel kept an arm around Penny, who wiped her eyes and sniffled. 'I hope I do ruin it!' Mariel said. 'I do not want this marriage.'

His mouth dropped open. 'You would wish your father dead? You ungrateful child.' He cleared his throat and spoke in a careful tone. 'This lover of yours must be prevented from causing any problems. Who is he?'

Mariel stood her ground. 'I will not tell you. It is my own affair and had nothing to do with you.'

Her father looked as if he might say more to her, but a sly expression came over his face.

He turned to Penny. 'You, girl!' he said in a mollifying voice. 'You will tell me who this man is.'

Penny's eyes widened again and she shook her head.

Her father swung back to Mariel, a snide smile on his face. 'Tell me, then, who is the man?'

'Do not do tell, miss,' Penny cried.

How could she tell? If her father let Leo's name slip in front of Kellford, it would definitely cost Leo his life. But she also could not allow him to use Penny to get his way.

'Out with it,' her father demanded, while tears ran down Penny's cheeks. 'Tell me the name of the man or you are discharged.'

'I will not tell you, sir.' Penny sobbed.

He pointed to the door. 'Then, go. Leave this house immediately. This instant!'

Mariel embraced Penny and whispered in her ear, 'Go to Walker. He will take care of you. Tell him what happened here.'

'Yes, miss.' Penny nodded.

Mariel gave her one swift hug before Penny hurried out of the room.

Mariel faced her father again. 'That was not well done of you, Father.'

Her father wiped his face. 'Tell me the man's name and she may come back.' His voice was more desperate than demanding.

She merely glared at him.

'Please, Mariel?' His breathing accelerated. 'Please do not ruin this. I'll hang, if you do.'

'At the moment, Father, I do not care.' She was still furious at him for sending Penny away. 'You have accomplished nothing but the injury of an innocent girl. I cannot stand the sight of you. I am going to my room.'

She did not wait for his permission.

By the time she reached the hall, Edward, who was just closing the door on Penny, waved her over. 'You have a message, Miss Covendale.'

Her father marched past her and snatched the paper from Edward's hand. He read it and crumpled it in his fist. 'Go up to your room, you ungrateful wretch.'

She reached for the note in her father's hand. 'I'll have my note first.'

He pulled it out of her reach. 'Go to your room.'

This was impossible to tolerate. The message was from Leo; she just knew it.

Edward approached her, standing between her and her father. 'I will carry your bag for you, miss. Penny took hers with her.' He winked, which was very unlike him.

She followed the footman up the two flights of stairs to her bedchamber.

At her door, he turned to her and leaned close. 'I read the note,' he said in a hushed tone.

'You read it!' Her heart beat faster.

He looked sheepish. 'Well, the seal broke.' He opened the door and put her bag inside her room.

She seized his arm. 'What did it say?'

'It said, *Arrived safely. Have plan. Do not worry. Take care.*' He lifted his palms in the air. 'It was not signed.'

She squeezed his arm. 'Thank you, Edward. It is enough.'

He bowed and started to walk away, but turned back. 'It was not right for Mr Covendale to dismiss Penny like that.'

'I agree, Edward.' It was abominable.

He nodded and hurried back to the stairway.

Mariel entered her room and closed the door behind her.

Bless Edward for being a busybody. The note was not nearly enough, though. It said almost nothing. Like her note to Leo two years ago. Had she written more carefully, he might have guessed her father's manipulation. But Leo's note might have been cryptic on purpose. If anyone—such as her father—confiscated it, it would tell them nothing.

But why had Leo told *her* to take care? Did danger still exist? It must or he would not have written that. She could do nothing but wait, not knowing at all what was happening outside these walls.

She lowered her face into her hands. Once again she was left waiting…and not knowing.

Penny walked through Mayfair with tears streaming down her cheeks. She was terrified. She had no employment and no references. How was she to find a new position?

Plus what would happen to Miss Covendale? Her father was so very angry. Could he force her to marry Lord Kellford, after all?

She hurried through the streets, clutching her portmanteau, all she had of her belongings. Would she even be able to get her other things from her old room at the Covendale town house—the pair of gloves from her father's shop, the garnet cross that had been her mother's? That was all she had left of them.

When she reached St James's Street, young gentlemen loitered on the corner. They made rude comments to her as she passed by. Her faced burned with shame at the words they used and the names they called her. She kept her eyes straight ahead and pretended she did not hear them.

Soon she could see the building where Mr Fitzmanning lived. She quickened her step and wiped her eyes before knocking upon the door.

There was no answer. Her nerves jangled even more. What if Mr Walker or Mr Fitzmanning were not at home?

Finally she heard Walker's voice behind the door. 'Who is there?'

'It is Penny,' she cried. 'Oh, please open the door for me!'

The door opened and he seized her arm and pulled her inside, putting her behind him. He glanced quickly out the doorway before closing the door again and turning to her. 'Why are you here? What has happened?'

He sounded angry and it frightened her. 'I—I had nowhere else to go.' Her voice cracked.

He wrapped his arms around her. 'Do not weep. Do not weep. I dislike seeing you so distressed.'

She clung to him. He was so strong and he smelled so nice and she felt so safe with him. He brought her over to a sofa and sat down with her.

Taking her hands in his, he said, 'Now tell me what happened.'

'Mr Covendale found out that my lady lied to him and he tried to make me tell where she went and who

she was with, but I wouldn't do it.' She took a shudder-
ing breath. 'So he discharged me and sent me away!'

His expression hardened. 'He discharged you?'

She nodded and tears filled her eyes again. 'What
will happen to me? How will I find another position?'

He held her again. 'You do not need another position.
I will take care of you.'

It seemed like he held her a very long time. He
soothed her with this talk of taking care of her. She
would be safe forever. She took a deep breath at the
satisfaction of that thought.

Finally he released her and handed her his handkerchief. She wiped her eyes and blew her nose.

'Why were you angry at me when you opened the
door?' she asked, holding the handkerchief in her hand
and vowing to wash it for him.

His expression hardened again. 'I was not angry at
you. There are men watching these rooms—Kellford's
men, I imagine—I merely wanted to get you inside as
quickly as I could.'

Her eyes widened. 'Where is Mr Fitzmanning?'

He frowned. 'I do not know. A note was here when I
arrived. It had been slipped under the door. It only said
he would be away.' He rubbed his face. 'Better he stay
away. I'm worried that these ruffians will nab him if
he comes near.'

'We can watch for him and warn him,' she offered.

He wore the nicest expression of concern for her. 'I
will fix you something to eat. No doubt they did not
feed you at the Covendale house.'

'We had just walked in when her father set upon
her.' She rose and moved to a chair with a view of the
window. 'Should I watch out the window while you
cook?'

'No need. He won't be home tonight.' He picked up a piece of paper and unfolded it. *'I'll be gone a day,* it says.'

'Where did he go?' she asked.

He looked at the note again. 'I do not know.'

'He'll be away all night?'

He nodded. 'I suppose.'

That meant she would be alone with Walker all night long. Like at the inn. The idea excited her.

Kellford descended his stairs, spying Hughes waiting below in the hall, twirling his hat in his hand. When he reached the bottom step, he gestured for Hughes to follow him into the drawing room. He checked his timepiece, a fine gold watch that he had purchased after a very lucrative spell of faro. In an hour's time he had an appointment with Mr Carter. The money lender undoubtedly wanted to be assured that he'd soon receive payment.

Kellford hoped Hughes would bring him news that meant Carter would have nothing to be concerned about.

'Well, what do you have to say?' Kellford asked. 'It had better be good news.'

'It is good news, you could say.' Hughes spoke with an edge to his voice.

It made Kellford uneasy. 'Out with it, then.'

Hughes pulled at his collar. 'We have not captured him, but we have the next best thing. He will not bother you.'

Kellford's blood raced. 'Did you kill him?'

Hughes averted his gaze. 'No...but let me explain.'

Kellford waved his hand impatiently.

Hughes cleared his throat. 'I spread my men throughout the city, anywhere Fitzmanning might go—at great expense, I might add.'

'An expense you will, of course, take upon yourself,' Kellford inserted.

Hughes inclined his head. 'As I was saying, my men were watching for Fitzmanning. Lo and behold, one of them spots him coming from his brother's house. There had been lots of activity there all afternoon. Footmen coming and going; two gentlemen and one lady calling. Nobody saw Fitzmanning go in, though.'

Kellford poured himself a glass of sherry. He did not offer Hughes any.

'After an hour or so, grooms bring four horses around,' Hughes went on. 'A little while later, out he comes. Fitzmanning. The duke is with him, giving orders to everybody. Two other gents are with them. They mount up, all these gents around Fitzmanning. There was no way my men could get to him.'

'Where did they go?' Kellford took a sip, feeling his nerves jangle.

'They rode out of town,' the man responded.

'How do you know they rode out of town?' Hughes asked.

Hughes looked self-satisfied. 'My men followed them, which was not too hard with all the other carriages and such on the streets. They did not travel fast. My men were able to follow them all the way to Westminster Bridge.'

Kellford felt his cheeks flush. 'You dolt! What if they merely had an errand in Lambeth?'

Hughes smirked. 'Well, in that case the men posted at the bridge will see them upon their return.' He stared at Kellford's sherry glass. 'I also left a man at the duke's house in case they rode back another way.'

Kellford nodded approvingly. 'That might do it.'

Kellford's confidence was restored. He would convince Mr Carter that all was proceeding without mishap.

He'd also make certain there were no surprises at the church. His wedding was a mere two days away.

When it was finally dark outside, Walker could tolerate no more waiting. He decided to leave the rooms and gather whatever information he could.

'I'll be back as soon as I am able,' he told Penny. 'Do not allow anyone to enter. Do not even respond if there is a knock on the door. Pretend you are not here.'

She nodded, her beautiful blue eyes wary.

'Go sleep in my bed. I'll take Fitz's when I return.' He put on a black coat, raising the collar to better hide his white shirt.

'I won't sleep until you return,' she said in a trembling voice.

He reached over and touched her arm.

Her eyes looked into his. 'You must be careful.'

'I will.'

She then did a very unexpected thing. She rose on tiptoe and kissed him. The simple touch of her lips ignited his senses. And made him feel valued.

He now possessed a reason to be careful, so he could come back to her. No more living for the moment, not caring what came next. In fact, he no longer liked the idea of the trade he and Fitz were involved in. When this was all over, he'd tell Fitz he wanted to do business on the up and up. He wanted to be a man deserving of Penny's sweet kiss. He wanted to spend the rest of his life making hers happy.

He climbed out a back window and dropped to the ground. Soundlessly he made his way out the small yard behind the building and onto the street. Hiding in the shadows, he spied two men still watching for Fitz. He wished he could warn Fitz before he returned and walked into a trap.

Walker hurried away, bound for the tavern where he'd met Kellford's valet. He walked in the place and ordered ale, thirsty after hurrying through town. He threaded his way through the tables, looking for the valet.

'Walker!' a voice called.

It was Kellford's valet, seated at a table alone. The fussy man looked uncharacteristically dishevelled. His clothing was wrinkled and he'd not shaved.

Walker approached the man's table. 'What has happened to you?'

'I hoped you'd come,' the man said, slurring his words. 'I've been given the sack. Summarily discharged without references or prospects.'

Like Penny, Walker thought. He joined the man's table.

The valet peered at him. 'Do you work for Mr Fitzmanning?'

No sense lying about it. 'I do.'

'And you wanted information from me?' He looked wounded.

Walker nodded. 'Fitzmanning is a family friend of Miss Covendale and does not wish to see her ill used.'

'Ah.' The valet's brow cleared. 'I understand perfectly. The poor lady. But you need not have engaged in deception.'

'I did not deceive,' countered Walker. 'I merely did not tell you the name of my employer.'

The valet waved a hand. 'Makes not a whit of difference now. I'm sacked because Kellford assumed I'd been the one to tattle about the bank clerk and his where-abouts.'

'I am sorry to hear it,' Walker said with honesty. 'Do you know where the bank clerk is at present?' If he could find the bank clerk tomorrow, there would still be time to ensure the clerk's cooperation.

'Covent Garden, but I do not know precisely where. Kellford's newly hired men took care of it.' He paused. 'Those men were hired to eliminate your Mr Fitzmanning. Kellford's sparing no expense.'

'We've been made aware of that fact.' Walker reached into his coat pocket and removed a calling card. 'This has my direction. Come see me. You've helped us and we will help you.'

Chapter Twenty

The next morning Mariel requested a bath, something she longed for, but also something that provided her an excuse to avoid her parents.

Her father had made her so angry the day before that she could not think straight. To send Penny away! It was unconscionable. To have no word of her—coupled with not knowing Leo's whereabouts—was driving her mad.

Perhaps Edward would pass notes for her. He'd acted as her ally before.

Heartened by this idea, Mariel was able to relish the clean water and the fragrant French soap that was her favourite. She bathed thoroughly and washed her hair and, with one of the housemaids to assist her, dressed in a morning dress.

The maid made a great effort to see that she was comfortable. The girl did not speak directly, but Mariel suspected all the servants knew by now that she did not want to marry Kellford and that she'd been with another man. It touched her beyond measure that the servants showed her sympathy rather than censure.

Combing the knots and tangles from her hair brought back the memory of the river and how close she and Leo had come to death. How much it had changed things for her. Nothing mattered more to her than Leo being alive and unharmed, but she could not know if he were ambushed or captured or…worse.

She held her head. Her mind was spinning as it had done two years before, consumed with fears and speculation, not knowing where he was, if he was safe.

Please let him be alive, she prayed. *Please just let him be alive.*

The maid knocked on the bedchamber door and opened it a crack. 'Lord Kellford to see you, miss!'

'Kellford?' What did he want?

'Edward said he is waiting in the drawing room.' The girl's voice showed the alarm Mariel felt inside.

'This is the last person I wish to see,' she muttered.

The housemaid nodded in agreement.

She took a breath and gestured for the maid to come over. 'Help me put my hair up into a cap.'

The girl twisted her still-damp hair into a bun and secured it with hairpins.

'My caps are in the second drawer in the chest of drawers.' Mariel stuck in more hairpins while the maid ran to find a cap.

She brought back one made entirely of Belgian lace, edged in a ruffle and embellished with a pink silk ribbon. It was the prettiest one in her possession.

She would have preferred to look dowdy.

She did not want to tarry, however. She wanted to hear what Kellford had to say, hear if he would speak of Leo.

When she entered the drawing room, Kellford was seated with her mother. Her father stood nearby.

Kellford immediately stood and approached her with

arms open. 'Good morning, my dear!' he exclaimed, placing a kiss upon her cheek.

It paid to be careful. This was a man willing to kill Leo on the mere chance he might spoil the scheme to marry her. She must not let on that she knew anything about that, nor that Leo had survived the attempt.

'Why are you here?' she asked, finding it impossible to be entirely civil.

Her father sent her an anxious glance.

Kellford chuckled good-naturedly. 'Why, to see my prospective bride. Why else? Only one more day to go, my dear.'

'It is so exciting!' her mother piped up. 'Tomorrow at this time we shall be at the church with several of our dear friends to share the day with us.'

Kellford smiled. 'Are you quite prepared for the wedding, my dear?'

She faced him without expression. 'Not entirely.'

He gaped at her in mock horror. 'My goodness! You had better get busy. I do not wish to be kept waiting at the altar.'

'She will be there,' her father said reassuringly. 'I will see to it.'

Kellford's grin widened. 'I trust you will, sir. I have never doubted your willingness to give away your daughter.'

'I do think she jests.' Her mother tittered nervously. 'Her bridal clothes are ready. All is in preparation for the wedding breakfast. I cannot see what more needs to be done.'

Kellford walked back to Mariel's mother and took her hand. 'I am certain you have personally seen to every detail. I could not be more grateful to you.'

Her mother had done more fretting than anything

else, but Mariel did not care about the wedding breakfast. She did not care about the wedding clothes. She
only wanted Leo to be safe.

'Mother,' she impulsively asked, 'would you mind
terribly if I spoke to Lord Kellford and Father alone?'

Her mother looked alarmed. 'Well…no… I suppose
not.' Kellford assisted her in rising from her seat.

Mariel's father glared at his daughter, but a twitching
hand showed he also feared what she might say or do.

She walked her mother to the door.

'You will be good, will you not, Mariel?' her mother
pleaded.

Perhaps her mother was more aware than Mariel
thought. 'Do not worry, Mama.'

When the door closed behind her mother, Mariel
leaned against it. 'I have a proposition for you.'

Her father braced himself against the back of a chair.
Kellford merely smiled, as if whatever transpired would
amuse him.

One last try, Mariel thought.

She walked towards them. 'As you both know, I do
not want this marriage.' She glanced at her father. 'But
I also do not want my father to be apprehended for theft
and I do not want scandal. I have a solution for all of us.'
She faced Kellford. 'I will pay your outstanding debts.
I will even double the figure.'

Kellford's eyes were cold. 'You have no money, my
dear, not unless you marry me.'

'I can borrow the money,' she retorted. 'In two years'
time I will be able to repay the debt.'

Offering Kellford this proposition was surely a for-
lorn hope, but she had to try.

Kellford slithered closer to her. 'See? That is why

I must marry you, my dear. You have no idea how to manage money. It would be foolish to double a figure when half the amount would do. And where would you get such a loan? I assure you no bank would lend to you.'

She straightened. 'Perhaps not a bank, but I suspect the Duke of Manning would.' Or his brother. 'I am certain my friend, his sister, would convince him.'

Kellford's eyes flickered, but he resumed his apparent good humour. 'Not without charging interest and then you would lose even more of your fortune. And to no good purpose, I might add.' He shook his head. 'No, you are no manager of money, my dear. You must marry me and let me take that burden off your shoulders.' He turned to her father. 'You agree, do you not, Mr Covendale?'

Her father nodded. 'Of course I agree.'

'Do not be ridiculous,' Mariel said. 'You want my fortune, nothing else.'

She had known this all along, of course, but could not resist one last attempt.

Kellford's eyes flickered with malevolence. 'I assure you, I want more than your fortune.'

Mariel shivered.

Kellford slid a glance back to her father. 'Mr Covendale, it is my turn to ask an indulgence. May I have a few moments with my lovely betrothed?'

'Certainly.' Her father could hardly be more agreeable. Anything to keep Kellford from reporting his crime, Mariel suspected.

Her father left the room and Kellford turned back to her. He was no longer smiling.

She stood her ground while he came so close she could smell his breath.

'I have had enough of you involving the Fitzmanning Miscellany in our affairs.' His voice lost all its charm. 'It stops now.'

She made herself stare blankly. 'Asking my friend to make the request of the duke is not involving the whole family.'

He ran his finger down the ruffled lace of her cap. 'Do not play innocent with me, my dear. I know you sent the bastard brother after the bank clerk.'

She did not flinch. 'Bastard brother?'

He laughed. 'You know perfectly well whom I mean.' He gave her a self-satisfied look. 'But you need not concern yourself further with Leo Fitzmanning.'

Her knees weakened. Had something happened to Leo? Or did Kellford still believe Leo drowned in the river?

'Concern myself? Are you jesting?' She made her tone indifferent, but her heart pounded.

Please let him be alive, she prayed. *Let him be alive.*

Kellford smirked. 'An unimpeachable source informed me that Fitzmanning and his brothers left town yesterday.' He stuck out a prideful chin. 'Rode away, all four of them, over the Westminster Bridge. They are gone, my dear. Perhaps I had some influence over their leaving. I would fancy I did.'

Relief washed over her. His brothers were keeping him safe. She could envision it—Leo's brothers discovering the attempt on his life and spiriting him away. They could be taking him to Ramsgate to catch a packet to Calais, for all she knew. He would be safe.

He wagged a finger in her face. 'So none of the Fitzmanning Miscellany will be riding in to rescue you. And, believe me, if they are looking for the bank clerk, they will not find him. He is in town, close by in case I need him.

As the housekeeper in his hunting lodge had told Walker.

Mariel must not appear affected.

She scoffed, 'You needed my father to leave the room so he would not hear that the Duke of Manning and his brothers rode out of town? You could only tell me this privately?'

He leaned close again. 'I wanted you to know that I have ways of eliminating people who become troublesome to me. If you value your friends, you will not allow them to cross me.'

'I am so warned,' she responded sarcastically.

'And you will not cross me, my dear,' he continued. 'Recall that once I have your fortune, your value to me will be greatly diminished.'

She understood that implied threat.

'Well…' she stepped back and pasted on a false smile '…we are done, then. It has been so charming to have this little tête-à-tête with you, Lord Kellford.' She extended her hand for him to shake. 'I will remember to pass on your fondest farewells to my parents.'

He shook her hand, then scowled when he realised she had manipulated him into it. And that she had dismissed him. He walked out with an angry step.

Mariel sank into a chair. She felt faint with relief.

Leo was safe!

It was good that he'd left town, she told herself. Good that he was seeing matters her way and honouring her wishes for him to stay safe. His brothers would surely see to it that he did not rush in to stop the wedding.

This was the best solution. Everyone she cared about would be uninjured.

She alone would pay the price.

The day dawned grey and overcast over Brighton, matching Leo's mood. He wanted to feel hopeful. His brothers' support and optimism ought to have helped, but when he woke in his room at the Castle Inn, a sense of foreboding washed over him.

Leo and his brothers had ridden to find Lord Doring. Stephen had heard he'd left London two weeks earlier for his country estate near Brighton. A horse breeder like Stephen, Doring wanted to be present to supervise the foaling of one of his favourite mares.

They'd ridden hard the day before, reaching Brighton at dusk. Leo felt buoyed by his brothers' company. Their support humbled him. At the inn, they'd stayed awake late into the night, talking, clearing the air between them. He'd told them some of what he'd been through the last two years. They'd listened.

It should have been enough to hearten him, but too much was at stake this day and he'd already experienced so much failure.

At midmorning the inn's stable boy brought their horses to them. Nicholas had provided Leo with a strong mare, one that Stephen had bred. Once on horseback again, in the weak sunshine, Leo felt his spirits rise and his determination grow. This time he could not fail. Mariel's happiness—her life—depended upon it.

They rode past the Brighton racecourse. According to the direction given to them at the Castle Inn, Doring Park was nearby.

'How fitting that Doring's estate is near the racecourse,' Stephen remarked as they rode by. 'He is passionate to a fault about horses. Worse than you and I ever were, Leo.'

It was hard to believe that anyone could be more passionate about horses than Leo had been. It seemed a long time ago, but, he had to admit, that passion was gone now.

Soon Doring Park's stately white mansion came into sight. Built on a gentle rise and surrounded by pasture, it became visible when they were still some distance away. When they turned onto the long, winding private road that led up to the house, Leo lagged behind.

This was a great gamble he embarked upon. He planned to tell Doring about his lord cousin's theft and to convince him to overlook it. If he failed at this, it would cost Mariel's father his life and create the ruin Mariel feared for her family.

As if reading Leo's mind, Brenner turned around and gave him a reassuring smile. All his brothers were full of confidence and that did reassure him.

Their approach was announced by a shrieking peacock who displayed his colourful tail. By the time they reached the front entrance, two footmen had emerged.

Nicholas did not even give them a chance to speak. 'The Duke of Manning and his brothers to see Lord Doring,' he said in an imperious voice that reminded Leo of their father.

The footmen's jaws dropped. Obviously dukes did not often call.

One footman collected himself quickly and bowed. 'Your Grace. I will announce you immediately.'

'Very good,' Nicholas responded.

Leo and his brothers dismounted.

Nicholas gestured to the horses. 'Have someone tend to the horses, as well.'

The other footman hurried to hold the horses.

'If your Grace would follow me,' the first man said.

They entered the house into a large hall with dark wooden floors and a sweeping staircase. Another footman appeared to take their gloves and hats.

The first man led them to an oval-shaped drawing room whose many windows made the most of what little sunlight there was that day. None of the brothers sat, nor did they speak much while they waited for Lord Doring.

Stephen gazed out the windows, watching grooms lead their horses away. Brenner stood next to the white marble mantel, glancing at the clock.

Nicholas clapped Leo on the shoulder. 'This will work,' he told Leo. 'I'm convinced of it.'

Brenner turned back and smiled. 'I agree.'

Stephen said nothing.

It seemed an interminable length of time before they heard footsteps outside the door, although the clock's hand had not even moved halfway round the dial.

The door opened and the footman stepped in again, announcing, 'The Earl of Doring.'

Doring, a vigorous man in his late fifties, strode in and walked directly to Nicholas.

'Your Grace.' He nodded respectfully. 'Forgive me for keeping you waiting. I was just in from the stables when you called.'

Nicholas offered a handshake. 'I understand perfectly.'

Leo, Stephen and Brenner approached and stood behind Nicholas, who stepped aside.

'Allow me to present my brothers.' He gestured towards them. 'I believe you know the Earl of Linwall.'

Brenner offered his hand. 'A pleasure to see you again, sir.'

'Mr Stephen Manning,' Nicholas went on.

'We are acquainted, sir,' Stephen said.

Doring also shook Stephen's hand. 'Ah, yes. We last spoke at Newmarket, as I recall.'

'Newmarket.' Stephen nodded. 'I recall it well.'

'You may not have met my youngest brother.' Nicholas moved on to Leo. 'Mr Leo Fitzmanning.'

Leo noticed Doring's eyes narrow very slightly. The man, of course, realised he was the bastard brother.

'A pleasure to meet you.' Leo extended his hand.

Doring accepted it without hesitation. 'Indeed. It is my pleasure, as well.' His gaze swept over all of them. 'I've ordered refreshment, but do sit down. Your Grace, I am eager to hear the purpose of this unexpected visit.'

The man was affable. That was in Leo's favour.

Leo allowed himself to hope. 'If I may explain, sir. You may have heard that your cousin's daughter is to marry Baron Kellford—'

'Of course I heard, but I do not care one way or the other about the affairs of my cousin.' Doring mollified his churlish tone. 'It should be good that the daughter marries, shouldn't it? I admit I am little acquainted with the man, but he is a charming sort.'

'He acts the charmer, it is true.' Leo met his gaze. 'But he will make a cruel husband. I have seen him inflict injury on women. It is how he receives pleasure.'

Doring's brow rose. 'Is that so? Well, my cousin's daughter is of age. Her father cannot force her to marry the man. Warn her against him.'

'It is not so simple,' Nicholas said.

Doring went on. 'My cousin is an idiot. He should oppose her marrying any man. In two years she will be wealthy. She will make a fine cash pot for him then. He has more of a chance to get money out of a daughter than her husband.' He threw up a hand. 'Enough talk of my tiresome cousin. Why does his daughter's marriage concern me?'

'Hear him out,' Nicholas said.

At that moment, a footman entered with a crystal decanter and five glasses.

'Ah!' Doring clapped his hands. 'Some sherry, gentlemen?'

Leo waited impatiently while the sherry was poured and glasses handed out. Leo took one sip and placed his glass on a table.

When the servant left the room, he faced Doring again. 'I shall explain why you are involved in this, Lord Doring.' He paused, collecting his words. 'Kellford possesses some very damaging information about your cousin. If Miss Covendale does not marry him, Kellford will disclose the information and your cousin—and his wife and daughters—will be ruined.'

Doring's colour heightened. 'I should have known. What has my cousin done this time? Reneged on a voucher? Cheated at cards? I am certain it is something reprehensible.' He pointed to Leo. 'Whatever it is, leave me out of it. I told Cecil I would no longer lift a finger to help him. He is the veriest leech, I assure you. He'll suck me dry with his gambling debts. I have cut him off. Washed my hands of him! I do not care if he lands in debtor's prison. I will do no more for him.'

Leo's gaze remained steady. 'It is not for his sake we are here, but on Miss Covendale's behalf.'

Doring stood. 'You cannot hold his daughters or wife over my head! I warned Cecil that he is responsible for them, not I. I told him I would do nothing more for him or his family. Nothing! My fortune was gained honestly and I do not gamble it away. Cecil plunders his estate and throws its profits into a roll of dice. It is none of my affair.'

'It becomes your affair—' Leo also rose '—because Covendale stole money from you. Kellford has the proof—'

'Stole money from me?' Doring blanched.

'He forged your name on a banknote,' Leo explained. 'He trusted that you would not notice and that your man of business would not heed it as something unusual.'

Doring began to pace. 'I cannot believe he would stoop so low. He will pay for this! My cousin will not get away with it. I'll see him hanged first!'

Leo blocked his path. 'That is why Miss Covendale is compelled to marry Kellford—'

Nicholas broke in. 'Kellford has proof of the theft and threatens to expose the crime if Miss Covendale does not marry him.'

Doring gave a sarcastic laugh. 'Well, tell her she doesn't have to marry the man now. *You* have told me about the crime. Soon the world will know, because I intend to prosecute. Nobody steals from me. Nobody.'

'That is what you must not do!' Leo raised his voice. 'Think of the man's wife and daughters.'

Doring whirled on him. 'My cousin should have thought of them.' He looked at each of the brothers. 'Why do you come tell me all this? Why is this any of your concern?'

Nicholas explained, 'Our family is closely connected to Miss Covendale. We grew up with her. She has always been a favourite of our sister Charlotte.'

'No.' Leo caught Doring's eye again. 'The truth is that I love Mariel. I am trying to save her from this terrible marriage.'

Doring threw up one hand. 'You've saved her, as I said. You've told me. But her father is a different matter—'

Leo spoke quickly. 'I will repay the money her father stole from you.'

'I will pay you interest,' Nicholas added. 'You will lose nothing. There will be no need to prosecute.'

'And wait for what my cousin will do next?' Doring laughed again. 'Steal from someone else, perhaps? No, the man must be stopped.'

Brenner rose from his seat. 'We'll keep him under control.' He walked up to Doring. 'You knew my father, did you not, sir?'

Doring shrugged. 'You know I did.'

'Then you know that I was successful at keeping a foolish gambler in check.' Brenner's late father had nearly lost the family estate by making bad investments until Brenner took over control of the finances. 'We will accept responsibility for your cousin.'

Stephen remained seated and looked lost in his own thoughts. His detachment annoyed Leo, even though he could not think of what Stephen could do to help the situation.

Leo tried again, turning to Lord Doring. 'I beg of you, sir. Spare Miss Covendale. And her mother and sisters. They are innocent in this.'

Doring shook his head. 'No. My cousin bears the burden of ruining his family, not I. I have helped him time and time again and he continues to rack up debts. I do not need the money. It is not a matter of money, but of respect. He has treated me with the greatest disdain. He deserves whatever fate a judge and jury bestows on him. This is the last straw.'

Leo lowered himself into the chair and pressed his

fingers against his forehead. His gamble had failed. Doring would not listen to reason, would not have compassion for Mariel.

He heard Stephen mutter, 'He cares more for his horses.'

Indeed. Doring's horses would be cosseted and indulged, but his own flesh and blood would suffer.

Leo glanced out the window.

'Can we not convince you?' Nicholas persisted. 'You must know my father was a great friend of the king. If you ever need royal favour, I am certain his Royal Majesty would bestow it if we asked.'

Doring winced. 'I have no wish to offend the king, but I cannot be swayed.'

Leo ached with each word spoken. He rose again. 'It is no use, Nick. We might as well take our leave.'

Nicholas nodded. 'You are right.'

Doring looked apologetic. 'Your Grace, I do regret that I am unable to comply with your wishes. I hope you understand my thinking on this matter.'

'I do not,' Nicholas snapped. 'But I will waste no more of my time with you.' He started towards the door.

Stephen rose from his seat. He and Brenner followed Nicholas to the door.

Leo remained where he was.

'Wait,' he cried when they reached the door. 'Stephen, you once offered me a breeding pair of horses from your stable. May I consider those mine?'

Stephen looked puzzled. 'Of course you may. They are yours.'

Leo swung around to Lord Doring. 'Then I have another proposition for you, sir. This is one I hope you will accept—'

Chapter Twenty-one

Mariel descended from the carriage in front of St George's Church near Hanover Square. Even though she had not fussed about her appearance, she supposed she looked like a woman about to get married. She wore one of her good dresses, a pale pink muslin, and a hat with a matching pink ribbon.

Black bombazine and black gloves would have suited the occasion better.

She noticed a couple of men standing outside the church. Kellford's men, she guessed. Were they the ones who had caused the carriage accident? Perhaps they were there to ensure she did not run away.

The day before had been agony. The nightmare of marrying Kellford had become very real and all she wanted to do was flee. During the night her fears were magnified. What would her nights be like from this day forwards? Would she be able to make this sacrifice?

It was still the best option, the only choice.

If only they had been able to stop Kellford. They'd come so close.

At least Leo was far away. She must console herself with that fact.

Mariel's mother hurried into the church. Her father lingered behind and walked with Mariel.

As they passed between the church's stone columns, her father whispered to her, 'You are not going to do anything foolish, are you?' He looked haggard with worry.

She did not answer him. Each step made it harder to stick to her resolve. Each breath became more difficult.

They entered the church where Mariel's mother was already busy greeting the guests, about thirty friends, members of the *ton* who had been invited to witness the vows.

Mariel held back, scanning the church. Did she hope to see Leo there, or did she fear it?

In a pew, several rows behind where the guests sat, appeared another of those rough-looking men. Next to him was a thin, sallow-faced fellow. The bank clerk! It must be. She ought to have known Kellford would bring proof of his allegations.

Someone approached her from behind. Leo? She whirled around.

It was Walker and Penny.

She clasped Penny's hand and asked Walker, 'Any news of Leo?'

He frowned. 'He left word he would be gone a day.'

'A day?' He must stay away until it was safe to return. Her anxiety for him returned.

'Come,' her father demanded.

She gave Penny a swift hug before her father pulled her away.

'Who was that gentleman with your maid?' Her father's voice was tense.

She merely returned a scathing look.

Her mother hurried towards them. 'We should start now.' She quickly made her way to her seat.

The organist began playing a selection from Haydn and her father nearly dragged Mariel to the centre aisle. There was nothing to be done but to walk towards the altar where Kellford waited for her, the very picture of an eager groom.

'Do not fail me, daughter,' her father rasped.

She walked up the aisle on her father's arm. Her father handed her over to Lord Kellford. Kellford's cold eyes glittered with triumph as she took her place beside him.

The organ music ceased and the minister began, 'Dearly beloved, we are gathered together here in the sight of God…'

Mariel did not heed the words. She could not do this! She could not do this! She could not shackle herself to this despicable man.

Her heart pounded harder when the minister said, 'Therefore if any man can show any just cause why they may not lawfully be joined together, let him now speak or else hereafter forever hold his peace….'

She drew in a breath, praying some miracle would occur and someone would speak.

All was silent.

The minister went on, '…if either of you know any impediment, why ye may not be lawfully joined in matrimony, ye do now confess it…'

She should open her mouth. Tell the minister to stop.

He continued, asking Kellford, 'Wilt thou have this woman…?'

Mariel's heart pounded so hard she thought it might be heard in the back of the church. She heard a roaring in her ears. Would she even hear the minister ask for her vows?

The roar changed and seemed to come from outside the church, like muffled voices. She heard the guests moving and murmuring among themselves.

She could not do this. God help her. She could not do this.

The minister turned to her. 'Wilt thou have this man to your wedded husband…?'

'No,' she protested, her voice catching in her throat.

The minister did not hear her. '…keep thee only to him as long as ye both shall live?'

She tried to speak louder. 'No.'

At that same moment the doors to the church opened and a man's voice shouted, 'Stop!'

She turned. From the shadows at the back of the church, the man appeared.

Leo!

He burst into the church, dressed in riding clothes, followed by his brothers. Walker had joined them.

Mariel ran to Leo, caring about nothing at that moment except that Leo had come for her.

He'd come for her!

Leo gathered her into his arms. 'We've done it,' he whispered in her ear. 'All is well.'

Leo was the miracle, the answer to her prayer.

By this time the guests were all on their feet. Mariel's mother was wailing and her father had turned deathly white.

Kellford took a few steps forwards. 'See here!' he cried. 'What is this? How dare you interrupt—'

'There will be no wedding, Kellford.' Leo released Mariel.

Walker and his brothers formed a protective shield around her.

Leo addressed the audience. 'Ladies and gentlemen, I know this is alarming, but my brothers and I have come to prevent a wrong.' He pointed to Mariel. 'This lady does not wish to marry Lord Kellford. He is compelling her to do so in order to gain her fortune.'

Kellford straightened. 'That is a lie! And I demand satisfaction from you for speaking such a falsehood.' He moved around the guests. 'This man is lying, I assure you. The truth is, I am protecting Miss Covendale and her family—'

'Say no more,' Leo warned.

Kellford looked wild-eyed. 'You have forced me into this, Fitzmanning.' He pointed to Mariel's father. 'He is the villain in this! He stole money from his cousin, Lord Doring—'

A voice from the back of the church boomed. 'Stole money from me?' The Earl of Doring strode forwards.

A collective gasp rose from the pews.

'Yes! Yes!' Kellford hurried towards him, pointing to the back of the church. 'See that man there?' The bank clerk shrank down in the pew. The man who had been sitting next to him rose and hurried out of the church. 'That man can prove I am not a liar. He knows Covendale forged a signature—'

Doring laughed. 'My cousin did no such thing.' He walked up to Mariel's father and patted him on the back. 'I recently loaned Covendale a large amount of money. Why not? I have the funds and he was in need.' Doring glanced over to the bank clerk. 'Are you going to believe that fellow over me? Is he known to any of you?'

'Indeed!' Leo spoke up again. 'It is as I have said. We have come to stop Kellford from destroying the good name of Mr Covendale and his daughter. To prevent him from plundering this lady's fortune.'

Mariel's gaze went from one to the other, trying to take it all in. 'How did he do it?' she asked Stephen.

He grinned at her. 'He remembered his passion for horses.'

No more than an hour later, Leo sat beside Mariel on the sofa in Nicholas's drawing room. Nicholas's wife had taken Mariel's mother under her wing, distracting her and consoling her. Brenner stood in serious conversation with Covendale and Doring. Stephen and Nicholas laughed over a decanter of brandy.

'Nicholas has sent for your sisters?' Mariel asked him.

'Charlotte, Annalise, their spouses, Justine and Stephen's wife, as well.' He smiled at her. 'I am afraid you will be joining a rather large family.'

She took his hand and squeezed it. 'My happiest days have been among your family. I shall look forward to many more.' She sighed. 'I only wish Walker and Penny had agreed to come.'

'I do, too,' he admitted. 'Give them time. I have a feeling Walker is destined for such success he will soon find the company of dukes and earls commonplace.'

She returned his smile. 'And I suspect Penny will be at his side.'

Leo still had not settled with Mariel whether she would marry him. There were no real impediments now. His business ventures would now be ones he could shout from rooftops, if necessary. He would accept the help his brothers could provide. If a duke, an earl and a second son rallied around him, who would dare consider him scandalous? He'd had enough of danger and the only risks he was willing to take now were financial ones.

And emotional ones. He would risk loving again. He loved Mariel and would do whatever he could to see that she was happy. If that meant marrying him, his spirits would soar to the heavens. If not, he would find some other way to ensure her happiness.

She rested her head against his shoulder. 'I am still trying to believe that it is all over. What will happen to Kellford, do you think?'

'He left the church in the company of some hard-looking men. I suspect the money lenders will lose no time in stripping his house of its belongings. If Kellford is lucky, he will be left with his life and little else.'

Likely Kellford would flee to the Continent to escape the rest of his creditors. It was not punishment enough for him, in Leo's view, but at least they would not have to set eyes on him again.

Mariel stroked his hand. 'What Kellford has done will certainly be the topic of much gossip. I am sure some disfavour will fall on my family. I wonder if it will be enough to compel my father to change his ways?'

He threaded his fingers through hers, glad to be able to touch her, to know she was now safe. 'I suspect Brenner is concocting some plan between your father and his cousin to keep your father in check.'

She raised their entwined hands to her lips and kissed his fingers. 'I still do not see how you convinced Doring to forgive my father. My father insisted he would be full of wrath.'

'He was,' Leo responded. 'He was precisely as your father depicted him and I thought I had made a terrible miscalculation by going to him.'

'Miscalculation?' she asked.

He looked into her lovely eyes. 'I thought I would become the cause of your father hanging. I thought you would never forgive me.' It had been a painfully low point.

Her gaze softened. 'I still do not understand how you convinced him.'

He'd remembered Stephen muttering that Doring cared more for his horses than his family. That was the key. Leo offered him the breeding pair of horses from Stephen's stables and suddenly Doring was willing to forgive all.

Leo glanced around the room at his brothers. He could not have saved Mariel without them. Nicholas, as only a duke could do, had provided clout. Stephen had provided the solution. And now Brenner would seal the pact and prevent future problems. He said a silent prayer of thanks for giving him this family. This woman he loved.

'How did you convince Doring, Leo?' Mariel asked.

He grinned at her. 'Horses, Mariel.' He leaned down and kissed her. 'Horses,' he whispered.

Epilogue

Welbourne Manor—October 1830

The house party at Welbourne Manor was not unlike those held there when Leo and his siblings were growing up. Small children ran through the house, chased by haggard governesses. Older ones brought in dirt from the gardens or played rowdy games in the upstairs music room. As in days gone by, there was plenty of noise, the noise of a family party.

Leo and Mariel had invited the entire Fitzmanning Miscellany for several days of family enjoyment after the christening of their newborn son, John, named after Leo's father. Welbourne Manor was Leo and Mariel's home now and had been for two years, a wedding present from Leo's brothers and sisters, a return to their father's original bequest.

At the moment, Leo and his brothers were in the library, hiding from the children. Walker had arrived, providing them a great excuse to avoid the commotion. Walker and Penny brought two more toddlers with them, their twins, now just over a year old, their contribution to the din.

'What did you find in Liverpool?' Leo asked Walker as soon as the men all had drinks in their hands.

Leo and Walker were now partners. Their ship had come in from that not-quite-legal investment they'd made two years before, the one that had brought Leo back to London and to Mariel. By mutual agreement, they'd decided to remain within the law afterwards. That decision had not hampered them.

'The railroad is a marvel,' Walker told them. He had travelled to Liverpool to see first-hand how the new Liverpool and Manchester railways operated. 'It can move thousands of people, carry the mail, as well as goods.'

'Are you and Walker going to invest in railroads?' Nicholas asked.

'We have already, your Grace,' Walker said. 'We are looking to develop rail transport from London west.'

Stephen's brows rose. 'This is a far cry from raising horses.'

'I have no wish to compete with you, Stephen,' Leo remarked. 'Think of it this way. Railroads can bring more people to the races. There's money in this for you.'

Brenner spoke seriously. 'Do not sink everything into railroads. It is always better to invest in several opportunities. That way if one investment loses, you still make money on the other.'

'Spoken like the wise elder brother!' Leo laughed.

Walker provided more details, speaking so knowledgeably that one would never have guessed he once had been a thief and a valet. When Walker had left Leo's service, the man who had once been Kellford's valet took his place. Penny said he looked more like a valet than Walker.

Mariel knocked at the door. 'Leo, may I see you, please?'

He went to her immediately. 'What is it?'

'I need you to come to the nursery.' She gestured for him to come with her.

Leo's worries grew. It was not like her to interrupt like this.

Instead of the children's wing, though, she led him to their bedchamber.

'I moved the crib in here temporarily, because the nursery is so full,' she explained.

Indeed, it had been quite a challenge to figure out the sleeping arrangements for so many children, their nurses and governesses.

'Is something wrong with the baby?' He hurried over to the crib.

She joined him, looking down at the sleeping infant, this miracle they'd created together.

The baby slept peacefully.

She put her arm around Leo's waist. 'Nothing's wrong. The baby is perfect, as always. There never was a more perfect baby. I merely wanted an excuse to be with you.'

The sounds of children shrieking, their feet pounding through the halls, reached his ears. A new Fitzmanning Miscellany, Leo thought, smiling to himself.

He remembered running with his brothers and sisters through these rooms. How many priceless vases had they knocked over? Suffered how many scraped knees? It has been a happy place. He'd continue to make Welbourne Manor a happy place. How could it be anything but happy when Mariel was at his side?

'I've hardly seen you since the christening.' She sighed.

He wrapped his arms around her, realising he had

missed her equally as much. 'Were you worried that I'd run away to the Continent?'

Something crashed and shattered. A child began to wail and soon adult footsteps could be heard running to see what had happened.

She settled against his chest where she fit so perfectly. 'With all the noise and commotion, I would not blame you.'

He broke away from her so he could look down into her eyes. 'I would not leave you.'

She smiled. 'Not even if someone told you I'd fallen for an earl?'

'Especially not then.' He grinned. 'Or, at least, I would chase you down and make you explain why you would ever do such a thing.'

She laughed. 'Very good, Leo! You have learned something.'

He kissed her. 'The most important thing I've learned is that I love you. I will never leave you.'

She kissed him back. 'I know.'

* * * * *

REQUEST YOUR FREE BOOKS!

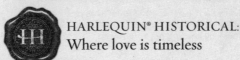

HARLEQUIN® HISTORICAL:
Where love is timeless

2 FREE NOVELS PLUS 2 FREE GIFTS!

YES! Please send me 2 FREE Harlequin® Historical novels and my 2 FREE gifts (gifts are worth about $10). After receiving them, if I don't wish to receive any more books, I can return the shipping statement marked "cancel." If I don't cancel, I will receive 6 brand-new novels every month and be billed just $5.19 per book in the U.S. or $5.74 per book in Canada. That's a savings of at least 17% off the cover price! It's quite a bargain! Shipping and handling is just 50¢ per book in the U.S. and 75¢ per book in Canada.* I understand that accepting the 2 free books and gifts places me under no obligation to buy anything. I can always return a shipment and cancel at any time. Even if I never buy another book, the two free books and gifts are mine to keep forever.

246/349 HDN FEQQ

Name _____ (PLEASE PRINT) _____

Address _____ Apt. # _____

City _____ State/Prov. _____ Zip/Postal Code _____

Signature (if under 18, a parent or guardian must sign) _____

Mail to the **Reader Service:**
IN U.S.A.: P.O. Box 1867, Buffalo, NY 14240-1867
IN CANADA: P.O. Box 609, Fort Erie, Ontario L2A 5X3

Not valid for current subscribers to Harlequin Historical books.

Want to try two free books from another line?
Call 1-800-873-8635 or visit www.ReaderService.com.

* Terms and prices subject to change without notice. Prices do not include applicable taxes. Sales tax applicable in N.Y. Canadian residents will be charged applicable taxes. Offer not valid in Quebec. This offer is limited to one order per household. All orders subject to credit approval. Credit or debit balances in a customer's account(s) may be offset by any other outstanding balance owed by or to the customer. Please allow 4 to 6 weeks for delivery. Offer available while quantities last.

Your Privacy—The Reader Service is committed to protecting your privacy. Our Privacy Policy is available online at www.ReaderService.com or upon request from the Reader Service.

We make a portion of our mailing list available to reputable third parties that offer products we believe may interest you. If you prefer that we not exchange your name with third parties, or if you wish to clarify or modify your communication preferences, please visit us at www.ReaderService.com/consumerschoice or write to us at Reader Service Preference Service, P.O. Box 9062, Buffalo, NY 14269. Include your complete name and address.

HH11B

*The mischievously witty Bronwyn Scott
introduces a brand-new trilogy,*
RAKES BEYOND REDEMPTION.

*Three deliciously naughty books, with three equally
devilish rakes. They are far too wicked for polite society…
but these ladies just can't stay away!*

*Read on for a sneak peek of book one
HOW TO DISGRACE A LADY.*

Available in September 2012 from Harlequin® Historical.

"**Y**ou're a beautiful woman, Alixe Burke."

She stiffened. "You shouldn't say things you don't mean."

"Do you doubt me? Or do you doubt yourself? Don't you think you're beautiful? Surely you're not naive enough to overlook your natural charms."

She turned to face him, forcing him to relinquish his hold. "I'm not naive. I'm a realist."

Merrick shrugged a shoulder as if to say he didn't think much of realism. "What has realism taught you, Alixe?" He folded his arms, waiting to see what she would say next.

"It has taught me that I'm an end to male means. I'm a dowry, a stepping stone for some ambitious man. It's not very flattering."

He could not refute her arguments. There *were* men who saw women that way. But he could refute the hardness in her sherry eyes, eyes that should have been warm. For all her protestations of realism, she was too untried by the world for the measure of cynicism she showed. "What of romance and love? What has realism taught you about those things?"

"If those things exist, they don't exist for me." Alixe's chin went up a fraction in defiance of his probe.

"Is that a dare, Alixe? If it is, I'll take it." Merrick took advantage of their privacy, closing the short distance between them with a touch; the back of his hand reaching out to stroke the curve of her cheek. "A world without romance is a bland world indeed, Alixe. One for which I think you are ill suited." He saw the pulse at the base of her neck leap at the words, the hardness in her eyes soften, curiosity replacing the doubt whether she willed it or not. He let his eyes catch hers then drop to linger on the fullness of her mouth before he drew her to him, whispering, "Let me show you the possibilities." A most seductive invitation to sin.

Don't miss book one of this seductive new trilogy
HOW TO DISGRACE A LADY

Available in September 2012 from Harlequin® Historical.

And watch out for:

HOW TO RUIN A REPUTATION
Available October 2012

HOW TO SIN SUCCESSFULLY
Available November 2012